Feminist and Abolitionist

The Story of Emilia Casanova

Virginia Sánchez-Korrol

Feminist and Abolitionist

The Story of Emilia Casanova

Virginia Sánchez-Korrol

PIÑATA BOOKS
ARTE PÚBLICO PRESS
HOUSTON, TEXAS

Feminist and Abolitionist: The Story of Emilia Casanova is made possible through a grant from the City of Houston through the Houston Arts Alliance.

Piñata Books are full of surprises!

Piñata Books
An imprint of
Arte Público Press
University of Houston
4902 Gulf Fwy, Bldg 19, Rm 100
Houston, Texas 77204-2004

Cover design by Mora Des!gn

Sánchez-Korrol, Virginia
    Feminist and abolitionist: the story of Emilia Casanova / by Virginia Sánchez-Korrol.
    p.   cm.
    Summary: A fictionalized memoir of Emilia Casanova, a Cuban woman who fought for independence from Spain and for freedom for the African slaves on her island home.
    Includes bibliographical references.
    ISBN 978-1-55885-765-0 (alk. paper)
    1. Casanova de Villaverde, Emilia, 1832-1897—Juvenile fiction. [1. Casanova de Villaverde, Emilia, 1832-1897—Fiction. 2. Cuba—History—1810-1899—Fiction. 3. Slavery—Fiction.] I. Title.
PZ7.S1949Fe 2013
[Fic]—dc23
                                                          2012044035
                                                                CIP

Printed in the United States of America
April 2013–May 2013
Cushing-Malloy, Inc., Ann Arbor, MI
12 11 10 9 8 7 6 5 4 3 2 1

To CRK
For a lifetime of love, appreciation and inspiration

Contents

Acknowledgments

Along the road to becoming *Feminist and Abolitionist: The Story of Emilia Casanova*, this narrative underwent several transformations. It began as a standard biography of Emilia Casanova de Villaverde set against the nineteenth-century Cuban liberation movement known as the Ten Years' War, but the evidence soon indicated that the format best-suited for telling this story was the historical memoir of imagination.

On this unexpected journey, colleagues, friends, acquaintances and family enriched my efforts to craft an imagined Emilia based on historical documentation. They gave generously of their time and ideas, read and re-read portions or the entire manuscript until the character evolved into someone they cared about and her life became believable. Their brilliant insights, frequent questions and suggestions gave me signposts to follow but it was their enthusiasm for the project that inspired me to continue the journey and write *Feminist and Abolitionist*.

My deepest, sincerest gratitude to Aura Sánchez Garfunkel who inspired me to write the book as a historical novel; to Asunción Lavrín who questioned critically and sharpened my historian's eye; and to Carlos A. Cruz, whose knowledge about Cuban history and literature deepened my focus. Elena Martínez found and shared obscure documents and illustrations; Antonio O. Nadal translated old Spanish terminology into modern English; Edna Acosta Belén, Vicki L. Ruiz, Lisandro Pérez and María Agui Carter engaged in

1

long, provocative conversations with me about research, interpretation and the creative process of telling a life story.

Nicolás Kanellos opened my eyes to Latino literature eons ago through the Recovering the U.S. Hispanic Literary History Project in Houston and had faith that I could write this book. His meticulous reading of the manuscript and suggestions enhanced it immeasurably. And Charles R. Korrol grew to tolerate the obsessions of a writer wife and still offered to read it and provide sage wisdom.

To these wonderful people, and to others I met along the way, I owe a huge debt of gratitude. There is, however, only one person to be credited with any faults, errors and omissions: that is me.

Virginia Sánchez Korrol, 2012

Prologue

An Unexpected Caller

1892

Tampa had a narrow escape from becoming a Cuban town when the cigarmakers began to move up from Key West, but the natural and healthy growth of the city was so rapid that the Cuban element did not have much chance for supremacy. The cigarmakers, who are all Cubans, are gathered in a suburb known as Ybor City about two miles from the Post Office.

The New York Times, January 31, 1892.

She stood with her back to the door facing the windows in the drawing room, a shimmering jolt of crimson and gold against the pale light of the winter's morning and, like an exotic bird of paradise, she brightened the sober antiquity of the room. It was the ringing of the bell that had awakened me with such a start. When the housemaid, Mary McDonald, knocked on the library door, I knew the last thing I wanted to do that morning was to attend to a visitor. The aches in my neck and shoulders from reading far into the night were enough to keep me huddled in my chair before the glowing embers in the fireplace, but she announced there was a young lady to see me in the drawing room and asked if I wanted to attend to her or not.

She turned to face me as I entered the room. Her sea-green eyes lit up, full of anticipation as she smiled and greeted me politely. I quickly glanced at her calling card, but even without my spectacles recognized immediately who she was.

"Señora de Figueroa, what a pleasure it is to find you here in my home after hearing so much about you. Please make yourself at home," I said and signaled for the maid to bring us some *café con leche* and sweet breads. "Please take a seat by the fire where it is warm and tell me how I can be of service to you today."

"*Por favor,* call me Inocencia," she answered in English with the lilt of a Spanish accent. She smiled again showing the promise of the young for whom every obstacle becomes an adventure. "I feel as if I've known you all my life. You, señora, have been my inspiration, my guiding light since I was a girl. Everything I've done in my life, you have led the way and I am honored to . . . but forgive me, I'm talking too much."

Inocencia, I thought. Innocence. Was I ever that young and innocent? Of course, I knew all about her, how she and her husband, Sotero Figueroa, had come from Puerto Rico three years ago imbued with the zeal for independence. He was a writer and publisher and had already begun to organize Puerto Ricans and Cubans into political clubs. She worked at his side, printing and proofreading and raising a young family in their flat by the print shop. Oh yes, I thought, I knew all about them. In another life they might have been my husband Cirilo and myself, raising our family and fighting for independence: organizing our clubs, writing and publishing, all in the name of liberation. I dwelled too long in past thoughts and she interrupted my musing by subtly shifting her head.

"Doña Emilia, may I call you that? I've come to see you today because I desperately need you, well, need your guidance. I want to organize a women's association to fight for the independence of Cuba and Puerto Rico. I need you, if you will be so kind, to help me, to show me how you did it, to teach me how best to inspire a group of women who will work for liberation in partnership with our men and our communities."

How dare she! How *dare* she ask me for such a favor. Does she understand that she is asking me to begin all over again? The words thundered in my head, sending a slight flutter to my heart. It is not that simple. She wants me to open old wounds, break my heart again over the disappointments, relive the sorrows. I'm not young any more. My husband needs me, the grandchildren . . . but she is so young and doesn't know about the pain of rejection, the slanders and the isolation. She doesn't know how it feels to have people cross the street when they see you walk toward them. She doesn't know what it is all about. She needs someone who has been there before to guide her. Maybe this time I can prepare her . . . maybe *this* time we can succeed . . . I studied her face for a long while and she began to get anxious. What a pretty little thing she is, I realized, with her light curls and dainty ways. But is she too dainty for the road that lies ahead?

After a while, I looked directly into her determined eyes and said, "Inocencia," sadly pondering the meaning of her name. "I do so admire what you want to do and wish you to succeed with your organization. But before you move in so perilous a direction, you must be certain. You must be tough. You could end up devoting your life to a cause which, in the long run, may be but a pipe dream."

"No, señora." She stood and faced me, grasping my arm with surprising force, her pale, white hand clenching the black crepe sleeve of my dress. "Not this time, señora. We've waited too long." She held her slender body firm and tall, full of determination, and continued, "Martí and my husband are organizing a new revolutionary party. There will be a newspaper, *Patria,* and all of us will be involved from Ybor City to New York, the whites, blacks, rich and poor, the workers and the intellectuals. And the women. This time, señora, we *will* succeed!"

Intensely moved by her dedication, I gently removed her hand from my arm and turned away for a second or so to regain my composure. "But my dear," I cautioned, "I must beg you once again to reconsider . . . Before you come to a decision, may I tell you my story?"

She sat before me like a young girl for whom a story is promised, curious about what I was about to impart as I eased myself into my favorite green velvet armchair. I then began a journey I had long ago boxed up with the other fragments of forgotten treasures of my life. I closed my eyes for a moment or two to summon the past. In the recesses of my mind I began to see it waving again against the brilliant sky. I began to remember . . .

The very first time I saw the flag, I was eighteen years of age. Startled awake by the shots from the rifles, I bolted from my bed to the window, trailing my bed linen across the floor. There I stared in complete disbelief at the most beautiful banner I had ever seen. Waving gently in the cool dawn breeze, the flag bore a lone white star embedded in a triangular field of deepest crimson from which three broad cobalt and two white stripes alternated to the banner's border. An overwhelming sense of excitement mingled with giddy elation filtered throughout my entire body. The long-rumored Cuban rebellion against the tyranny of Spanish rule had begun in earnest. From this day forward, I secretly vowed, I would forever be devoted to that flag, that beautiful banner and all it stood for. It was the 19th day of May, 1850 and this . . . is my story.

Part I
Cuba
(1832–1853)

One

Wednesday's Child: My Early Life in Agrarian Cuba

The sugar plantation is no grove, or garden, or orchard. It is not the home of the pride and affections of the planter's family. It is not a coveted, indeed, hardly a desirable residence.

Such families as would like to remain on these plantations are driven off for want of neighboring society. Thus the estates, largely abandoned by the families of the planters, suffer the evils of absenteeism, while the owners live in the suburbs of Havana and Matanzas, and in the Fifth Avenue of New York.

Richard Henry Dana, Jr.
To Cuba and Back: A Vacation Voyage, 1859.

"*¡Es hembra!*" The *partera* held up the newborn baby, deftly counting fingers and toes, and placed the swaddled child into my mother's outstretched arms. "You have yourself a feisty daughter, Doña Petrona, a fussy, squirmy bundle of joy."

"*Pobrecita. No llores, que Dios siempre te bendiga, mi Emilia,*" my mother responded kissing my tiny clenched fist. "Poor little thing, don't cry, may God always bless you, my Emilia."

Piercing the high heavens with baby wails, as if I already knew of the great injustices that awaited me, my cries were a counterpoint to the distant drone of slaves chanting as they cut cane in the hot, sun-drenched fields of our plantation. From that very moment, I'd like to think we announced our alliance to the rest of the world.

They say I arrived kicking and screaming on a Wednesday morning during the dry season of the harvest, the 18th day of January, 1832. As if to justify my infant complaints and sense of outrage at the world, that very same year a fierce hurricane struck the northern coastline of Cuba, uprooting giant Royal Palm trees like match sticks in a robust wind, destroying everything else in its path.

My family suffered losses to properties in Guamutas, the small hamlet where we lived at that time in Matanzas Province. But the disaster brought us the opportunity to move to Cárdenas, a fertile agricultural and seafaring region that progressed over the decades, as did we. Since I was brought to Cárdenas as an infant, I would proudly proclaim it as my birthplace, although the town would not always proudly claim me as a favorite daughter.

I was the first in a roster of Casanova offspring that followed in quick succession. Manuel, Andrés and José arrived soon after me. In all, the close-knit and caring family would constitute sixteen siblings. Papá and Mamá, known to others as Don Inocencio Casanova and Doña Petrona Rodríguez, prospered in producing a healthy family and a productive livelihood. At a time when children often died in infancy, eleven of us thrived beyond our fifth year.

The Casanova good fortune went far to shield all of us from the uncertainties of life in the tumultuous Cuba of the nineteenth century, if not always in the political mine fields we encountered. We owned several large sugar plantations in the region. An army of free and enslaved laborers worked our fields and cared for hundreds of head of our cattle. We owned warehouses, mills, forested and cleared land, wharves and a dockyard. Of houses, we had several in neighboring towns, including the family homestead damaged by the hurricane, Finca Caimito, where I first saw the dawn of day, and the two-story stone house in Cárdenas, where I matured into a young woman.

By any account, our family was wealthy. We children were raised in privilege, instilled with a sense of justice and compassion toward others who were far less fortunate. We were expected to honor civic and familial responsibilities, care for one another and maintain the impeccable reputation of our Casanova lineage. Our parents shared a close matrimonial union for more than half a century despite revolution, exile, relocation and persecution. It also weathered the oftentimes obstinate natures of their children. Nowhere was this more apparent than in our liberal political inclinations that would one day bring the family to the brink of despair. As I recall those early days, I do believe we managed to live up to our parents' expectations and they, in turn, learned to live up to ours.

My father was slim, of medium height, olive-skin toned and sported a thick head of wavy black hair, but it was his bushy moustache I best recall when I think of him during my childhood. I was fascinated by the way the ends of his moustache turned up when he smiled and, to my mind, encouraged little crinkles to appear at the corners of his eyes. He had been born in 1804 in the Canary Islands, an archipelago belonging to Spain just off the northwest coast of Africa. At sixteen years of age, he came to live with relatives in Cuba, who helped establish his roots in the sugar industry. Ten years later, he married the beautiful Doña Petrona, my mother, when she was a young lady of sixteen. Government land grants, livestock and implements, along with Mamá's dowry and generosities that flowed from the Rodríguez family, secured his place among the planters of Matanzas Province.

I remember that sometimes, when the *cocuyos* began their firefly dance in the cool of the evening and the shrill song of the crickets enveloped us, I'd sit on Papá's lap on the veranda, and he would tell us stories about his island home. Manuel and Andrés vied for the children's rockers nearest Papá. The younger children, José and Pedro, had been taken off to bed by their nannies. Rocking in her delicately carved wooden rocker by the hurricane lamp, her hands expertly creating intricate stitching on a baby's baptismal cap, Mamá would glance up at father and with a slight smile signal to him to begin a story.

"In the northwest," he'd begin audibly clearing his throat, like a singer about to launch into his favorite song, "it is always green and lush with lots of vegetation. The days are long and hot in las Canarias . . . but the evenings—ah, the evenings—are like ours . . . a bit drier, with soft breezes."

Father told the same stories over and over, the same jokes, the same dramatic pauses enhanced by a chuckle or two, but I loved leaning against his chest, feeling the soft vibrations of his deep melodious voice as he shared with us his childhood memories. His eyes took on a dreamy quality and I could see how pleased he was to re-visit his homeland, even if it was only in his mind.

"My family grew grapes, you know, for wine making," he'd continue, "and the part I liked the best was the time of the *cosecha*, the harvest. Before dawn, when the mist began to rise like a blanket of smoke, the whole family would come together, even the children, whose small hands could easily reach the bottoms of the bushes to pick the grapes. In one long day all the grapes would be harvested and crushed. Then, our family, our workers and their families, and everyone else who had helped, would gather together on the patio at long tables laden with huge bowls of rice, vegetables and meats, fruit, breads and, of course, bottles of our own wine, for the best dinner of the year! That is how we celebrated the harvest."

"But, Papá," I'd insist with childish perseverance, sitting up tall on his lap so that I could look directly into his eyes, "tell me why you came *here*?" I knew the answer, of course, but I would always ask the question because it prolonged the protective rapture created by the storyteller.

"Yes, Papá," yawned Manuel, his younger brother was now fast asleep in mother's arms, "why?"

"When business declined, it was time for some of us to make our own way in the world, especially if, like me, you were one of the younger sons of the family. My father, your grandfather, *m'ijita*, told me that the government offered incentives to Canary Islanders willing to come and settle in the Indies, and so I came here." He paused and looked at me, searching my face for understanding. "If I had not come to Cuba," playfully pulling at one of my dark, corkscrew curls, he whispered, "I never would have met *you*, my love." As the oldest and only girl in a family of boys, at least until Cecilia arrived in 1840, I relished Papá's special attention.

As the story was told to me, father boarded a ship for Havana, following in the path of other Canary Islanders who sought their fortunes by migrating from one region of the Spanish empire to its possessions in the Caribbean.

Like them, he was lured by expanding opportunities to be found in sugar cultivation and, like them, he discovered similarities between the Canaries and the Cuban climate and culture. Before long, he understood the ways of working the soil and making it yield a productive harvest. His decision to relocate was a good one and it proved to be beneficial for us all.

Papá became a successful, respected planter and businessman, owner of several sprawling plantations. He cared for and managed hundreds of free and enslaved workers, the people who made everything function in our lives. The harvest, milling the sugar crop and trading agricultural products such as sugar, rum, molasses and tobacco, for goods like furniture, machinery, flour and other foodstuffs were Papá's major occupations.

In these matters, he traveled far and wide from Guamutas to Cárdenas to oversee his extensive properties, or further west to Matanzas, or to the island's capital city of Havana, all in the course of a season's work. Commercial transactions, selling and buying, negotiating prices and catching up with the political and economic news of the world were important to a man of many business affairs. And Papá was indeed such a man, a man of business negotiations and deals.

The backbone of the country's economy were the plantations. Planters' families, like ours, could live comfortably on the plantation but most of us preferred to live in the towns or cities away from the isolation of the countryside. Already, within my young lifetime, there was talk of plantations becoming such huge enterprises that they'd require enormously large numbers of enslaved men and women to make them productive. I knew this because Papá often told me so.

What I remember best about our plantations during my childhood was that they resembled a separate world, a small village where hundreds of people lived. Among them, aside from the field workers, one would find carpenters, priests, blacksmiths, barrel makers, stable keepers, oxherders and accountants. The managers and overseers ran the estates for my father. You might ask how I, a mere girl, learned all about our plantations at such an early age. It was because father frequently encouraged me to accompany him on his rounds.

"Emilia," he would say at the evening supper the night before such a long trip, "you must be up with the roosters tomorrow if you are to help me complete the day's chores."

"Yes! . . . Oh, yes, Papá! I'll be awake *before* the roosters," I'd squeal, running to my father, arms outstretched in anticipation of a giant embrace, to the consternation of Manuel who felt deprived of the privilege. He was less obedient than I, more likely to court trouble and often clashed with Papá over simple orders. For me, these adventures alone with Papá marked the highlight of a childhood otherwise brimming with demanding brothers and babies in an active household of relatives, nursemaids, servants and slaves.

Sunrise would find me riding my small horse next to his larger gelding over dusty red roads still wet from the morning dew.

Wrapped in a warm shawl, bonnet and gloves to ward off the coolness of the morning, I'd imagine a strong kinship blossoming
between us as if we alone were about to enter a secret covenant
known only to the two of us. I recall how much I loved to be with
him, mostly, I think, because he never treated me like a child.

"Look at the fields, my love. Notice the size of the cane," he'd
say. "This is called *tiempo muerto*, the dead season, because the
cane needs to rest and time to grow."

"Papá," I'd ask plying him with more questions, "why do the
bibijagua ants make holes in the leaves? Why don't they just live
in the dirt like other ants?" And so our conversation would continue . . . until I tired of the complicated answers he gave, often
filled with more information than I cared to know.

Once we reached the plantation, I'd have free reign of the place,
even though father made sure to entrust my care to the *mulata*,
Seña Aurelia. Her daughter, a light-skinned girl named Geneva,
became my favorite accomplice, but she was a willful girl. If I said,
"Geneva, you must do this or that," she'd often reply with a snob-
bish toss of her curly light hair, "only if the mistress *orders* me, but
not because I want to." Seña Aurelia would threaten to box her
ears, warning her to do exactly as the mistress commanded.

You should know that as a willful child myself—I shudder to
admit this—I took advantage of Geneva because she was a *mulata*
servant on our plantation. I, on the other hand, was the white
daughter of the owner: her mistress. But in our young adolescent
years, Geneva and I became like sisters, sharing confidences and
forming a close friendship that blossomed beyond the boundaries
of race and social class. I grew to love Geneva, the closest person
outside of my family on whom the sun rose and set.

On the plantation, I was confined to the manor house set
some distance from the sugar mill and the palm-roofed dwellings
of the slaves. The house slaves smothered me with treats: fried
plantains, cigar-shaped corn sticks and bowls of succulent *yuca* in
broth seasoned with lots of salt. I had abundant sugar cane to

suck, which I shared with Geneva until the two of us became giddy with laughter and began to drool sugary saliva all over our arms and aprons.

While father conferred with his workers, my time was spent with Geneva, seeking adventure in spite of the fierce heat of the day. First, we'd leave the manor house unseen through the kitchen door. Then, we'd dare one another to run past Mamá Conchita, a black woman said to cast spells on her enemies. We'd dash uneasily past the old *santera,* afraid she'd give us the evil eye, as she squatted outside the kitchen barrack plucking feathers off scrawny chickens. Holding a lit cigar in her mouth, she would glare at me as I ran by. To this day, I still feel a chill whenever I think of her.

One day as she turned to look my way, I noticed the pinched, whitish skin of a scar running from ear to jaw across her right cheek. Too frightened to ask what had happened to her, I simply ran away. But I remembered the horror of that puckered white scar on her ancient, weathered face for years to come. Whenever I was hurt or frightened, the image of Mamá Conchita would haunt my dreams.

Geneva would challenge me to race to the small, cool chapel where we found safety from the old *santera* and solace from the searing sun. We'd make our way up the rickety ladder leading to the trapdoor of the nursery to play with the babies. No two babies looked alike. Their skin color ranged from the deepest black to almost white. *Las viejitas,* the old grandmothers, took care of them while their mothers worked in the fields or the kitchens. Some buildings, where danger lurked within, I was strictly forbidden to enter the storage rooms; or the workshops, the infirmary, the maternity room, and especially the boiler house.

By late afternoon, Papá and I mounted our horses to head for home and the game of questions and answers would begin all over again in playful companionship. As the burnished golden sun began its slow dip into the sea, we rode in silence, side by side, enchanted by nature's beauty. I remember those afternoons as father's little helper, like small gems of treasured memories. By the time I was sixteen, I knew as much about running the business as did my brothers and I became father's assistant. I kept the household accounts, the purchase ledger and answered correspondence.

Two

The Age of Reason

*. . . How could she not love them if from the age of reason until
her marriage she was in her paternal home, the keeper of the
keys, the administrator of the estates, the family counselor, the
real lady of the house, the healer for all, the nanny for the
younger children, the angel on guard, in a word, in the home, she
was the protector of the numerous slaves . . .*

Apuntes biográficos de Emilia Casanova de Villaverde
escritos por un contemporáneo. New York, 1874.

If you asked me when I first became an abolitionist, I'd probably
say it began when I was still a young girl. My childhood experiences around the plantations, on our *quintas,* or properties, conditioned my earliest uneasiness about holding people in bondage.
As I became older, I sensed the lot of the African and Afro-Cuban
laborer, supporting the luxurious lives of planters, would never
change unless they were set free.

How, I wondered, could anyone reconcile the oppression of
one group of people by another? Papá, I discovered, shared similar sentiments as my own, deciding long before any legislative
actions required him to do so, to free the children of his slaves at
birth. I began to believe slavery could come to an end only when
we, the free citizens, fought hard enough for abolition. I resolved

to be among the first liberators to stand up and shout *"¡Presente!*
I'm here! Lead me to the battle!"

That is what I'd say if you asked me when I first became an
abolitionist. But in my mind I can still envision Geneva's beautiful,
laughing, thirteen-year-old face encircled by a halo of sun-filled,
light-colored curls . . . the golden girl with the willful spirit.

In truth, I became an abolitionist the day Geneva was murdered for denying the overseer her favors . . . and I, in spite of all
my privileges, was powerless to save her.

It was the lot of the slaves to work from sunrise to sundown every
day of their lives, but the harvest on our plantations, as I recall it,
was the most grueling. Sugar mills spewed unrelenting fires
extracting a physical toll on the health and energy of the workers
in exchange for their labor, day and night. I'd hear the whip crack
incessantly. Its sharp thud filled the air, punishing double-yoked
oxen teams for their slowness and often falling upon the bare,
sweat-glistened backs of the slaves themselves. Pulling heavily
loaded carts of cane to the mill, one row of oxcarts brought in the
cane for grinding while a reverse row returned to the fields for
more. In the boiler house, it was as if the mill's bone-weary workers were condemned to a life of interminable toil. "That," I once
remarked to Papá, "was surely what Hell looked like."

I noted, as well, the rare occasions when the slaves were given
permission to celebrate, allowed to beat the African drums calling
down their deities and recalling their former homelands. One
could see and hear snatches of the African past and the Creole
present: Spanish and African dialects, drums pounding out Creole
rhythms. Dancers swayed their hips, stamped their feet and called
out responses to the rhythm of the drums, scrapers, maracas and
song. All of this had a momentary healing effect on the slave community, bringing it from a place of drudgery to a spontaneous outpouring of merriment. If fortune shone their way, the slaves could
roast a pig or a chicken raised especially for the occasion. As if it

were yesterday, I still recall how their rituals fascinated me, how I trembled on the periphery of their closed society, observing and absorbing their humanity.

The more I learned, the more sympathetic I became. I imagined such celebratory moments could call up silent memories in their hearts, memories of: forced separations from loved ones, newborns yanked from their mother's breasts . . . inhumane deaths, and the abuses women endured simply because they were women. Frivolity could not mask the dire, oppressive enslavement under which they lived.

To think, this all had to do with your place in society, your social class or the color of your skin! The truth was that color and class mattered enormously in Cuba. It mattered whether you were born in the colonies or in Europe, in the countryside or the towns, because your place of birth, like your family name, molded your aspirations and social position. Race and class determined your place in our society, and within the many categories one could occupy, women always answered to the men of their class.

I could see, early on, that in our society my parents were powerful people. They were well-respected, people of means and impeccable reputation. And they were white. At first, I did not question my privileged good fortune, nor considered the limitations of social movement or intermingling among the races. What cause had I to do so? That was knowledge one acquired as one went along taking life, with all of its social peculiarities, for granted as one often did when growing up. But once I began to harbor abolitionist sentiments, I also began to challenge the notion that women were subservient, not fit to occupy positions equal to men, to make decisions or speak their minds in public. And all my dissatisfaction, in years to come, I'd lay at the doorstep of a government that denied its citizens the right to bring change to their way of life.

Despite the fact that she was a woman, Mamá was important. She was second in command, my father being first in all matters, of what to me was the entire world, our home. And because she was important, she carried a great deal of authority for making decisions. Sometimes, loud banging on our front portal awakened the entire household in the middle of the night, frightening us children into imagining looming catastrophe. I especially listened for telltale sounds of danger, strained to learn the whereabouts of my parents and our servants because, as the oldest child, it was my duty to care for the younger ones. Frequently, the commotion signaled a domestic situation, someone seeking mother's attention, as she was often called upon to tend to a sick person or some other emergency that required making decisions.

In matters of illness, Mamá took immediate charge, called upon the *curandera* to bring the healer's carefully selected plant and herbal cures, because diseases like the dreaded cholera or smallpox sprang up and spread at the most unexpected moments.

Throughout my childhood, I longed to become a Doña Petrona in miniature. Being strong-willed, a child who challenged restrictions placed on her because of her youth or her sex, I often fell short of achieving ladylike conduct. And yet, I'd strive to become my mother's shadow, for in mother I had the best of teachers. She taught me what was expected of a young lady, in spite of my obstinacy. And I, in my young, eager-to-please years would copy everything she did, emerging like a butterfly from its cocoon, her miniature duplicate.

I'd often wrap myself in Mamá's enormous Spanish silk shawl with the embroidered red and yellow roses in the center and shiny black frills running along its borders because that is what my mother did. Some days I quietly studied her at her work table when she thought no one was looking. Absentmindedly twirling a lock of dark hair around her finger, she appeared to be far away, mentally exploring worlds I knew nothing about. I'd wonder, is she remembering life as a little girl learning at her mother's knee, as I am trained at hers?

"The role of a 'lady' is complicated," mother would sternly intone while trying to hide the amusement in her eyes. "She is to organize the household. She is to set the weekly calendar, plan the meals, supervise the pantry and the children. But Emilia, you must never forget, the actual work involved falls upon the shoulders of the slaves or domestic servants. You, *m'ijita*, despite your heart of gold, must learn how to properly train and reprimand them." Behind serious faces, Mamá and I would look at one another for a moment and spontaneously spill over into contagious peals of laughter as we recalled the many bejeweled "ladies" we knew who preferred to perfect the art of lounging rather than that of supervising anything or anybody.

On the shaded, Spanish-tiled veranda that surrounded the inner courtyard of our large stone house, I'd play at being a lady. Intensely absorbed in the game, I'd dismiss the wisps of black curls stubbornly clinging to my forehead in the heat and humidity of the day, ignore the teasing of my brothers and coax my sister Cecilia to play my baby. I'd plan pretend activities with baby Cecilia and my China dolls, just as mother did for our real family. I'd reprimand the dolls, pretending they disrespected me, frightening Cecilia into copious tears. As I was often told, I had a flare for the dramatic, but Cecilia was still too young to appreciate it.

On some days I'd play at being a saint, sacrificing my life for the good of others, like the martyrs in our catechism, or devoting myself to good deeds for the sins of the poor. I'd dress the statues of the saints in church, like my maiden aunts did every Thursday, and organize charitable projects until it was time for the afternoon meal. I'd play at such games because those were the obligations that befell my mother and aunts.

If Mamá showed me the ways of a lady and what one was required to know to run the household, Papá taught me to consider a world beyond our boundaries, the differences between Cuban and American cities, and the islands where he experienced childhood. I learned about commerce and history and how it was important to set high principles, speak your mind and never lie.

"I fully intend to become a lady who always speaks her mind and never lies," I promised myself aloud, as if I were reciting my evening rosary. Simple childish promises sometimes had the habit of becoming true.

"If I had to choose between life on a plantation and life in a town like Cárdenas, guess, Mamá, which would I choose? . . . I must admit, I'd choose Cárdenas," I confided to Mamá, answering my own question before she had the chance to speak. It was one of those rare afternoons when I had her all to myself without meddlesome siblings. We strolled like ladies, arm-in-arm, across the Plaza Mayor heading toward the cathedral. Turning to look at her, a silly smile on my face, I noticed that my head already reached above her shoulder.

"Well, of course *m'ijita*," she responded gracefully with an amused smile that lit up her pretty face. Mother had the blackest, shiniest hair of all her sisters and surprisingly warm, honey-colored eyes that seemed to invite you to be friends with her. "For young people, life in the towns is much more exciting than in the countryside, where the day practically ends at sunset. I should know. I grew up in a rural village and was fortunate that your father found me at all."

I thought about it, never once imagining I'd ever be forced to leave my home for parts unknown. Cárdenas had an abundance of social activities available to us that made our seasons interesting and we had the means to indulge in them. Of course, I loved the opera. Touring theatrical companies never failed to make Cárdenas a port of call. And I liked to spend an evening at a private home listening to interesting discussions, poetry recitations or musical ensembles. Then too, ladies were often invited to teas, but I considered those rather silly affairs, the purpose of which was mainly to gossip and show off one's jewels and finery.

On December 2, 1853, Cárdenas was officially declared a "Villa" by royal proclamation of Queen Isabel II. The promotion from town to Villa, a great honor, rewarded Cárdenas for the progress it had achieved since its founding in 1836. In our town of 6,000 inhabitants, official celebrations involved a number of festive events, and this one was no exception. People descended upon Cárdenas in droves and prepared to celebrate the Villa's good fortune without restraint.

The Casanova and Rodríguez kinfolk arrived at our doorstep for the celebration, bringing the gift of gossip, the latest social and family scandals, current fashions and other observations about their lives. Amid a whirlwind of embraces, room assignments and directives to the servants for the comfort of the guests, mother admonished the men to lay aside the burning political or commercial issues of the day. Her first words in greeting uncles, brothers and other relatives as she welcomed them to our home were "There is to be no talk about liberation movements or slave uprisings during these festivities." And for a while, the relatives contained themselves from such matters.

Our guests plunged eagerly into revelry as the atmosphere crackled with music, dances and culinary delights; horse races, cock fights and all sorts of betting games. As the days of revelry came to an end for the relatives, they mounted horses and *volantes* to head for home, satiated with camaraderie and the private deals they managed to make behind Mamá's back.

As pleasant as it all was, there had been much discussion about the current political state of affairs in our colony. The specter of slave uprisings could not go long unnoticed among a family of planters. I had learned on my way to becoming a woman in a Cuba of slavery and repression that festivities in my native land carried an undertone of political cynicism, intrigue and unrest that never failed to dampen its gaiety. This revelation was not part of my mother's teaching, nor was it taught to me by either my father or the English governess my parents employed as our tutor, but would form, nonetheless, an important part of my destiny: my long absence away from the homeland.

And that is how I remember my early years . . . a pleasant childhood nurtured by loving protective parents, strong and wise enough to navigate the winds of change that threatened to engulf us in the social and political conflicts that would, in years to come, ultimately overtake us. But first I needed to become an educated lady.

Three

My Education as an Unruly Girl

... Girls are not admitted into the institution after ten years of age: and being entirely supported there they are completely separated from their parents ... until the time of their final removal from the establishment has arrived. They are taught the various branches of needlework and dressmaking, and receive such other instruction as may sufficiently qualify them for becoming domestic servants, house maids, cooks or washerwomen ...

John George F. Wurdemann. *Notes on Cuba.*

I was a rather unusual girl for my times. At eight or nine years of age, I was tall and thin, like the reeds one found growing in the marshes. My long, black, wavy hair I wore pulled back and tied with a red ribbon at the nape of my neck, complementing a golden brown complexion that was a direct result of my love of the outdoors and extraordinary passion for sports and athletics. I seldom wore head scarves to protect my hair, or carried a parasol to ward off the sun's rays, but I did carry a shawl to place over my shoulders when I remembered to retrieve it from the ground, a bench, a tree limb, the stables or various other sites of my escapades.

For the life of me, I cannot count the numbers of times I was admonished for my passions and seemingly unbecoming conduct.

While at times I thought mother and father were being unreasonable in their expectations of my behavior, I suspect they worried a great deal about me.

"Emilia," they would say, "those passions of yours are scandalous, unsuitable behavior for young girls of our station in life on their way to becoming young ladies! You will never attract a suitable husband and people will talk." But try as they might, their Emilia was climbing up the wrong tree.

Raised as I was in a privileged world brimming with restrictions because of our place in society, but primarily because I was a girl, my most memorable adventures were those that defied convention and allowed me to roam at will without adult supervision. My mare was a wonderful co-conspirator. Braced by salt-laden sprays on my uncovered skin, I remember cantering at a fast clip through long stretches of foamy green surf. Since I was old enough to ride a horse, I loved to ride mine out into the open countryside, passing orchards of gnarled fruit trees, green fields and lush forests. We'd jump the hurdles in our path, my horse and I, pretending to flee a drove of dangerous, fire-breathing dragons intent on stopping us in our tracks. I'd squeeze tight on her reins as her long mane whipped across my face in the wind, the horse exhilarated that I gave her the freedom she craved.

My sweet-tempered chestnut Sueño had some Paso Fino in her bloodline, but she was docile and smart and seemed to know me better than most humans. I made up all sorts of rhymes or chants to keep time with her movements. A slight touch of my leg and she came to associate certain words with a particular gait. A trot often accompanied a children's rhyme, but a gallop was something more serious, and I knew she listened for my familiar chants to really let go.

"¡A la rueda, rueda, rueda . . . dame pan y canela!" I'd chant in unison with her sleek, even-paced, muscular movements. "¿Qué quiere usted . . . ?" I shouted shrill nonsense syllables into the wind as we played our game, "¡ma-ta-ri-le-ri-le-ri-le . . . !"

Besides the daily outings with Sueño, I remember the thrill of slicing through the open sea in swimming meets that I secretly arranged with neighborhood children and one or another of my brothers. A good swimmer, I was one of the few girls who dared to engage in that sport. Following my brothers' examples, I'd been perfecting strong, even strokes that cut across the glimmering water with hardly a ripple in my wake. While I was quick to challenge anyone to a race, few moments were as pleasant for me as floating lazily, close to the surf and seeing nothing above me but a brilliant sun against a field of blue sky and white, billowy clouds. I felt like I was one with nature. I was a fairly good athlete, as I recall, at a time when the education of girls neither included nor considered sports important enough to be part of the girls' curriculum.

But Mamá, Papá and the English *aya* they brought to Cuba to be our governess did not appreciate my skills, regardless of my budding proficiency! Rarely did I see them glow with pride in my athletic achievements. Instead they often scolded me for what they labeled "Emilia's exhibitionism" or "Emilia's unladylike behavior."

Inappropriate as it may have seemed, no one stopped to consider swimming, horseback riding, running and imaginative play as positive enhancements that helped to counter-balance the intellectual side of learning. They did, after all, build strong character and values. Fair play, loyalty to your teammates, responsibility and commitment to the task at hand were simple values—these have guided my actions into adulthood and continue to do so to the present.

My governess, Miss Clark, was a middle-aged spinster in her forties. The diminutive, sad-eyed lady came downstairs from her bedroom every morning dressed in shades of gray, high-ruffled collars and long, bouffant cotton sleeves in spite of the Cuban heat. As I was growing up, she was a source of curiosity to me. She wore her brownish hair center parted in the English style and gathered in a bun at the back of her head to cope with the unfamiliar Cuban humidity that stuck to your skin like a layer of adhesive. Later in life, I grew to love and appreciate her courage. It took a special person to leave the familiarity of her homeland in England, perhaps never to return.

To my despair, she always addressed me in the English language, which placed me at a distinct disadvantage because it was the language in which I was least fluent. When reprimanded by the trio of ogres, my parents and the governess, I remember stuttering, " . . . but, Miss Clark" or " . . . but, mother . . . or please father," all to no avail, since I didn't have the English words to defend myself nor did the adults allow me to indulge in much of a defense.

Our "unruly Emilia" conversations frequently took place in the drawing room, which should have been the most splendid of receiving rooms in the entire house but was instead the most dismal and austere chamber. Regardless of the amount of light that filtered into the space through the curtained double doors that led onto the inner courtyard, or through the doorway leading into the dining room, the interior's dark decor and furniture kept the room somber. To a girl of nine, the drawing room meant serious business made even more serious if mother or father happened to join Miss Clark in her moments of retribution.

On more occasions than I cared to remember, I'd demand my rights. "But Mamá," I'd argue, "you don't understand. I need to tell you what happened *myself* . . . "

I'd plead my right to explain myself, to come and go as I pleased, arguing as if I were a young lawyer in the making. Short of becoming disrespectful, I'd stamp my foot on the ground and resort to an arsenal of childish accusations, but my primary weapon was sarcasm, for which I discovered I had an intuitive talent.

Despite my noblest efforts, I received a penalty for my actions, which often meant that I was confined to my room or within the house and its immediate surroundings. Contrite, downcast eyes and pursed lips, I'd beg forgiveness, wiping my tear-streaked face and making promises to change my ways.

Afterwards, I'd reflect for hours on the incident in question, imagining that Mamá or Papá would realize the errors of their judgment and beg *me* to show them my mercy. I'd sometimes consider that there might possibly be two separate sprites, one contrary, the other docile, that lived side-by-side in my head. These mythical pixies engaged in a never-ending tug-o-war. They debated my every movement, smothering me in feelings of guilt whenever I displeased my elders.

I was home-schooled as were most of the girls in my social circles. When my parents engaged Miss Clark as a teacher, the Casanovas joined legions of other first families who enhanced their social standing by employing an English governess and showing they could afford to expose their children, daughters included, to some degree of formal schooling.

Miss Clark taught by rote, as that was the conventional method for education. She instructed me in the languages and literatures of the English and the French. I learned writing, geography and history, music, drawing, dancing and needlework, and spent an inordinate number of hours practicing the manners expected of my social class. I did not learn anything about Cuban history or literature, unless it was included in the study of Spain, which was rarely the case. That part of my learning came from my own observations and interests.

Because our governess subscribed to the latest English educational journals, she practiced the current trends. She was against "dulling the intellect" and open to the idea that boys' curriculum could be adopted for girls. And so she added modified calisthenics to our learning because girls, as much as boys, needed to build strong healthy bodies. A daily walk perfected our postures, and dancing gave us the beauty and grace that promised to enhance our appearance.

And yet, in spite of her progressiveness, I found I did not have the inclination, nor the compliant nature, to accept everything the *aya* taught without questioning her motives and challenging her ideas. Among the litany of "dos and don'ts" and "one must or one mustn't," a polished young lady of my era not only excelled in the art of fine needlework and intricate embroidery, she also mastered the domestic arts, performed religious duties and displayed lady-like temperaments—at all times! Instructed in singing and playing the piano, she was encouraged to appreciate classical music and literature but warned against losing her head over amorous tales.

So much of my so-called "formal" education was meant to transform me into an accomplished young woman that I soon became rebellious and cantankerous at the thought of it. What would I have given for an afternoon completely on my own, concealed in a secret alcove in the garden or shielded by blossoming bushes on the veranda without the benefit of intrusive siblings or a sad-eyed governess? There, I'd lose myself in my books, reading stories about a past chock full of larger-than-life women in history who then became my imaginary soulmates. I'd replay in my mind the stories of Joan of Arc, savior of the French monarchy, or Inés Suárez, *conquistadora* of Chile, imagining myself to be their loyal companion in arms. Above all else, my secret ambition was to take up a saber and defeat the enemy in the name of justice. These thoughts I shared with no one for fear that I'd be ridiculed.

Knowing that adventures awaited me at every turn, I'd find new ways to indulge in them that did not require subsequent "unruly Emilia conversations" with my elders. A clever and strong-willed girl in a large family where the younger children required more supervision than I, these circumstances encouraged me to search for opportunities of escape from home. And so early on, I learned to plot small, but effective, little jaunts. And like an inconspicuous little sparrow, I'd fly away from the nest to seek adventure.

Offering to run errands or entertain a young sibling for a few hours gave me time on my own, and no one added up the hours required for my voluntary services. Visiting a friend sometimes worked, but that required a servant, a sibling or an adult to accompany me. Helping in the kitchen was a blessing because inevitably someone would complain that I was less of a help and more of a hindrance, and I'd be forced to get out of the way and left to my own designs.

It was not unusual to find three large empty clay jugs lined up on the ground beside the courtyard cistern, where "unruly Emilia" had left them instead of bringing in water for the kitchen. Another concealed escape route, the carriage entrance near the *volante* and the stabled horses was often left wide opened during the day. But my favorite ploy was blending into a group of women on their way to market. That was ideal because no one seemed to notice that the small, curly-topped girl among the serving girls was not one of their own.

With neighborhood playmates I'd share imaginary games, plot mischief, run races chanting rhyming songs to pace myself the way I did with Sueño, or play at hiding. In these activities, I found it remarkably easy to act as a leader, to persuade my friends to join me in swimming races or other tests of ability. As girls were rarely allowed the chance to become the leaders, that gave me an enormous feeling of accomplishment. I felt a sense of pride which I attempted to suppress with false modesty, but that did not always work. The more daring the task I set for my followers, the more satisfaction I felt in its execution. In recalling this phase of my unusual "education," I've wondered to this day if that was not the training ground for the political activism of my later years.

Sooner or later, I'd return to our classroom, the pleasantly large alcove with a desk and six red calfskin, straight-backed chairs in the ground-level room reserved for father's accounting. While mentally deciphering the street sounds coming through the window in the room, I'd recite memorized English verbs. I'd ponder the good fortune of being a boy, whose education was markedly different from my own. Even my younger brothers, whom I envied, had an easier time of it. Young ladies, I reasoned, while spouting aloud the dreaded conjugations, were seldom permitted in public without a companion, but young men were encouraged, indeed expected, to leave home to study abroad in the United States or Europe. Often by themselves.

By the time I became an adolescent, young Cuban men had already been educated in American schools by the hundreds and were returning to Cárdenas with new customs and ideas shaped more by the American experience than by the Spanish. Young men became lawyers or engineers, studied medicine or were apprenticed to trusted mentors in the counting houses of major cities, like New York, where they learned to speak English fluently (without suffering conjugations) in preparation for managing the family business.

But young ladies were educated in preparation for a suitable marriage. Expectations to marry early and have many children set the prevailing criteria for a dutiful woman. Many of us, even those as rebellious as I, soon incorporated the mantra as our life's ambition. We would bear the children, nourish and raise them, teach them as we were taught, and pass on our class and cultural values. No one questioned the ebb and flow of this universal expectation, but I felt there had to be more than that in store for me.

When I reached my eleventh year, I could easily pass for fifteen. That was neither good nor bad as far as I was concerned, because girls naturally matured early in Cuba. What was of graver concern to me was that by the time we reached fifteen, we were considered to be marriageable. Even my most level-headed female friends learned, early on, to play up their domestic or artistic skills, coquettish ways and good postured appearances to attract the best suitors among the eligible young men.

As I blossomed from a child into a young woman, I found myself comfortable enough to turn away from my childhood pursuits, but not because I was drawn to the notion of marriage and family. Instead, I ached to march to the drumbeat of change associated with nationhood, abolition and liberation that was becoming more pronounced in my immediate social circles. My rebellious nature and love of freedom, my innate desire to live in a just world would find fitting outlets after all. I was certain of it.

As I grew into young womanhood, some among my friends and family believed I was attractive enough to find a husband. I was of medium stature and shapely form, attributes for which I credited my penchant for athletics. My friends admired my sable-colored eyes, light skin tone, long, wavy hair and my outgoing personality. "How interesting," I'd think to myself. "My friends take stock of my outward appearance but neglect to note my intellect, feelings, thoughts or ambitions. Haven't they learned that there is more to life than outward appearance?"

Aside from my sisters and brothers, who may have thought me to be plain and prudish, friends did like to spend time with me. Being young and carefree, I loved to dance, craved having fun at all sorts of social events, liked to pay visits and looked forward to group activities with my friends. But while I liked the company of young men, I was not ready to look for a husband, and none among my immediate circles interested me. Despite the eager prodding of girlfriends and family, I stood firm on my decision.

Looking back, I think I went out of my way *not* to attract male attention by flaunting my athletics and competitiveness. Never one to hide my intelligence, I loved a lively, articulate political discussion, while most of my female companions remained mute. Rejecting the notions of the period that women were helpless and witless, I went so far as to take on controversial issues that boiled my blood and stirred my spirit into action, like the abolition of slavery or the liberation of Cuba. Shock, disapproval, ridicule and oftentimes snickering were the ways some people reacted to my ideas. But rather than focusing on the negative, I felt emboldened to undertake greater preparation for the next debate. I refused to give in to the chorus of "poor Emilia, she is so misguided."

I believe that much of my supposedly progressive ways were also conditioned by the fact that I lived in a town on the cusp of modernity in the 1840s. The town led in the production of sugar at a time when the trade in Cuban sugar sweetened the profits of a world market. Cárdenas fostered thriving agricultural and fishing industries, and ships of every nation entered and left our harbor. It was known as the "American City," a center for international trade that encouraged numerous Americans to make their homes there, giving it a cosmopolitan flavor.

Besides the upper- and middle-class Spaniards and Creoles, there was already a growing population of free blacks and mulattos who excelled in the artisan trades. Artists, tailors, seamstresses, musicians and writers shared their colored community with urban laborers, carriage drivers, servants, messengers and vendors. I was exposed to a thriving diversity of talented people and occupations that allowed women of certain classes to emerge as entrepreneurs, especially among the mulatto and working classes. I glimpsed the possibilities for progress, if not the tensions among the races.

As an abolitionist, I was delighted when I read or overheard enlightened merchants discussing the merits of wage labor in opposition to slavery. The rail system that linked Cárdenas to Corral de la Bemba, a small town that would, in days to come, become the important railroad hub station, Jovellanos, was a sure sign of progress. Indentured Chinese had set the rails. For thirty British kilometers of track, the railroad connected the Villa of Cárdenas with the countryside, bringing opportunity and prosperity to the entire region. When I spoke with Americans about their impressions of Cárdenas and they compared our transportation facilities favorably to what existed in New York, I must admit, I took great pride in my town.

At the tender age of twelve, I did not pay particular attention to issues of public education because I was home schooled. I was too busy debating the merits of my homebound curriculum with my governess. But that was a time when the Villa began to explore public education for its young citizens. As a young woman, I could appreciate that this, too, was a sign of progress in our town not always available in other villages. The Villa established a number of primary and secondary schools, seven in all by the time that Cárdenas was given Villa status in 1853.

There were, to be sure, schools run by the Casa de Beneficencia or the Catholic Church in Havana and a few of the other large towns, but my country generally held a poor record when it came to educating its youth.

Charitable institutions did provide limited opportunities to learn a trade or develop skills for free blacks or mulattos and poor white boys and girls under the age of ten in urban areas. They learned to sew, cook, keep house or improve their manual skills so that they could become employable and not have to beg to make a living. But realistically, aside from the well-to-do, most young people simply did not go to school. They never learned to read or write and never had the freedom to express an opinion. In Cuba, the poor were almost as bad off as the slaves.

Part II
Cuba
(1842–1854)

Four

My Years of Discontent

A court marshal presided over by Brigadier Velasco, was yesterday held at the Real Carcel, and passed sentence on the prisoners Edward Facciolo, Juan Anastasio Romero, Antonio Bellido Luna, Florentino Torres, Juan Antonio Granados, Felix Maria Gasard, Antonio Palma, the lawyer Ramon Palma, Antonio Rubio, Ladislaz Urquizo and Idelfonso Estrada y Zenea, denounced by the mulatto Johnson as authors, printers and accomplices in the publication of the clandestine subversive paper, La Voz del Pueblo . . . .

"Threatening Aspects in Cuba."
New York Herald, September 21, 1852.

"**F**or a people to be free, they only have to truly want it," I'd repeat *ad nauseam*, arguing in favor of the underground liberation attempts cropping up throughout the country. We sat, all five of us, in the grapevine-shaded inner courtyard of our house. Surrounded by sweet-smelling orange and fig trees, we argued about politics and sipped cool drinks made from oranges, *guanábanas* and other ripe fruit of the season. For my brothers, José and Manuel, their childhood school friend, Alfredo Castellanos, his sister, Concepción and I, politics was the altruistic bond that drew us together, and we became close friends who guarded one another's secrets and political persuasions.

An avid and effective debater, I'd fetch my arsenal of facts to make my case, pointing to the smallest detail in the monumental deeds of Latin America's great liberator, Simón Bolívar, or his compatriate, Luisa de Arismendi, a woman who suffered torture and imprisonment under the Spanish in Venezuela. I'd call upon the glorious exploits of the Argentine leader of the army of the Southern Cone, José de San Martín and the brave *colombiana*, Policarpa Salavarrieta, the rebel spy and my personal inspiration. La Pola, for that was also her name, gave her life to the cause of independence before a firing squad with inspirational words. Melodramatically, I'd place my arm across my forehead and recite, "Although I am a woman and young, I have more than enough courage to suffer this death and a thousand more. Do not forget my example!"

"Seriously, without their leadership and enlightened ideas, without their unrelenting commitment to the cause of liberty, where would independence be in Latin America today? These heroes set attainable goals for their countries that we could easily set for ours," I'd argue, throwing my arms up in the air to make my point as I swaggered in my imagined imitation of a brave leader, and daring, just *daring* anyone to oppose me.

The stories of illustrious Latin American leaders spread like an unstoppable wildfire in conversations among my peers, in the letters we wrote to one another and within the circles of our families at the dinner tables. As young adults, we felt we had come into our own, wise and sophisticated; committed and intelligent enough to solve the problems, if not of the whole world, then certainly of Cuba.

The examples set by the Latin American patriots in our sister colonies became our religion, nourishing us with a burning love for Cuba that was all-embracing. Ever watchful for opportunities to serve the cause of freedom, we devoured the radical newspapers and journals for news of impending rebellions and liberation efforts. We exchanged subversive materials, shared verbal information about the insurgent leaders and counted the days until we were old enough to join them.

At first, these were merely brave words spoken without much action. The truth of the matter was that by mid-century we were living in a country alarmingly under siege. Fear and repression lurked everywhere, in every corner of every town, every village and countryside. The laws that governed us today changed tomorrow at the whim of the captain general, whomever he might be at any given moment. Newspapers that printed opinions contrary to government policies, or questioned the island's colonial status, were shut down from one day to the next. Laws prohibited assemblies of any kind, and the most enlightened among our Cuban intellectuals were incarcerated, exiled and sometimes executed. The best among our future leaders were not even to be found in Cuba. They were living in the United States or other countries, forced into voluntary exile.

In those days, I found myself in constant disagreements with my father over the state of affairs in Cuba. If I was to be kept by conventions of womanly behavior from doing so, I wanted him to take up the sword to defend our cause. But he was the most restrained, infuriating individual I'd ever met! In my young and immature eyes, he had become the epitome of arch conservatism. "Where was the forceful patriarch of my youth," I'd comment under my breath, "the leader and risk-taker, the champion of the enslaved?"

"But, Father." Our discussions, like the well-worn, iron rim of a carriage wheel, always followed in the same back and forth manner. Tossing a string of newspapers across his desk for added emphasis, I'd begin my argument. "If you want to form an intelligent opinion, you need to weigh both sides of the argument. For that, father, you cannot rely on the *Cárdenas Boletín Mercantil*, or that Havana paper, *El Diario de la Marina*. You need to read *La Verdad*, the newspaper for independence I told you about, the one published in New York and smuggled into Cuba. Or read the so-called treasonous literature of our ever-growing exiles who now write from New York, or Boston, or Philadelphia, or New Orleans."

I would set *La Verdad* where he could easily see it whenever it came into my hands. He would come home from his travels or after visiting the plantations and glance at the paper, but he would not pick it up and read it. Its headlines never became the topics of our conversation and, when I would refer to an article or a commentary in the paper, he would simply respond, "Now, Emilita . . ." and proceed to caution me to show restraint, fearful that my youthful impertinence would be discovered outside the walls of our family compound. Intent on not raising the ire of those individuals who wielded the power in town or state government, he managed to maintain a low profile. A very low, unremarkable profile, in my opinion.

He would never speak out against the government and, except for the fact that he'd free the children born to our slaves, my father's compliant nature did not change. I would not realize until many years later that his impeccable reputation as supporter of the status quo was the thin shield that stood between the colonial government and the Casanovas.

"If only our blind country would shake itself from its long slumber to awaken freedom and glory." I'd recite José de Heredia's words dramatically, my personal rendition of his poem, *To Emilia*, pretending it had been written for me. But the sobering thoughts behind his words, the exile's lament for his lost country, shattered my heart into a thousand pieces and blanketed my spirit with an unrelenting dark cloud of desolation. And for an impatient young woman such as I, there was no indication of the slightest change on the horizon.

My brothers and I personally knew of friends and acquaintances who were tortured and incarcerated because of their political beliefs. They were imprisoned in the dreaded Spanish fortress in Ceuta in North Africa. Known for its harsh treatment and impenetrable fortifications, its name alone struck fear in the hearts of those accused of crimes, if not in those about to commit one. The political prisoners were abused, starved and chained in forced prison labor gangs, and their families never knew if they were dead or alive.

As José, Manuel and I secretly supported Cuban independence from Spain, we did what we could to help our imprisoned friends. At one point, I wrote to them in Ceuta but never knew if any of my letters were received. I mounted a fund-raising campaign among our family members to raise money for the Cuban political prisoners, not knowing whether or not they would actually receive the funds. You see, it all depended on whom you knew and could be trusted to deliver the messages, monies or goods. Given the undercurrent of unrest, bribes were hard to resist, and you never knew if and when your own name would appear on a government roster of suspected traitors.

Believe me, in those days I was not näive despite my youth. Accepting the discord within my own home and my lack of power to bring about any sort of change, I immersed myself in serious study of the issues that brought our country to such a disastrous state. Anxious to make sense of what was happening in Cuba, I created a comfortable setting for reading and contemplation. Away from the family in the quiet solitude of my bedroom, I reclined on the yellow cushioned bench beneath the balustrade window, where I first saw the flag of liberation. Every chance I had, I retraced the experiences of my past and contemplated the ways that justice could prevail.

I'd recall ordinary scenes that in my youth had not been burdened with political implications. On the few occasions, for example, when my brothers and I ran errands for father along the wharves, the stench of rotted flesh and human waste often reached us before we actually saw the slave ships at anchor. I remember the cargo holds thrown open to the air, filled with less than half of the hundreds of Africans initially captured from the dark continent. Sailors brought up rows of shackled Negroes on deck, poured buckets of salt water over their emaciated bodies, carelessly stinging the festering open wounds beneath their restraints, in order to rinse off the filth of their bodies to make them presentable for auction. The overwhelming stink hung heavy in the humid air.

"Bundles, they call them," my brother Manuel had said with a sneer. "Not Africans, not black people and certainly not poor souls, but bundles like piles of wood or tobacco. Would that the English had a thousand more ships to block these slave vessels on the high seas, and that Cuban merchants were cursed instead of rewarded each time a slaver made it to port."

I sat frozen still in the carriage, my arms crossed tightly across my chest, and stared at the tragic scene unfolding before me but could not blink nor tear my eyes away from it.

At sixteen I had become father's assistant in matters relating to the household. I kept accounts of what was needed and allocated a budget for purchases. On days when we worked together in his study, we'd calmly discuss political matters, exchanging ideas and learning from one another in a civilized manner.

"What strikes fear in the hearts of those who support the Spanish authorities today," I'd say to Papá as I recorded figures into the accounting books, "was first fueled by that revolt in Haiti. You remember it? It ended slavery and colonialism and transformed the country into a free black republic. That rebellion almost on our own doorstep helped pave the way for wars of independence in Latin America . . . left Spain with the two colonies in the hemisphere: Cuba and our sister island Puerto Rico."

"Don't forget, Emilia, other examples like the north American Revolution. That war, and the one in France, stressed brotherhood and equality. In time, rebellions began to spark like fireworks out of control right here, in Cuba, out in the open, until they became too large for the Spanish authorities to contain. In 1841, and again in 1842, you were just an inquisitive girl more interested in your horse, Sueño. That was when rebellious slaves set the cane fields aflame, burning them to a crisp in anticipation that mass conflagration would become contagious and ignite the spirits of fellow slaves to join in the fight for justice."

As young as I was, I did remember. Many of the rebels escaped into the mountains, but captured slaves were so cruelly punished that just glancing at the articles about the situation in *El Diario de la Marina* sent shivers up my spine. I paused, momentarily closing my eyes to consider this long panorama of madness in all of its inhumanity. I could not really grasp how it all happened, but a sense of pride in the people fighting for their own salvation mixed with fear sent shudders throughout my body.

"To set examples!" I whispered in a low tone. "Imagine that, just to set examples for the rest," and I tried desperately to dismiss a mental image of our faithful slaves and workers in such a human hell.

"I can understand why the planters are frightened to the core," I told my father nonchalantly, speaking calmly to avoid an argument. "A number of Cuban families in our region are of French origin. They witnessed the Haitian Revolution firsthand. That horror must have shattered their comfortable world, for it left them to barely escape with the clothes on their backs."

"The planters worry that Cuba *could* become another Haiti, Emilita, you must understand that . . . where rebel slaves succeeded in overthrowing their white masters, because, as you well know, our enslaved population already outnumbers the whites and has for some time."

"But, Father!" I found myself breathing faster, my heart beginning to pound in my chest. "You, of all people, must agree that our measures to avoid the Haitian experience are inhumane. Without thinking twice, those planters imposed the severest punishments imaginable. Under lock and key, they kept men, women and children captive in their barracks every night, ordered unwarranted whippings, cut their food reserves, mutilated their bodies and engaged in unspeakable kinds of maltreatment. Father, you just cannot condone that behavior!"

Father did not respond, his lips sealed in a straight line unwilling to brook a word. But I sensed, or rather I hoped, he was considering my point of view.

I reasoned to myself, it all comes down to whether or not the planters acknowledge the humanity of the enslaved people. Slave owners delude themselves by thinking the slaves have neither human feelings nor spiritual souls; they are animals, the Cubans rationalize, and therefore inferior to white men and women. This is probably why they dread intermingling among the races, even though the mulatto population is proof that it frequently takes place. And the white people think the slaves cannot possibly feel or suffer in the same way that they do.

There is no doubt that money is a basic component in this game, I mused, focusing on the tallies on the pages of the heavy ledgers. The planters are the wealthiest in our country, and therefore the group that has the most to lose. A fleeting image of my own father came to mind. "But he is not like the rest," I whispered under my breath and quickly glanced up at his kindly face and discarded the suggestion of depravity in my dear father.

"If the planters worry that an alliance of black slaves and Creoles could easily overpower them, why don't they consider abolishing the system," I asked. "The trade in slaves has already been abolished in other enlightened societies throughout the world, like England, and yet business continues to profit because they pay their workers decent wages. At least I imagine they are paid decent wages.

"Do the planters not believe," I continued, "in the teachings of the church? Do they not believe that it is against Christian principles for one individual to own another? To their way of thinking, this institution of slavery must be protected at all cost. Rather than considering Christian teachings, the planters have come to believe the cure for their maddening dilemma is clear cut. Their salvation is annexation to the United States, a stronger, slaveholding nation that can offer protection. If you ask me, annexation is just another form of subjugation; it does not hold a candle to freedom, and I, for one, will never support it."

"Emilia," my father responded as he calculated, pen in hand, the last sheet of expenses for the plantations in the countryside. "You will understand, in time, that the planters must have the workers to make the land productive. It is our livelihood. Some argue that England had no right to abolish the slave trade for all countries."

I knew from my readings that the United States of America had tried, on several occasions in the past, to buy Cuba from Spain. Cuban and American merchants seemed to be favorably disposed to such a purchase. For the Americans, Cuba was to be a market for unloading their goods. I knew American expansionists believed the destiny of the United States was to extend its borders from the Atlantic Ocean to the Pacific. It was called their "Manifest Destiny." Speculators hoping to increase their wealth from Cuban exports also supported the idea. In fact, some slaveholders in the U.S. felt that Cuba would be a welcome addition to their roster of slave states, increasing the number of representatives in their congress based on their common interests.

I recalled that in 1844 all the talk among the merchants, including my father, was about yet another major conspiracy, and this one was perhaps the most threatening of all. Everyone felt the impact of what the authorities feared the most: some fifty to sixty Creoles, working together with free and enslaved Afro-Cubans, plotting to overthrow the Spanish government. Until now, most uprisings originated either from the Creole sector or from slaves, but this time, both groups saw the mutual benefits of uniting with one another.

The Spaniards called it the Conspiracy of the Ladder because dissidents were tied to a ladder, whipped and tortured. The authorities took great pride in that the rebellion was quickly suppressed. It was in all the newspapers. But in my opinion, the downfall of Spanish colonial rule began right then and there, with the Conspiracy. This time, their actions backfired. Instead of gaining approval for their actions, the government brought about sympathy for the rebel cause. Although they may not have won this battle, the Creoles had won the hearts of the people.

As had become our practice, Father and I continued to work together on household accounts, gradually beginning to respect one another's point of view. Once, when my brother, Manuel, unexpectedly entered the room looking for the figures of one of the plantations, I noticed, perhaps for the first time, how mature he had become. Old enough, I thought, for rebellion! I began to feel that recent uprisings were finally on the right track, that changes were on the horizon after all.

I think, as I look back, it was that knowledge that gave me the courage not to abandon my beliefs and, for the first time in a very long time, I felt my spirit come alive. I remember needing to feel close to my father, to perhaps make amends for the many disagreements we had encountered with one another. I crossed the room and sat beside him, opening an overlooked ledger to record recent purchases. I studied my beloved father's serious expression and smiled as he leaned over and pointed to a figure I'd entered incorrectly in my ledger. It was to be a beautiful day, after all.

Five
A Flag Waves Over Cárdenas

"My death will not change the destiny of Cuba."
General Narciso López, September 1, 1851.

It had been four nights in a row that I dreamt about the flag. This was a recurring, frustrating dream where the annexationists always left Cárdenas without declaring victory over the Spanish army. But in this dream, I was determined to change the ending. López's army would finally triumph! I was again a beautiful, floating guardian angel, dressed in a shimmering gossamer gown, not unlike the many stars I could see in the jet black night sky above me. I hovered weightlessly over the battle scene and could see for miles around, even into the tiniest recesses of the buildings surrounding the Plaza Mayor. Shivering ever so slightly at the coolness of the pre-dawn dew upon my bare arms, I strained to hear the cock crow, because I knew . . . somehow I knew that when the rooster crowed twice, the invasion would then be well on its way.

At first, the general's men resembled tiny specks, like red ants climbing laboriously up the slippery side of a hill. Moving ever so slowly in a ponderous, languid fashion, they inched toward the railroad yard, filling the Plaza Mayor and then gliding up the right hand side of Calle Real. There they became rugged-looking Americans clad in red shirts, their beards sharply defined in the blush of the dawn light.

I knew all about them, could recall the names, ranks and nationality of each of the officers. I must have read about them in the newspapers, I reasoned in my angel mind. In the same mysterious way, I knew all about the sacred silk banner, the emblem of liberation they carried; I knew it had been stitched together by the *criollas* of New Orleans and presented to the Louisiana regiment just before the invasion.

What I could not grasp in my sleep-induced state was how to encourage this irregular army of Cuban and American mercenaries. They were willing to violate their nation's neutrality laws to liberate Cuba, so why would they leave without claiming their victory? I wanted to swoop down and stop them, lift them up by the handfuls, but was unable to move my arms and legs. I soon awoke, trapped in a swirl of bed linen, my heart pounding wildly in my chest. In a momentary flashback, I remembered a title from my dream. It appeared to be emblazoned on the brown leather binding of a book carried by one of the American officers. In bold red letters it read: *A Flag Waves Over Cárdenas.*

Since the day I first saw the flag of liberation fly over the Capitular House, I was reborn a revolutionary. My life led me in new directions and nothing but independence would temper the passion to right injustice that burned in my heart like a new religion. When our beloved General Narciso López and his army mounted assaults in Trinidad and Cienfuegos in 1848, the story was carried like raging flood waters, far and wide, pouring into every nook and cranny of the island before the year came to an end.

Everyone was talking about the charismatic General López, whose words were committed to memory among his most ardent supporters. The general's proclamation of 1850 " . . . to do for your Cuban brothers what a Lafayette, a Steuben, a Kosciusko and a Pulaski . . . " have done for your country, encouraged me beyond belief because it meant that the Cuban struggle had now garnered American support.

Fresh from the war between Mexico and the United States that ended in 1848, and hungry for the wealth found in California's gold mines discovered the following year, veterans responded eagerly to López's offers. A private's pay, rations and five acres of land, as López stressed in his recruitment documents: "gold already dug and coined for which you fight."

And I *personally* witnessed the siege of Cárdenas led by López and his army of 610 mercenaries! Their Jennings rifles and other modern weaponry in firing positions, they were a force to contend with, quickly defeating the Spanish soldiers from the garrison right close to my home. Engaging the enemy, the López-led forces succeeded in taking over the Capitular House, headquarters of the lieutenant governor, setting it on fire and virtually holding the city in rebel hands. I saw all this from my bedroom window on the second story of our large stone home in Cárdenas.

As day crept into night, close to a hundred Spanish soldiers and forty Americans lay dead. The townspeople supposed to leave their homes and joyfully support the uprising failed to do so. Many did, in fact, run off to outlying areas while others sought refuge in the cellars of their homes. My family remained in our home and I fully believe father would have given his help to anyone who needed it, be they Spaniard or mercenary. As evening approached, the general and his army abandoned the city altogether and returned to their ship, the *Creole*. They retreated just in time to avert engagement with a regiment of the King's Lancers on its way from a neighboring town.

Eight days before the Cuban flag of liberation flew over Cárdenas, its sister image flew over New York City. I was elated to read newspaper accounts about New Yorkers who awoke that morning to see the strange banner waving on high from on top of the *New York Sun* building on the corner of Nassau and Fulton streets in lower Manhattan. The *New York Sun's* owner, Moses J. Beach, and Jane Cazneau, a writer for the *New York Sun* and editor of the pro-annexation newspaper, *La Verdad,* staunchly supported the annexationist movement. They believed Cuba should and would one day become part of the United States. Hoisting the liberation banner was the signal for a small group of Cuban exiles to begin a march, accompanied by a band of musicians, through the main thoroughfares of the city. This was Moses and Cazneau's bold statement: the time had come to wrest Cuba from Spanish hands even if it took military force to do it.

On the first day of September 1851, atop a ten-foot scaffold in Havana's central plaza, General Narciso López was garroted to death. When I heard the news, the blood in my veins ran cold.

Six

Forced to Flee

*"Countrymen, I most solemnly in this last awful moment of my
life, ask your pardon for any injury I have caused you. It was not
my wish to injure anyone, my object was your freedom and
happiness . . . my intention was good, and my hope is in God."*
    Lopez died instantly without the least struggle.

"Monthly Record of Current Events."
Harper's Magazine, October, 1851.

We were now caught in a web of tightening government control and increased repression. Our leaders and young intellectuals were forced into exile. Restraints were placed on what we
could do and say in public, and we feared being branded as traitors.
In the seclusion of my chambers, my thoughts flitting from one
thing to the next, I suddenly realized, just how much anger and
hostility I felt toward the Spanish authorities—not all Spaniards,
you understand, just those who perpetuated injustice against our
citizens. Lately, even the strains of adored Spanish favorites played
with gusto at the Philharmonic made my blood boil.

Nothing seemed to tweak my interest. Not the current fashions, nor books, nor public events, not even the opera, which I'd
always loved. Not even afternoon rides in the *volante*. Everything
made me nervous to think of the precious time it took when I
needed to do other things. But what those other things were, I

could not say. Weekend balls featuring the finest musicians bored me to tears. My loving friends, resplendent in their gowns and the cornucopias of feasts of fish and fowl, soups, sauces and sweetmeats, served at the stroke of midnight by an army of slaves and domestics, seemed to me a colossal waste of time. Those amusements I lay away with the rest of my innocence.

For some time now, I had decided to wait no longer to put my feelings into action by openly declaring my defiance of the Spanish authorities. "*Cuidado*, Emilia, *cuidadito*. Proceed with caution," I'd repeated over and over to myself. Others had begun to notice my expressive disdain of all things Spanish. Officials in our local government and others were beginning to whisper behind closed doors about Don Inocencio Casanova's contrary daughter. Not to be taken lightly, I understood that any sign of disrespect to officials and administrators could be cause for confiscating one's properties or worse, sending one into exile and their relatives left to rot in shame and shambles.

One special evening in October, I dressed for a *soirée*, a victory banquet given in the home of the lieutenant governor. Except for the sounds of the crickets and the occasional bullfrog, the house was unusually still. Only the rustling of my off-the-shoulder, white, full-skirted satin gown whispered softly with every move I made. Adding the finishing touches to my hair, which I had arranged in a swirl of curls that cascaded down the back of my neck, I knew that its dark hues contrasted nicely with the creamy shades of my gown sashed by a band of soft blue. Except for the small scowl of annoyance that I found difficult to get rid of, I also knew I'd attract the attention I wanted this evening. Pleased with myself, I looked every inch a lady. An adult look and an adult demeanor. And now, I was totally prepared to face the evening that lay ahead.

As I prepared to join my father, who'd grown tired of waiting for me at the foot of the stairs in the lower vestibule, I suddenly thought of the flag: that glorious flag, my joyous moment of patriotic awakening. I raised my gaze to the spot outside the window where it had flown and vowed in my heart to wait no longer.

The banquet was very special because the new governor of Cuba, Don Manuel Fortún, was to be in attendance. I was no stranger to such affairs, having attended dozens of balls among my intimate circle of family and friends, but this night it was just to be my father and me who represented the Casanova family. Before stepping up into the *volante*, father turned and offered his hand to help me step up to the carriage. His face held the strangest look as he sadly sighed, "Emilita, my dear . . . please do not say or do anything obnoxious that might be construed as imprudent behavior."

I took a sharp breath. Had he guessed my secret thoughts?

The Spanish officials, be they civil servants or crown appointees, loved to celebrate their victories, flaunting military prowess with pomp and extravagance, showing off their sumptuous dwellings, fine crystal, elegant furnishings and other luxuries. Such occasions served another purpose as well. They were a constant reminder to the invited Creole guests of who really wielded the power in Cuban society.

That evening, there was a great deal of talk about crushing slave uprisings; fear would be struck into the hearts of any upstart Creoles or Negroes who might be lurking within earshot. Officers congratulated one another on the execution of General Narciso López that September, as if they had personally tightened the garrote around his neck. They patted each other on their backs, and uproarious laughter could be heard coming from their small clusters.

The celebration vibrated with music, dancing, the clinking of wine glasses and undulating waves of conversation as the evening wore on. It had rained that afternoon and several hours into the festivities the anemically drifting breezes on the veranda could no longer contain the oppressive humidity. I became aware of the many sounds surrounding me. The neighing of horses hitched to the carriages outside of the mansion; the stomping of military boots as couples quick-stepped to the fast-paced music; the click, click, clicking of the pearl and ivory handled fans of the ladies who sat on porch rockers trying to catch the last bits of the evening's coolness. Their fans seemed to quicken as if paving the way for the highlight of the evening. And I murmured under my breath, "Well, Emilia, let the game begin."

The hour arrived to toast the Spanish hosts and a multitude of *¡qué vivas!* and *¡Brindis!* and other similar cheers filled the air. One after the other, Spanish victories over insurgent uprisings and the good health of all those present were celebrated until I thought they would never end. And suddenly, there was a short lull in the good wishes . . . and without a moment's hesitation, I took center stage, raising my own glass in a toast. All eyes were drawn to me, but I pointedly stared at the one Spanish officer who happened to be facing me, as if he were the incarnation of corrupt Spain.

"I toast for the liberty of the world," I proclaimed in a firm, fearless voice. I felt, but did not see, the crowd growing uneasily quiet around me and in the stillness of the moment, my sainted father, poor dear, audibly held his breath, " . . . and what is more, I toast for the liberty of Cuba!"

In one brief moment, my world as I knew it, came crashing down. My shocking, outspoken behavior brought the evening to an abrupt end as frenzied guests rushed to assure the governor and his officials of their loyalty. News of my outrageous behavior spread like a raging inferno coming out of the bowels of the earth. Friends and acquaintances stood ready to condemn me to whatever punishment the authorities saw fit for such treasonous disloyalty. My innocent family, my one regret, experienced the first signs of social rejection from those they had long considered friends and allies.

I was told that my tender age, sex and the high esteem accorded to my father saved me from severe punishment that night, for in those times of indiscriminate repression even comments from well-bred young ladies could provide the tinder for revolution.

My so-called "madness" tainted the entire family, which was now regarded as suspect, antagonistic to the Spanish presence, despite my father's sincerest apologies and proven record of loyalty. The Casanovas were shunned, ostracized from social and political circles. My father seemed to age overnight, his long beard growing whiter than ever. But it was the sadness in his eyes that most frightened me. Fully at the end of his patience, he begged me to recant, but I could not; I would not. . . . As a result, I was virtually sentenced to remain in my room, a captive under my own roof or on Casanova property for almost a year, for fear that another such outburst would end in calamity. Instead of feeling remorse, now more than ever before I was committed heart and soul to liberation: the cause of *Cuba Libre*. It was too late for me to turn back.

In an attempt to alleviate the situation and because there was no doubt that he loved me very much, father reduced my domestic restriction and decided we would take an extended voyage. He planned to enroll me in an American boarding school to complete my education. Along with my oldest brothers, José and Manuel, we would leave for New York City in the summer of 1852. Arranging a series of visits to historic places in various American cities, my father hoped that he could, once and for all, wipe the toxic topic of liberation from my mind. After what I considered semi-incarceration, I probably would have left Cárdenas for Calcutta or any other place in the far reaches of the earth. That did not mean I learned to tolerate life under scrutiny any better.

"Would the wise Don Inocencio Casanova take his liberal-minded offspring to visit New York City if he knew it was a hotbed of radical Cuban politics?" I'd question sarcastically within hearing distance of my parents and brothers. "Or did he plan this trip *precisely* because New York, as well as Philadelphia and other places in the north, are centers of Cuban expatriate communities? There, heaven knows," I'd intone annoyingly, "American freedoms would protect them to safely express their opinions about Cuban repression. . . . "

No one responded, choosing to ignore my provocative games. But while such utterances frightened Mamá, the rest of the family remained at ease, quietly ignoring my sarcasm, which they attributed to boredom. Interestingly, I thought, in such an atmosphere as New York's, I would find the safe haven that I did not have in Cuba. A father could protect a daughter in ways he could not in his own homeland.

It didn't take very long to answer my obnoxious questions. It came, unsurprisingly, in bits of conversation related to the upcoming trip. Comparing the political environment in our country with what we could expect to find in America, father revealed himself to harbor his own wishes for Cuban liberation. He sternly opposed the monarchy, he said. Shrewd in matters of domestic and international business, he noted that politics and economics shaped nations. However, as a man who abided by the law of the land in which he lived, he would never actively conspire against Spain in Cuba unless he or his family were threatened, as we were at that very moment. He did not, in any way, believe in government by repression.

"Everyone," he said, "is entitled to justice and freedom of expression, both of which have been grossly abused by the current regime in Cuba."

My father believed in hastening the abolition of slavery, even though he was the master of many slaves. On our family estates, it was well-known that he granted liberty to all new-born children of slaves, but I did not realize that, at one point, he had devised a plan to gradually free all enslaved people throughout Cuba. Although the plan was presented to the liberal-minded Captain

General Serrano, it failed to gain momentum, largely because of the opposition of the powerful planter class. Cuba was, after all, a colony whose wealth derived from sugar, and sugar production rested on the sweat of captive or indentured labor, the African and the Chinese. Even our progressive rail system would not have been possible without the controlled labor of the Chinese.

Well, I thought, I guess we were all in the same predicament. Father was a covert republican, my brothers openly supported the liberation movement and I was now, according to the prevailing wisdom, in the camp of the revolutionaries. It became clear to me that from the time we were infants, the Casanova offspring had slowly been absorbing many of our father's liberal points of views. Ironically, it was a double endowment; we received silent messages from our parents but we assumed that we had come to discover them completely on our own. There was no doubt about it: These tough acorns were definitely the ones intended to have fallen from that parental tree.

Part III

New York City

(1852–1871)

Seven

A Gathering of Exiles

While she [Cuba] remained uncultivated, depopulated and poor she suffered all that it is possible for men to suffer from ignorance and misery. By-and-by she reached a certain state of civilization and aggrandizement by which she learned her rights and her strength and aspired to independence.

. . . The undersigned contend that they have deserved the confidence . . . and that they are sufficiently authorised to represent, sustain, promote and carry on to a successful termination the interests and views of their revolution.

Gaspar Betancourt Cisneros, President; Mantel de J. Arango, Vice President; Porfirio Valiente, Secretary; Domingo de Goicouría, Treasurer.

"Cuban Affairs." Manifesto of the Cuban Junta.
The New York Times, October 20, 1852.

"Everything is in perfect order," I assured my overly con-cerned father. Within three days' time my devoted Papá and brothers, Manuel and José, would be in Cuba after having left me and my serving girl, a thirteen-year-old *mulata*, all alone to fend for ourselves in New York City.

We had spent an entire glorious summer attending concerts at Castle Gardens, viewing the work of new artists at the American Art Union and visiting public parks, such as Brooklyn's Greenwood with its array of lakes and monuments. Friends opened their doors to us and took us on tours of historical sites, but we had reached the point to prepare for my family's return to Cuba. My father asked again if everything was ready, and I responded, "Yes, Father, for the hundredth time, it is."

Running through my mental list, I enumerated the tasks at hand. The boarding school selected, check; funds converted, check; residence secured, check; and a wardrobe of fashionable dresses designed to my specifications, check. "All that is missing," I beamed at Papá and my brothers, "is a hint of autumn in the air to herald the beginning of a new academic year, and I can't do anything about that." I gave a nervous laugh that I hoped would ease everyone's anxiety, especially my own.

"I will surely miss this family," I muttered more to myself than out loud as I handed father and my brothers last minute trinkets to place into their valises. The books were meant for the younger children, handkerchiefs and accessories for the older. Mamá would get the jewelry and the girls would receive the colorful ribbons. Diligently, I wrote their names on the gift cards, each name bringing to mind a vivid image of an individual sibling, his or her distinct personality traits intact. I wondered how I'd ever adjust to life without their noisy playfulness and incessant chatter. My younger siblings, I decided as my eyes misted over with affection, brought so much joy into our home. They embraced life with all of its contradictions.

The plan was simple. I would remain in the city for a short spell before classes began to accustom my ear to the harshness of spoken English. Although I'd studied the language in Cuba with my English governess, it sounded completely different as spoken in New York. Slightly nervous at the thought of my new situation, I calmed the flutters in my stomach by focusing intensely on the impressive wonders I'd had the good fortune to visit on this trip.

I remembered my initial reactions to the progressiveness of American cities like New York that raised beautiful, costly monuments to honor their revolutionaries and the sense of freedom that seemed to infuse the very air you breathed. Niagara Falls, the roaring cataracts dividing Canada and America and Saratoga Springs, known for its curative mineral waters, impressed me with their majestic beauty and natural wonders. But the fast-paced, clipped hustle and bustle of congested city life in New York quickened my pulse with its unbounded energy, noise and electricity.

Just to walk the streets was a marvelous feat. In this city teeming with immigrants from all over the world, it was a wondrous sight to behold, to smell and taste exotic foods, remnants of an old world culture, even as these new Americans embraced the strange language and customs. The city exuded an air of progress so strong that I could almost feel it seeping into my very being. A walk along the wharves to catch a breath of cool air was a feast for the eyes as clippers from as far away as China, steamers or barques from South American ports and packets, brigs and other vessels flew a veritable circus of colorful flags of all nations.

Every day these vessels brought new people and goods to this city. In turn, imported commodities, including Cuban sugar and cigars, found eager buyers beyond the Hudson through a network of roads, rail and waterways. It seemed that everything came to and left from New York City. An account in *The New York Times* about a new carrier service, Wells Fargo & Company, announced plans to deliver mail, packages and freight across the country, connecting New York to California. "Now that," I thought, "was truly the height of an impressive network of communication." Imagine the time and expense merchants would save by not having to sail around the tip of South America! Oh! I was *completely* in love with this city!

But there was an even stronger reason why New York City quickened my pulse. Like Philadelphia and New Orleans, the city offered safe haven for expatriates: political exiles, dissidents and insurgent intellectuals from the Latin American republics, from

Cuba and Puerto Rico, forced, by necessity, to seek asylum in this country.

As I discovered an array of boarding houses and barber shops catering to Spanish-speaking people, I began to identify the Caribbean presence in the city. Every now and then I'd pass the open doors of a cigar factory and hear *lectores* reading aloud in Spanish from newspapers or giving dramatic readings of novels translated into the language. It was said, and I tended to agree with the observation, that cigar workers were among the most liberal and enlightened within the working class because they were exposed to such a wide variety of ideas. This custom of reading out loud to men and women working on the various stages of making cigars might be a tradition only among Cuban and Puerto Rican cigar workers because I did not think other cultures followed the custom.

My brother, Manuel, became my cheerful and trustworthy companion for brisk walks along the city streets, congested as they often were, and sometimes we braved exploration of the rough and tumble, seedy sections of the waterfront or even less desirable streets not suitable for visits by ladies. Bundled up in my crimson cloak against the first nips of autumn winds, I was surprised to find Spanish-owned boarding houses tucked amidst dark alleys, on narrow streets or right on the waterfront, that advertised room and board for seamen. But many of the merchants and their families, Manuel informed me, lived in lower Manhattan or in the city of Brooklyn not far from the docks. Popular boarding houses for Spanish-speaking people were found in Chelsea, on W. 14th or 15th streets, or Greenwich Village, on Waverly Place; others frequented a boarding house on West 29th Street. The prankster among all my brothers, Manuel comically mimicked my look of surprise when I marveled at the large population of compatriots who lived in this city. I was even more surprised to learn that a merchants' association, the Sociedad Benéfica Cubana y Puertorriqueña, had opened its doors as early as 1830 to offer services, information and, I suspect, much sought after fraternity.

Enthralled by the multitude of book stores and their related publishing houses that seemed to be cropping up all over the city, I'd learned it was the center for Spanish-language publishing of all sorts of materials: prose and poetry, pamphlets, children's story books, religious tracts, primers and of course newspapers that found an eager readership both here and abroad. And, imagine that, no one was waiting to denounce their actions or beliefs, to ban their books because their ideas might challenge the current system of government. Presses weren't shut down on a whim, and people were not under constant surveillance. I couldn't help but compare how restorative life in New York was in those days for our insurgents, in contrast to the widespread, arbitrary oppression they faced in Cuba.

On occasion, when I'd accompany father to a business-related social event, I'd have opportunities to converse with some of the *viejitos,* the old-timers. Well-known among the city's merchant circles, they traded in sugar, rum and molasses or imported prized Cuban cigars with all the relevant paraphernalia: cigar boxes, cigar bands and the artwork long associated with the trade.

Sporting a Havana in one hand and a glass of rum in the other, they would compete with one another to tell me fabulous fables of bygone days, about the earliest Cubans to make the city their home. Stories about the famous and infamous, scandals, tragedies and daily struggles encountered in an unfamiliar city were not only grist for the anecdotal mill, but stories meant to impress me.

"Some Cubans," a jovial, bearded merchant from Oriente told me, "came as apprentices to the counting houses, or to work in merchant house affiliates. They came to learn the trade of their fathers, you understand, and to become fluent in the English language. Others desired an education, sought matriculation in the colleges like St. Joseph's. But quite a few, you see, were fleeing Spanish justice because, if you remember, the Creoles favored progressive ideas, like free trade and abolition. You probably don't know," they'd address me as if I were an uninformed school girl, "the first newspaper to call for Cuban independence was *El Habanero*. Two or three sheets of tiny print . . . I remember how difficult it was to read it when the print blurred or the paper fell victim to rain. It was published in Philadelphia around 1823, but later, in New York City. That newspaper was the genius invention of the great abolitionist, Félix Varela."

Of course, I knew all about the expatriate hero, Father Félix Varela. Even as a child, I had heard his name, for he was frequently praised as one of the best educators at San Carlos Seminary in Havana. Father Varela advocated for Cuban independence and abolition. I knew he represented Cuba in the Spanish parliament but I knew *nothing* about his role in the United States as an ordained clergyman!

He struggled alongside a handful of Catholic prelates to establish churches and schools for the predominantly Catholic Irish immigrants who had fled the devastation of the potato famine. Varela founded the city's fourth parish, Christ Church, on a vacant lot belonging to Trinity Church in 1827. Surprisingly, this remarkable man was as much a figure in New York's history as he was in Cuba's.

Added to the series of curious happenings I'd already experienced in New York, on the eve of my father's departure he received an unsettling letter from my mother. I was afraid that someone had fallen ill or worse, and also that our plans would be altered. Father read the letter to us, and I became more deeply troubled. My mother wrote that she missed me terribly. She longed to be with her first-born once again, the one closest to her heart. I could understand Mamá's desire for my companionship, since my sister, Cecilia, the next female after me, was merely a twelve-year-old girl. It was now safe for Emilita to return home, mother wrote, as the gossip about her political tendencies had died down. And as for that incident of the toast, well, mother assured my father, it was hardly remembered by anybody anymore.

My hands trembled as I picked up mother's letter to read it for myself a second time. It was difficult to remain calm. My throat constricted, and tears welled up in my eyes preparing to spill down my cheeks. Trying to focus rationally on my mother's depressed state, I began to fear the worse. Was there something she was not telling us? Right then, I'd decided to return to Cuba with my brothers and father. Father did not argue against my decision and proceeded to cancel my arrangements. To make sure the situation was as safe as mother described, father requested written guarantees for my safety from the Spanish Consulate in New York.

When I recall this episode in my life, I'm reminded of the old saying, "*no hay mal que por bien no venga*"—there is no misfortune that doesn't bring some good with it. While we waited for the official documents guaranteeing my safety, there was one more thing I wanted to do before I left New York. I had read an article entitled "The Manifesto of the Cuban Junta" printed in *The New York Times* on October 12, 1852. The article lauded the brave deeds of General Narciso López and recalled with absolute praise his planting the flag of liberation at Cárdenas. At the mention of both the flag and General López, I felt the article was intended directly for me. How could I have possibly felt otherwise?

"Cuba desires to be free," wrote the organizers. "She has manifested this desire conclusively, and she repeats it now through our voice." The Junta's goal, they reported, was to spread their political ideology far and wide, casting an expansive net to gain as many converts as possible. Through a proliferation of flyers, pamphlets, newspapers and broadsides, they hoped to win supporters to the cause of *Cuba Libre* from both Cubans and Americans. They had, without expending a great deal of language on the subject, already won my full support.

The Junta Cubana's treasurer, Domingo de Goicouría Cabrera, was an old family friend. A wealthy Cuban known for his liberal positions, he was also known as a staunch supporter of General López, generously financing the latter's expeditions to free Cuba. Using this connection, I contacted the Junta but did not inform my father or my brothers about my actions. Because Goicouría Cabrera had known me since I was a child, he was well aware of my sentiments on liberation. He suspected that I would jump at the chance to help the Junta in any way possible, even if it involved undertaking a dangerous mission. He studied me carefully when we met, probably calculating whether anyone would possibly suspect a well-bred young woman like me of subversion.

Aware of my imminent return to the island, the Junta invited me to join their revolutionary efforts.

"I must ask, Señorita Emilia, if you would be willing to perform a favor," Goicouría said, the sly smile on his face fortified by his pencil-thin moustache, "just a small favor you understand . . . if you could perhaps see yourself willing to deliver some papers to friends in Havana . . . "

The "papers" which I was to deliver were clearly contraband materials: documents, manuscripts, propaganda, sealed folders and bonds. Stunned by this unexpected request, I gulped quite audibly and most unladylike. Hoping it was not too noticeable, I relied on sheer will power to appear as calm and composed as possible.

"Of course," I responded, casually adjusting my suede gloves as if I intended to leave the premises. "But as everyone knows, such materials are strictly forbidden entry into the country by the Spanish authorities, and persons caught trafficking in subversive materials will be branded as traitors."

There was no response to my comment, indicating that, clearly, the decision was mine to make. Here, I thought, was the golden opportunity I'd longed for: a chance to be in the thick of things, to leave the sidelines of inactivity and strike a blow for liberation. Ignoring an onslaught of doubting demons that suddenly invaded my thoughts and pretending the thunderous beating of my heart was quite normal, I gave in to youthful bravado. I did not, for one more second, hesitate to accept the mission.

Back in Cuba, with the discipline of a professional spy, I set out to honor my commitment, but it was not as simple as it had appeared in New York when I willingly ensnared myself into a web of intrigue. In Cuba, I was still under parental restrictions for my previous behavior in front of the governor. For simply walking the streets of Cárdenas without a chaperone, I had acquired a reputation for audacious behavior. Now I'd be courting open defiance of authority. Unaccompanied señoritas might leave their homes in a group riding in a *volante,* but seldom left their homes unnoticed, and I had to be especially sure that I did not attract unwanted attention that would jeopardize the mission.

Carefully considering and discarding alternatives, I fantasized dozens of scenarios. To be seen in public speaking to young men could damage my reputation even further . . . and . . . "More important," I said to myself out loud, "my family will surely bear the brunt of this." Yet the cause of *Cuba Libre* was my destiny; it was in my blood, far outweighing any unfortunate obstacles placed in its path. Before long, I devised a viable strategy to carry out the mission, silently praying to a multitude of saints that the damage to the Casanova name would be minimal, if at all.

First, I befriended Cuban conspirators, making sure we met within the confines of a routine setting or right in my own home. I absorbed their seditious propaganda like a prisoner thirsting for water. Hoping to further the cause, I also shared pamphlets and newspapers with trusted friends, like Alberto and Concepción Castellanos, whose help I eagerly sought. Then I enlisted my two liberal-minded brothers in my crusade; in one way or another, they had already expressed their willingness to promote the mission.

Far more ambitious, my second objective was to plant the seeds of insubordination among the local military men in the garrison that guarded the Villa. A simple step, I thought, as the garrison stood within walking distance of my home. One could casually saunter by and engage the guards in frivolous conversation, therein judging their suitability for further interaction. After that, we'd share propaganda with them and solicit their support for liberation.

Fraught with danger, the second phase of the agenda proved to be the most difficult of all. It not only involved sharing contraband materials in clandestine meetings where secret discussions would take place, it also meant openly promoting conspiracy against the Spanish government. What was I to do? Surely the Casanovas would be branded as subversives, regardless of father's sterling reputation.

Despite my misgivings, the plan began to bear fruit. We convinced one or two recruits to join our efforts. But it did not take very long for a newly converted soldier, a youthful conspirator imbued with revolutionary zeal, to expose the Casanova strategy of indoctrination. The soldier pointed a finger at Manuel, and I thought that I would faint from fear. My brother was the Casanova most fervently committed to the cause. He was forced into hiding before the authorities could capture and imprison him for treason. Shortly thereafter, Manuel made his way on board a ship bound for the United States.

In the wake of my brother's escape, father acted with lightning speed. He lost no time in gathering the family together and laying out the necessary steps to leave Cuba immediately for the safety of the United States.

We sailed on board the barque *Luisa* directly from Cárdenas to Philadelphia. The ship made port on the 6th of May, 1854. "How appropriate," I thought, "that we should land in Philadelphia, the American city of brotherly love, but how much love and care had I really shown my own brother?" I prayed that Philadelphia was an omen of forgiveness. Arriving in Philadelphia, our family consisted of fourteen Casanovas, one domestic servant and several relatives. Counting from me, the eldest at age twenty-two, to one-year-old Concepción, six Casanova girls and seven young men made the voyage. On the ship's manifest, my mother listed her occupation as "gentlewoman." Her "gentleman" husband did not appear on the passenger list at all, because he traveled on another ship.

For more than a year, my family remained in voluntary exile. Perhaps sensing the current political situation would pose a continuous threat to our lives, on the 29th day of November, 1854, my father petitioned for American citizenship in the Common Pleas Court of the County of New York. That cold, overcast day, in which the buildings and the sky appeared to be cast of the same molten lead, seemed a harbinger of the ill winds rushing in our direction. But we celebrated when American citizenship was ultimately granted to him on July 17, 1860, by the Superior Court of the City of New York. From then on, father would acquire properties in New York and divide his time between Cuba and the United States, spending the winters in Cárdenas and the summers in New York.

That year in exile proved to be an extraordinary one for us all. I feared for the relatives left behind and for the welfare of my family. But I adjusted to life in *el exilio*. Eventually, my days began to show the promise of a rosy future. The 8th day of July, a warm and beautiful summer afternoon, I married Cirilo Villaverde. The year was 1855.

Eight

My Partnership for Life

"At last I am resting under the wings of the American Eagle. It may be that you are already apprised of my miraculous escape from the prison of Havana, where, as a man guilty of high treason, and accused of a capital crime by the District Attorney (Fiscal) I was lately watched with the greatest diligence. I see myself free in the land of liberty; and I can hardly believe what I see and touch."

Cirilo Villaverde, *The United States Magazine*
and Democratic Review. 1849.

It was an ordinary day, not one you purposefully set out to remember, but it was the day I met my husband. When I met Cirilo Villaverde in Philadelphia in 1854, he was working as a teacher of Spanish language and literature. Initially, I must be honest, I was attracted to him because of his reputation as a writer and a revolutionary—mostly, the latter.

Every inch the distinguished gentleman he was reported to be, his doleful eyes shielded by heavy eyelids offered hints of compassion and sadness. I sensed, looking into those proverbial windows of the soul, an honest and wise man. His fair complexion, slightly dusted with pale rosiness around the cheekbones, complemented a full gray beard. At about five feet, eight inches, he stood a few inches taller than I. His smile was genuine, almost shy.

Flushed with excitement from the moment we were first introduced, I regretted that on that particular day I had paid scant attention to my dress and wished I'd selected something more complementary to my skin tones and hair color. Perhaps something in pastel shades or in red to match my flighty mood. Amused at myself, I'd suddenly realized I wanted him to like me. I wanted that very much.

Warmed by the sunlight streaming in through the tall, bay windows that framed the far wall of our formal parlor facing the street, we sat politely for our afternoon tea, hardly aware that other family members were in the room. The extra logs thrown into the fireplace earlier were not needed. The room felt small and stuffy to me, in spite of its high ceiling. I gathered my skirts and moved to a sofa away from the windows. To my surprise . . . Villaverde followed me.

At some point in our conversation, Mr. Cirilo Villaverde politely leaned over to listen to my animated rambling about compensating slave owners after abolition. That was the moment I realized that he was genuinely interested in what I had to say. He appeared to value my opinions for their merit, conversing with me as if I were his equal, in spite of his vast knowledge and experience.

It did not take very long before we recognized that we shared similar ideas. As we engaged in conversation, shrewdly taking the measure of one another, I said to myself, here is a man committed heart-and-soul to the very ideals I believe in . . . here is a man . . . I could easily grow to love.

In later years, Cirilo would recall that he thought of me as beautiful, an extraordinary woman passionately committed to altruistic values, who was to be commended for never leaving his side, except for the briefest of periods. That summer of 1855, when the rest of the Casanova family returned to our home in Cárdenas, I prepared to make a new life with my husband in New York City where, as he would write at a future date, I would "share with him the bitter bread of expatriation."

As you can well imagine, I knew a great deal about my husband's past, having read his writings and listened to others sing his praises, but I wanted to discover much more. What precious stories defined his boyhood, his ideas and what personal thoughts shaped him to become the person he was? I did not discover the answers from one day to the next. But over time, our mutual interests and conversations revealed more and more about his experiences, his nature, thoughts and intimate perspectives that I was delighted to find were so very much like my own.

He was born on October 28, 1812. His father was a physician on the Santiago sugar plantation near Pinar del Río. Like me, Cirilo had witnessed the atrocities of slavery and valued the humanity of the enslaved people he got to know. He described the suffering of the slaves to me as if he, himself, had lived it. I could easily understand his life-long commitment to wiping out the practice, because I felt the same way. We'd often discuss the way abolition could be accomplished in Cuba, never once anticipating that we would personally experience the effects of a bloody civil war, brother against brother, a nation torn asunder, right here in New York City.

Like me, Cirilo believed that the power of the pen to raise awareness and change the hearts and minds of the people was the path toward social change. One evening, we debated that issue after reading *Uncle Tom's Cabin or Life among the Lowly,* taking turns in reading chapters aloud to one another, as was our practice after supper. Closing the book on the last page, we contemplated the story for a minute or two, finally breaking our silence to marvel at what the Connecticut author, Mrs. Harriet Beecher Stowe, was able to accomplish with her pen.

A morality tale of man's cruelty toward man and the destructive effects of slavery on America's social fabric, the book's popularity spread across the nation like ripples on a tranquil lake. Every evening, in homes just like our own, hundreds of American families gathered to hear the story read aloud, multiplying the numbers of people influenced by Mrs. Beecher Stowe. Stage versions, performed by traveling theatrical companies, rivaled all-time favorites like the perennial *Rip Van Winkle,* and played to full houses everywhere. "Now, that was exactly what we needed to do in Cuba," I thought, replaying our conversation over again in my own mind.

Cirilo believed that the written word required a strong commitment of activism to be effective, even if it meant sacrificing your life for your beliefs. I realized, perhaps for the first time in my entire life, that if Mrs. Beecher Stowe could inspire an armed struggle through her writing, I could do the same.

Cirilo Villaverde, himself, was an accomplished writer. He was schooled in law and received his credentials in 1832, but chose to become a creative writer of short stories and essays instead. Journalism called to his sense of justice, and writing for the radical press, crafting pamphlets and essays, gave him the platform to advocate for those issues most dear to him. The contraband bi-weekly, *La Verdad,* undoubtedly the paper of note on annexation, was distributed secretly by him. Later, in New York, he edited the newspaper and wrote articles and editorials aimed at American and Spanish reading audiences. I mentioned to him that *La Verdad* was required reading for budding revolutionaries, like myself, in Cárdenas. He smiled broadly at me and said he was delighted to know his work had born fruit.

I had read a number of his short stories, but especially loved *Cecilia Valdés* for its romance and authenticity about ordinary life in Cuba. The first versions of that tale appeared in print as a two-part story in 1839. We did not know then, in those early years of our marriage, that *Cecilia Valdés or the Angel's Hill,* as he would title the book, would place Cirilo in the pantheon of eminent writers. A tragedy of star-crossed lovers, a beautiful woman of mixed blood in love with her half-brother, a white man, during the first decades of the century, the story depicted Cuba as an integrated culture, distinct and unique with its own social classes and traditions. This in itself would be revolutionary because my husband, demonstrated that Cuba was essentially different from Spain in many respects and that it chafed under a destructive administrative system.

I knew my husband by reputation as an annexationist and advocate for Narciso López, but he was also a devoted educator who loved to teach. He believed in exposing young minds to the great writers and philosophers so that they, too, would learn to reason and think for themselves. He worked long hours to produce political tracts almost daily, edited and translated English classics, like Charles Dickens' *David Copperfield,* and still found time to teach in a school he founded in Weehaukan, New Jersey. His goal, Cirilo once remarked to me as I made my first attempts at writing essays, was to unambiguously state the pros and cons of a political argument to his readers and provoke them to think about alternatives for Cuba's future. He sought to engage the reader in the present crisis and to provide first-hand accounts of the true history, as he knew it, for future generations. I remembered how the sad Miss Clark had tried and failed to teach me. But through discussions with my husband, I, too, became one of his most dedicated pupils.

Six months into our marriage, Cirilo and I sat in a drafty compartment of a New York Central railroad car on route to the International Suspension Bridge that would bring us into Canada. We were celebrating our mid-year anniversary in spite of the wintry weather. Engaged in quiet conversation, I related my story about the flag of liberation and my fleeting encounter with General López and his army. I imagined my flushed face and luminous eyes, the result of reliving such a vivid experience for me, inspired him to tell me about the conspiracy of Cienfuegos.

As his story goes, in 1848 he had aligned himself with Narciso López, taking a highly visible role in the annexationist movement. In the middle of the night, he woke up to find himself taken prisoner, "confined like a wild animal to a dark, damp cell for six consecutive months." After that long wait, he was tried and condemned, first to death and later to a sentence of life in prison. Planning and plotting his way to freedom, he engineered an escape worthy of one of his short stories.

With the help of a sympathetic guard, on April 4, 1849, a date he would never forget, Cirilo simply walked out of the prison along with the turnkey and another criminal and boarded a sailing ship bound for Apalachicola, Florida. From there, he made his way to Savannah, Georgia, and then traveled overland to New York City, where he was finally able to freely pursue his political objectives.

Already a mature man, my husband related how in those days he found himself at a crossroad in his life, seriously considering what he would do with his future. His decision, to put aside his passion for writing, consciously stifling his creativity as a novelist for a new, politically oriented, albeit often frustrating way of life in New York, was reached after careful deliberation. In his own words, he had "passed from a world of illusions to a world of realities."

As a great admirer of General López, he was the general's military secretary in New York. After the general's execution in 1851, my husband wrote a stirring account about López and his soldiers. Cirilo detailed the events of the general's life, his dedication to the cause and the unbounded courage of the predominantly American mercenaries in defying their nation's neutrality laws to bring freedom to the Cuban oppressed. A powerful indictment of Spanish aggression, the essay was published as a pamphlet that sold for twelve and a half cents. Clearly intended for broad distribution, I asked if it was also intended to shore up support for annexation. But my husband dispelled that notion with another story.

The year before we met in Philadelphia, he lived in New Orleans in the heart of the annexationist community, where he published and edited his own newspaper, *El Independiente*. Evident from the name he chose for it, "the independent one," he wished to convey individual choice in matters related to political ideology and reforms. The paper clarified my husband's own thinking, now that the idea of annexation was beginning to wane in favor of a future for Cuba that was not integrated into the United States. He shared with me the article wherein he wrote, "We are opposed to the purchase of Cuba either by Cubans or by Americans. We believe that Cuba can yet gain her independence by force of arms." After reading the article, I smiled discretely. Fortuitously for the future of *our* union, that point of view found instant favor with me. Once committed to complete liberation, I was a person of steadfast values.

We settled in Manhattan in a community surrounded by a growing presence of well-to-do expatriates and other immigrants. In those days, the elite among Cuban émigrés lived in well-appointed residential neighborhoods in the village of Greenwich, Washington Square or lower Manhattan, where they rented rooms or apartments in some of the city's most desirable townhouses. Working-class families often took less expensive housing where they could rent three-room gaslit flats, warmed by coal stoves with an indoor sink but shared bathrooms located in hallways. In congested neighborhoods like Five Points, a jumble of dank streets and alleyways in lower Manhattan, the stench-filled sewers of crowded squalid tenements, often home to the city's most impoverished immigrants, reeked of destitution and illness, and made you wonder if any of these wretched people would ever find the better life they had come for.

Added to the city's woes were multitudes of horse-drawn public vehicles, such as omnibuses and double-decker stagecoaches. Of the two, I preferred the omnibus because it ran on tracks along Fifth Avenue on a regular schedule, and you could be assured of reaching your destination in a somewhat timely fashion. But peddlers' wagons and carts, livestock and stray chickens filled the streets at all hours, and private Broughams and Hansom cabs, neither of which guaranteed saving any time, were affordable only to the rich. All blocked the major thoroughfares so completely that traffic was often snarled for hours.

We newlyweds, however, viewed our shared city life through rose-tinted lenses and found in New York a virtual cornucopia of opportunity. I sang the praises of the city as a mecca for the Spanish-language publishing business. At first, I relied on the *Guía de los Estados Unidos para Viajeros Españoles*, a guide published right here in the city, which became my personal compass for traversing the neighborhoods. But soon, I was boarding cabs and carriages to travel the city as if I'd been born here.

The numbers of Spanish- or English-language international newspapers, like *La Verdad, El Mulato* and *El Eco de Cuba* flourished, providing an ever-growing literate population of Spanish readers, a place to state opinion and find local and international news. Generally, these papers ranged in size from two to four pages, each page jampacked with four columns of small print.

The presses were kept alive by subscribers and advertisers. You could find classified ads about embarking and disembarking ships, Cuban tobacco shops, printers, tailors, seamstresses, shoe makers, schools, pharmacies, doctors and surgeons and almost anything else you wanted. *La Verdad* lasted for several years, but others did not last more than a year. Yet, one could always count on the spontaneous birth of new newspapers, given the diversity of opinion found within the expatriate community.

Without fear of reprisal, debates regularly appeared in print about the best political course to take in Cuba. Articles actually offered strategies for military interventions originating in the United States. But that was no surprise because there was already a strong feeling that the first volleys for Cuban liberation would originate in the United States.

"It seems to me," I remarked to my husband one morning, "that freighters and passenger ships from the Caribbean disembark more Cuban and Puerto Rican immigrants in the city every day." As if ordained from above, dissidents exiled in previous years, escaped prisoners from the Spanish garrison of Ceuta, or political refugees from all parts of the Antilles and Latin America, soon found their way to our home in the city. That was, to me, a most welcome surprise! Before long, the Villaverde home became the central gathering place for lively discussions on strategies to break the chains that bound our beloved Cuba in colonial servitude.

"Cubans must take steps toward creating an independent state," I'd declare to energetic guests, "ruled by justice and respect for humanity." This would give way to everyone speaking at once, eager to plot the next steps in our agenda. If the topic weren't so serious, this bumbling of would-be statesmen would have been hilarious. Fortunately for us, we lived in a city where the right to assemble and free speech was protected. Given my personal experiences in the homeland, this was something I'd always cherish.

As a gathering place for all sorts of dialogue, once word got around that a writer of a certain book or article would be visiting our home, our parlor became a standing-room-only forum for invited and some not invited guests. On one such occasion, our good friend, Miguel Teurbe Tolón, editor of the Latin American desk of the *New York Herald*, agreed to make a presentation of a recently published anthology, *El laúd del desterrado*, (The Exile's Lute). *El laúd* was a collection of poetry written by some of the best-known expatriate writers. The poems covered a variety of subjects but stressed, above all, nationhood and were incendiary enough that the collection could only have seen the light of day in New York's free press.

An animated discussion followed Teurbe Tolón's interpretations of *cubanidad*—the essence of what it meant to be Cuban—with comparisons to the American founding fathers whose, separate sense of self ultimately led to separation from Great Britain. It could have gone on all night had Cirilo not taken the lead in ending the evening. He simply informed our guests that he had an early morning meeting and excused himself. As if on signal, one by one the guests began to take their leave, perhaps to resume the discussion at a local beer hall.

After everyone had departed, I sat by the dying embers of the spent logs in the fireplace, quietly reflecting on the evening's discussion. I wondered if Cuban identity could indeed be molded from afar by writers and thinkers living in the United States. Have they played such an important role in forging a separate sense of self simply through the written word? As I thought about it, this need for an identity could become a powerful reason for independence and abolition.

As I began to appear more and more in public places in New York, I commissioned a dressmaker to design two fashionable ensembles with figure-enhancing bodices, full skirts, ruffles at the neckline and on the sleeves and just a hint of military detail. That special feature was my personal reminder that I was an active revolutionary. Befitting my new status as the wife of an important writer, the clothes gave me the confidence to speak in public in what was unmistakably a man's world.

I was taken seriously in New York, unlike my past experiences in Cárdenas. I began to feel a strong kinship with many of the hero-women I had read about in the past who had struggled for their own countries' liberation. As a young girl in Cuba, those were the stories I had found most intriguing. And now, here I was following in their footsteps. I began to think of myself as a woman who could become a serious leader.

Public meetings, lectures and rallies brimmed with a freedom of movement that did not depend on one's sex. I railed against oppression openly, argued for the abolition of slavery in both Cuba and the United States without having to resort to silent fuming. At political rallies, I'd applaud progressive points of view and outline my own proposals for liberation. I'd encourage Cirilo to resume his work on *Cecilia Valdés*, offering to edit, read and discuss its progress. And I'd taken up my own pen to write letters to the editors of numerous newspapers in the city, political tracts for publication and viable agendas for the liberation movement.

But in 1858, unexpected events disrupted our harmonious lifestyle. Drawn to the idea of returning to Cuba because the government, in a conciliatory moment, offered amnesty for all political refugees, Cirilo and I decided to leave New York. Pregnant with our first child, we'd agreed I'd give birth on our native soil, surrounded by the women of my family.

On the 8th day of September in 1858, our son Narciso was born and quickly became the epicenter of our existence. With his black wisps of curly hair and honey-colored eyes, he reminded me of his grandmother. We lived in a lovely house on Galiano Street in Havana, and Cirilo, once again, began work as publisher of a newspaper. His novel, *Dos Amores*, was reprinted, and he began to recast *Cecilia Valdés,* a task that gave him an enormous, long awaited, pleasure. In the warm bosom of family and friends, our days seemed idyllic at first, but before long, the far-reaching tentacles of the government, extended by the recently re-appointed Captain General José de la Concha, wrapped themselves around the sacred core of our harmonious home with insidious signs of repression.

"That wretched Concha, who gloried in the capture and public execution of General López, has set out to complete the degradation of the Cuban people he was not able to accomplish the first time," Cirilo railed angrily, scattering his precious work all over the tiled floor.

I was as thoroughly disgusted with this turn of events as was my husband, but the final blow came when *El Diario de la Marina* published a letter I'd previously sent to the *New York Herald.* Deemed offensive to the Spanish government, Cirilo and I found ourselves the targets of suspicion. Concerned for our safety and that of our small son, we decided there was no other recourse but to leave Cuba. Our decision to leave the homeland, perhaps the last time we would ever set foot on its soil, was unavoidable. We wrapped our boy in his blanket and embarked on the steamer, *Quaker City*. We arrived in New York on the 20th of August, 1860, less than eight months before the Confederate Army attacked Fort Sumter.

What followed were four long years of civil war, race riots, draft rebellions and overall strife and deprivation in our adopted city. A myriad of inescapable tragedies brought us to understand the enormous price a nation must pay for self-determination and abolition. The one silver lining in the overall gloom was the joyful birth of our beloved daughter, Emilita. We welcomed the respite from the liberation movement and tried to survive the war, providing for the needs of our growing family. Cirilo attempted, once again, to complete the revisions of *Cecilia Valdés*.

I supervised our small household with the scarce wartime provisions available to us and poured my energies into raising the children. I never wanted to be like those Cuban women I'd known in elite society who gave their children to be raised and cared for to a retinue of nurses and nannies. Since Narciso's birth, I took great pride in nursing and raising my own children, tutoring them myself until they were old enough for outside tutors or sent to school. But in all the times I hugged and kissed them, I do not ever recall holding them as long, or as tightly, as I did on the afternoon of July 14, 1863.

On that day, the children and I listened to horrendous screams and rioting by hordes of angry and irrational men, women and children, who protested the Union Army's order to draft some 30,000 New Yorkers to meet the city's military quota. The burden of conscription fell upon young immigrants and laborers, generally poor, huddled in the Five Points and other depressed pockets of the city. The wealthy could easily buy their way out of the draft for the sum of $300. But the impoverished, barely able to make ends meet, carried the weight of war on their undernourished shoulders.

A spontaneous protest without leadership suddenly erupted into a mob out for blood. Some used pitchforks and axes; others took to knives and makeshift weapons to achieve their goals. For four days, the city was set on fire, torn apart with indiscriminate killing and maiming. This contagion of evil—I can't call it anything else—overwhelmed the city with wanton looting, burning, physical assaults and lynching of innocent people. No one was safe in the streets, especially if you were black, as the struggle for abolition was thought to be the major reason for the war.

In our barricaded home, Narciso's big brown eyes filled with tears and, although he tried to be brave, he clung fiercely to me. "Mamá, will the bad people find us?"

When we were told by our coachman that the Colored Orphan Asylum on Fifth Avenue and Forty-Third Street, a shelter for 233 Negro children, had been burned to the ground, I held on to both my children as if our lives depended on it.

Nine

Shots Heard from the East

To: Señores of the Comité Republicano de Cuba y Puerto Rico.
Gentlemen and Esteemed Compatriots,
Please accept and remit to its destiny at your first opportunity,
the enclosed flag of Cuba Libre which fluttered first in Cárdenas,
place of my birth . . . I send it as a token of the admiration and
enthusiasm inspired in me by the heroic compatriots who today
struggle to bring our land liberty and independence, above all,
Carlos Manuel de Céspedes, the first to break the chain of
ignominy with which Spain binds us, and to whom I humbly
dedicate it. Your attentive servant,
E. C. de Villaverde. Nueva York, Enero 1, 1869.

"**B**ut, Father!" I implored, as hot, angry tears threatened to make their way down my cheeks. "Everything points to it! There *will* be revolution and you must, with all due haste, transfer your assets to the United States. Otherwise, what will become of our family? We will lose everything if you do nothing but wait for Spanish concessions!"

How clearly I recall the intense encounters I'd had with my father over our family's safety as the unrest in Cuba escalated. My parents had chosen to divide their time between New York and Havana, making their yearly excursion to the north accompanied by no fewer than three daughters, and two or three servants. On this particular occasion, no sooner had he set foot into our foyer when I began to voice my concerns. Poor Papá! Hoping to escape the brutal heat of Cárdenas, he was hardly prepared to entertain the manic ravings of a frantic daughter, but I continued to plead my case nonetheless.

At thirty-five, I was no longer a young woman and, in fact, I was in the final stages of a difficult pregnancy. "Did you think that the formation of the Sociedad Republicana de Cubanos y Puerto-rriqueños two years ago was a frivolous act? That was not intended to be a social club. It was organized by our leading thinkers. *We are preparing for war!*" I hoped my intensity would move him to agree with us. "We are now in the spring of 1867. How much longer do you think we have before taking a stand?"

I was convinced that we would be at war before long. Holding Emilita on my lap, I could feel the child had a low grade fever again. I caressed my daughter, pushing her damp black curls away from her face. That year, she seemed to come down with some malady every other week. But I attributed it to childhood illnesses, dipped my pen into the inkwell and began to write a series of letters to close friends in Cuba, warning them, as well, of the potential confrontations on the horizon.

The Sociedad, I noted, was a step in right direction. I pointed out that the organization was under the leadership of Juan Manuel Macías and the respected Puerto Rican abolitionist, Dr. Francisco Basora. Both were known for their integrity and as the founding editors of the newspaper, *La Voz de América*. I was confident, I wrote, that the Sociedad would flourish because at that time many in the expatriate community recognized the newspaper as the voice of the liberation movement. I signed my name with a flourish that conveyed more confidence than I actually felt and guided my drowsy daughter to her bed.

On August 21st, our son, Enrique Cirilo, was born. Like his mother, he arrived on a Wednesday. In my mind, I'd often change the fortune of Wednesday's child in the nursery rhyme to "fair of face," because it suited Enrique, who was, indeed, a beautiful baby. That summer turned out to be unbearably hot and humid, causing the iceman's wagon to become a permanent fixture on our street. A contented, alert baby, Enrique lay in his crib, his finely stitched white batiste, linen cap and gown soaked with perspiration, but he did not seem to mind the still, heavy air that hovered over New York.

"My precious boy," I murmured and began the strains of a lullaby that seemed to delight him. "If we were in Cuba," I said in a singsong voice, "I'd let you lie naked in a finely woven hammock out on the veranda like the black babies used to do on our plantation. . . . " It seemed as if there were an invisible bubble-shaped shield preserving the putrid smells of rotting fish and overrun sewers hanging in the city's humid air . . . and there was no escape.

I was so relieved when father finally heeded our warnings. During the summer months, he deposited a little over one million dollars in several New York banks. Arrangements were underway to sell some properties in Cuba and to transfer control of others into the hands of my brothers.

José and his family would run the plantation *Armonía*. As an American citizen who had once served as U.S. Consul in Guayaquil, Ecuador, it was taken for granted that he would not be harassed by the Spanish authorities. Manuel, Pedro and Ricardo became partners in another Casanova venture, a commission merchant house entitled Los Hermanos Casanova. This firm produced large profits and paid equally large taxes to the government. Father, in his wisdom, reasoned that the authorities would not want to lose the taxes and would, therefore, not trouble the business. He was satisfied that all the legal precautions he had taken would safeguard his sons in Cuba. Justice, as we would soon discover, did not always favor the just.

It was on the first of November, 1867, that father unveiled his finest surprise. There was to be a new home for the Casanovas! Father had purchased a large estate on Long Island Sound some nine miles north of New York City in an area known as Mott Haven or sometimes, Oak Point. Before the Civil War, it belonged to Benjamin Whitlock, an avid, southern sympathizer who poured over $250,000 into renovations, intending to make it the grandest, most beautiful home on the Sound. Sadly, the estate had fallen onto hard times after the war, and Whitlock's widow sold the property to my father for the sum of $150,000.

It soon became known as the Casanova Mansion. A winding road led the visitor to massive bronze doors inscribed with *Soyez le Bienvenue* on a coat of arms. Constructed of brownstone, the imposing house was enhanced by beautifully kept gardens and statuary. The property sat on fifty acres overlooking the Sound from a hillock on a small islet. On first impression, the house was a formidable four-story building, looking more like an institution than a house. But the inside had scores of amenities suitable to a large family like ours.

There were about one hundred chambers with exquisitely designed windows that allowed beams of sunlight to dance in shimmering patterns on the dark wood floors. The rooms had high ceilings adorned with intricate sculptured moldings and beams, massive wrought-iron chandeliers, a ballroom with an exquisite, multifaceted crystal chandelier and a secret chamber containing a large safe. Only the best of materials were found throughout the house. I noticed carved cherry, oak and mahogany woodwork, gold doorknobs and interior decorations imported from France. The library, paneled in warm mahogany from floor to ceiling with a surround of elegant, built-in bookcases, sported a bank of ornately carved windows overlooking the gardens. Pull cords sounded dainty bells that connected every room with the downstairs kitchens. The view of the woods and the sea beyond the house was spectacular.

There was a drawbridge flanked by massive iron gates to access the grounds when high tide made carriage wheels difficult to maneuver. Triggered by underground springs, the portals opened and closed as if by magic. However, the feature that most attracted my attention was the enormous network of underground tunnels that led to a cove, making for easy sailing in and out of Long Island Sound. Down there, there were cellar vaults that could be used to store weapons and ammunition.

For several weeks Cirilo, the children and I had been living in the Casanova mansion. So sure was I that the clean country air would have healthful effects on the children that I pressed my husband to arrange the move as soon as the house was ready. I was wrong. In the final days of 1867 when families gathered together to enjoy the blessings of the season and to celebrate the birth of the child Jesus, we lost our beautiful Emilita. She had not yet reached her seventh spring.

A blanket of fresh snow covered the grounds of the Casanova Mansion as far as the eye could see. From the depths of my heart, I was grateful for my husband's care during those difficult times but I did not have the wherewithal to tell him so. I lacked the energy for conversation, found myself staring into space for long periods of time, entering a room and not knowing what I meant to do there. Some days I didn't want to leave my bed, or after my morning ritual, wanted to crawl right back into it. I dissolved into tears for no apparent reason and Narciso, . . . poor Narciso . . . my big boy almost ten years old, looked unhappily to his books for companionship. He hardly talked or laughed anymore, afraid he would upset me.

Eventually, I stopped blaming God for taking Emilita away from me, afraid that catastrophic punishment would befall our other children. Gloom inhabited every nook and cranny of this enormous house. The bare trees were solitary sentinels against the steel gray skies. The raucous squawk of the seagulls, crisp in the sea air, deepened my feeling of desolation. Cirilo felt I would also fade away into the nebulous landscape. He prayed that the rebirth of spring would nourish my soul into a new awakening.

On the 10th of October, 1868, a shout for independence, *El Grito de Yara*, exploded like a burst of thunder and we were finally at war! In late October, a messenger from Cuba brought the news to us at the mansion, where almost my entire family had gathered to celebrate Enrique's baptism and honor the memory of our beloved Emilita. It did not matter that the first blow for liberation had failed to originate from the expatriate community, as we all thought it would. Instead, it exploded, like the rising sun, out of the east from Bayamo, from the mountain landowners of Oriente Province, from lawyers and other professionals schooled in the liberal ideals of Europe, from farmers, from enslaved and free blacks and from Chinese laborers who joined the rebel cause! Overwhelmingly burdened by taxation and repression and not tied to the commercial sugar interests of the east, these *Mambíes*, as they called themselves, this hybrid group of guerrilla fighters, had declared Cuba's independence from Spain at the town of Yara.

The messenger, barely able to catch his breath, informed us that a similar shout in Lares, Puerto Rico, *El Grito de Lares* had led to an uprising that was brutally crushed by the military. Thus, the Cuban Creoles and the Mambíes were left to face the military might of Spain on their own against 40,000 regular troops, an unbeatable fleet of warships and hundreds of paramilitary *voluntarios!*"

When the messenger finished his tale, he was escorted by the butler to the kitchen for a well earned meal. I began to prance about the room. "I am ecstatic!" I repeated over and over to the consternation of baby Enrique, who no longer felt very secure in my movable arms. "What does it matter where the war began? The important point is that we are finally at war and we must prepare

to join the rebellion." I raved a bit like a lunatic, finding it difficult to contain my composure. "Now we are free!," I chanted and
danced around the great room embracing my husband, our parents, the children and my siblings. "Here we have our revolution.
It is most welcome!"

The younger children joined in the dance, thinking, perhaps,
that it was all a grand new game, but my parents and adult siblings
remained motionless, somewhat disturbed. One of my sisters
began to shed silent tears in the emotion of the moment, perhaps
recalling a a special gentleman left behind in Cuba. Mother quietly reached out for my father's hand, while my adolescent nieces
and nephews could hardly wait to run out the door and take up
arms.

Our house guests, a Spaniard married to a Cuban woman,
were momentarily forgotten, but Cirilo, who always kept his wits
about him, noticed that they had quickly gathered their belongings and were quietly headed for the front door. He went to bid
them farewell. None of us stopped to think of the terrible consequences of war—it was much too soon for that—but the downcast, pensive look on father's face already hinted at depths of sacrifices that we could hardly imagine.

The leader of the insurrection, I soon learned, was the son of
an Oriente landowner, Carlos Manuel de Céspedes, a native of
Bayamo. An attorney, Céspedes organized the Yara conspiracy
from his own plantation, *La Demajagua*. The lyrical name alone,
as you can well imagine, assumed epic proportions in our minds.
Apparently, Céspedes had already created a temporary government under a new entity, the Junta Revolucionaria de Cuba. He
issued a manifesto, formed a local militia and called all supporters
to a convention to form a new constitutional government in the
town of Guaimaro.

It would be at Guaimaro where a *cubana* patriot, Ana Betancourt Mora, would issue her famous declaration comparing the
status of women to slavery. "Cuban women," she remarked, "have

waited patiently and resigned in the dark and tranquil corners of the home for this sublime hour . . . you have destroyed slavery based on color. Now the time has come to liberate the women."

When I first read the letter from my brother, José, that carried her declaration, I could not help but feel the hairs on the back of my neck stand on end. At that moment, tears of joy glistened in my eyes and a compassion born of camaraderie stretched across the seas to Doña Ana and others like her, who had been at the forefront of changing women's legal status in Cuba. I made a silent promise to the brave Betancourt Mora that I, too, would do the same for our *patriotas* in New York.

As fate would have it, I had the opportunity to meet her in New York in later years. She'd given a speech at one of the lecture halls. Afterward, I humbly thanked her for her inspirational act.

I remember the frenetic activity in the city following *El Grito de Yara*. It did not take long for the expatriate community in New York to fall in step with the revolution. The Sociedad Republicana de Cuba y Puerto Rico was reborn as the Junta Revolucionaria de Cuba y Puerto Rico. My only concern was that I'd felt, I'm not sure I can explain it, somewhat uneasy about subdued rumors that the new president of the Junta, Morales Lémus, was willing to entertain the idea of annexation. . . .

Looking back, I can say that my own life was radically altered by this turn of events as I was now committed to travel into the city every day. I had much to do related to the war effort, so that I hardly had the time to think about anything else. At seven in the morning, I'd dress for a day of business in prim bustled skirts, hems lightly brushing my button shoes. I had breakfast with Cirilo and the boys, even if it was just to have a *cafecito* with a teaspoon of sugar and a slice of freshly baked bread. Then, I assessed my appearance before the mirrors in the front foyer, adjusted my hat, slipped on matching gloves and climbed into the carriage that took me to the Casanova Railroad Station.

Within the hour I'd arrive in the city and board an omnibus to my place of business, a rental I'd arranged especially for the war effort. Then my workday began in earnest. There would be visits to the local establishments for donations of shoes, clothing, anything they could supply that could be used or sold to raise funds for the war effort. Two days of every week, I reserved for forwarding the donations by messenger and carriage to the Junta headquarters.

On one bitterly cold day, the kind you could see your breath in front of you in small vapors, a young woman, improperly dressed for such weather and holding the hands of two small children, perhaps the same age as Narciso, approached me as I entered the office. "Señora," she said speaking to me in Spanish. "I am told you help those in need."

I knew immediately that she was a Cuban from her accent and that she was a stranger in the city. Seated in the relative warmth of the office, a steaming cup of tea in her hands, she related a horror story about how the *voluntarios*, the paramilitaries of her home town, set fire to the plantation where her husband worked as caretaker. He was captured and beaten to death, for it was rumored he had helped supply food to the Mambíes. She and the two youngest children managed to escape with their lives. They hid in the sugar cane fields all night, fighting off the rats and insects. The third child had found refuge in the home of a friend. When the woman was able to gather her wits, she set out on foot for the coast. There she boarded a ship leaving Havana. Ultimately, she made her way to New York.

I gave her all the money I had in my purse and sent her to seek refuge at St. Bernard's Catholic Church, which would help her find room and board. But for the rest of the day, the image of that woman and her young children would not remove itself from my mind.

She was just one of so many, I can still recall, can see their faces in my mind's eye. We were already beginning to witness the first exodus of refugees arriving at New York and Brooklyn piers, war casualties fleeing the homeland with only the clothes on their backs. Among these unfortunates were the first clusters of widows and orphans.

The owners of cigar factories in Havana had transferred their businesses to Key West and New York, and refugee cigar workers now flooded this city looking for work. And of course, as everyone understood, the intellectuals were the first to be ousted. Because of Lares, the purge of Puerto Rican rebels became intensely brutal, and they, too, had begun to make their way to New York in more visible numbers.

That afternoon of my encounter with the refugee and her children, I'd made arrangements to negotiate support for the rebellion with some influential people whose donations would be beneficial. Having accomplished that task, I dashed to a lecture at Hardman Hall where, quite unexpectedly, I met Dr. José J. Henna, one of the Puerto Rican conspirators and the learned Eugenio María de Hostos, who had recently arrived in New York. I was heartened to hear these seasoned patriots speak of their experiences, which, if nothing else, solidified our commitment to the armed struggle.

Brimming with animosity toward the Spanish regime, Hostos lost no time in joining the editorial staff of *La Revolución* where he railed in writing against the colonial government. An ardent proponent for a federation of the Caribbean Antilles, Don Eugenio confided in me his fears that undeclared factions existed in the expatriate community that could destabilize support for the rebellion. He was particularly concerned, as was I, about the bitter differences of opinions between Cuban separatists and annexationists, but also among Puerto Ricans who refused to understand that both struggles were one and the same. In later years, I'd come to believe that more than anyone else Hostos deserved the credit for unity, for his was the critical voice that called for Cuban support within the Puerto Rican expatriate community. For that, I'd always be grateful. But on the day we met, all I could say was, *"Un millón de gracias,* Don Eugenio."

By late afternoon, I'd find myself at the brink of exhaustion, yet strangely exhilarated. Returning to Oak Point in time for the evening meal with Cirilo, I'd share my day with him, unable to stop talking about the refugee and her children or any other peculiarities that took place that day. He encouraged me to believe our difficult road was not in vain. On days when he was not with me in the city, Cirilo motivated our revolutionaries with his scathing political treatises. Those fleeting moments when we shared our days' events had become our own private time, jealously guarded from outside intrusion.

As it was often close to the children's bedtime, I'd quietly make my way to their third-floor bedrooms listening for signs of movement. I'd first enter Narciso's room, sit a while and talk to him about his day. Narciso was old enough to understand why it was necessary for me to spend so much of my day away from home. Enrique, however, was still a baby whose young world consisted of milk and honey. For him, I'd sing silly rhyming songs as he nodded off to sleep.

Leaving the children's rooms, I'd turn my attention to the invisible satchel that had accompanied me throughout the day on the bus, the train and the carriage ride home—an accumulation of mental notes, plans and ideas yet to be accomplished.

In the seclusion of the library, I'd reach high to adjust the gaslight and prepare to face a mountain of correspondence and letters to the editors that patiently awaited me. Hours later, when the silence of the evening cushioned the house in velvet slumber, I'd complete one more task before retiring. In the quiet comfort of my bedroom, I'd place a few coal nuggets on the dying embers, wrap myself in an oversized white cotton shawl and settle into the wing-backed chair that faced the fireplace. I'd open the sewing basket on the small adjacent table and carefully remove the roll of smooth cobalt blue material. How silky it felt against my fingers,

I marveled; how beautifully it contrasted with the red and white, I thought, as I stitched a white star onto the crimson triangle. I'd imagine how it would inspire the army of the new provisional president of Free Cuba—*Cuba Libre*—Carlos Manuel de Céspedes, when he unfurled this banner on high and led his army of liberation into victory.

Ten

Organizing the Women

To: C. José Morales Lémus

The committee of the society Liga de las Hijas de Cuba, informed
that you have been authorized by the patriot leader, Carlos
Manuel de Céspedes, as his representative in this country, have
the honor to address you, . . . since the 6th of February, various
ladies constituted themselves in formal association, the Liga de
las Hijas de Cuba, under written by-laws . . .

E. C. de Villaverde. Secretary. March, 1869.

The irony of it all was that for a woman whose childhood dream was to brandish a sword in the fight for justice, the rebellion in my native land was both frustrating and out of reach. Oh, to be sure, in my letters to the editors of the local newspapers, I was gaining a reputation as an outspoken opponent of the Spanish regime. Before long, I had made enemies: those who wrote to refute or criticize my support of the rebellion or those who felt that, as a woman, I had no right to an opinion. You see, neither in my speeches nor in my writings did I engage in innuendo. Instead, I named names, denouncing persons and actions deemed contrary to my point of view. But I'd not allow myself to be drawn into endless argument with those critics whose only claim to fame was that they refuted the writings of a woman, for I considered such encounters a waste of my time.

To be honest, in playing my small part as a writer, I'd found limited gratification. Cirilo seemed content to fight the war by brandishing his pen, but I needed to engage in something more tangible, more immediately beneficial to the war effort. What I needed, I thought, was to raise my own sword and lead an army! And that was when I decided to form a women's patriotic association to aid the Mambí Army of Liberation.

As we all learn in due course, organizing people in a common cause extracts its own pound of flesh. My plan was to develop support for the rebellion from the ladies in New York. After discussing the matter with my husband and family, I decided, for better or for worse, to plunge ahead with it.

"These are my plans," I excitedly explained to Cirilo on an unusually foggy morning in the middle of January in 1869. We were finishing our morning coffee in the relative warmth of the library, our favorite retreat during the winter months. The room was a large rectangular space with a high sculptured ceiling and a bank of majestic floor-to-ceiling windows on the wall overlooking the gardens and beyond to the winter-gray waters of Long Island Sound. In one corner of the room, my husband's desk was angled to catch the natural light and to face the entrance. The seating area held comfortable sofas cozily arranged in front of the large stone fireplace in which the servants maintained a crackling fire throughout the day. Three paneled walls of the room accommodated bookshelves filled with all sorts of books to the ceiling; a step ladder was used to reach the very top.

"Do you think the idea is enticing enough to attract the women?" I asked Cirilo. "I've been thinking about this for some time and am convinced that an association of women committed to raising funds for the liberation army's sick and wounded will be effective. If we can manage to send money and provisions to Cuba, then we'll become vital to the rebellion and not just interested bystanders from afar."

I read over his shoulder as he sat in his favorite wing-back chair and studied my detailed plans.

After a short while, Cirilo gathered my papers together and said, "I don't see why your idea wouldn't work, Emilia. It's not unlike the political clubs already organized by men to help support the rebellion. You would, or course, need to have a solid set of by-laws . . . and the women must be selected carefully. They must be willing, from time to time, to make independent decisions on their own." He continued thoughtfully, "You must also select women of means who can and are willing to use their resources to mount costly and effective projects sure to bring in funds. And they must be loyal patriots to our cause . . . and to you, my dear. What I don't want," he continued, "is for you to become disillusioned or hurt in anyway."

At hearing his words, I felt a spontaneous burst of affection and appreciation for my husband. He rose from his chair and looked out the window at the fog drifting in from the Sound. Linking my arm into his, I joined him. At the far end of the drab garden wall a flash of red suddenly caught my eye. Oh, I realized, It was Narciso! Bundled up to his nose against the wintry weather in his bright red Christmas scarf, our son tossed a stick and ran after a fluff of black fur, the new puppy the boys had received as a gift.

Turning to me, my husband chuckled with an almost imperceptible twinkle in his gray eyes. "You, my dear, should have no problem convincing the ladies. Is not the art of persuasion one of your strongest assets?"

He seemed to enjoy his little joke immensely but didn't tell me anything that I had not already considered. Nonetheless, for me it was important to have his opinion and endorsement. After the children were attended to and household chores discussed with the housekeeper, I sat at the desk in my chamber to draft the by-laws of the women's association I intended to name "La Liga de las Hijas de Cuba" (The Daughters of Cuba League). The purpose of the group would be to raise funds through bazaars, raffles and cultural events like dances, art exhibits, theatrical presentations and concerts.

Pen in hand, I arranged my note paper and reflected on a mental image of Emilita for inspiration, while deciding what exactly Las Hijas could do. Oh! I thought, adding new details to the list, we could have auctions of art work. I noted . . . *fine furnishings, crafts and jewelry*. The money we raised would be sent to the *Cuba Libre* government in New York, the *Junta Revolucionaria*, but we needed also to budget separately for our own expenses. We needed stationery, postage stamps, maybe travel funds, and we might have to pay a fee for a meeting place if none of the ladies had adequate space in their homes. Funds for producing an event also should be included in our expenses.

I recall how exuberant I felt, my mind flitting from one thing to the next. And, of course, we would not forget the needy, the widows and orphans, the wounded and the destitute that crowded the city streets in greater numbers every day, refugees from the battle zones. We'd want to generate donations from some of the small clothing stores that had cropped up in the vicinity from 14th to 23rd streets. A number of establishments sold ready-made clothes, and their donations would be useful for the women and children. In a few months, I recalled, a new Cast Iron Palace Department Store was slated to open for business along the cobblestone streets of the Ladies' Mile. We should target that establishment. Anything and everything that was donated could be sold for medicines, lint and bandages. What else could we do? Think, think harder, I commanded myself, still giddy with excitement.

If we raised enough funds to buy weapons and ammunition . . . a shudder of excitement ran down my spine, we could send Remington Rifles or pistols! That would surely be appreciated by our men on the battle front. And if we were really successful, we would be able to mount our own expeditions. Outfitting and sending an expedition of men and munitions would not be difficult because the mansion had ample subterranean space for weapons and equipment in its underground cells and also had easy access to Long Island Sound. From there, a ship could reach the Atlantic Ocean in no time . . . no time at all. Oh, I had such high hopes for the work of the Liga. If only it could all spontaneously take shape, if as by magic.

But magic played no role in the hard work that lay ahead. The next two weeks were spent shoring up support for the organization. It meant I'd personally make it a point to visit the wealthiest ladies in our community to convince them to join our association. They needed to be strong women who had minds of their own, and did not depend on their husbands' approval for every detail. I envisioned myself on long treks from the mansion to the city in nasty winter weather as worthy sacrifices for *Cuba Libre*. I tried hard not to dwell on icy cold fingers and wet feet, visions of drafty train compartments and poorly heated Hansom cabs.

First on my list was Señora Eufemia B. de Macías, a lovely, gentle and wealthy woman with sparkling hazel eyes who didn't have an enemy in the world. She received me graciously in her Washington Square home. From the window of her formal parlor I could see a group of men who looked like surveyors, taking measurements for what would soon become a park on Washington Square.

"The noise and the controversy over that small plot of land has been enormously unsettling for those of us who live here," Señora de Macías confided, clasping her hands together as if she were begging for respite. "But now to the business at hand. You want to form an association to aid the rebellion and want me to be president? I'll really have to think about that, but I can tell you, my dear Doña Emilia, that it is an exciting idea." We spent the rest of the hour pleasantly reviewing plans for the association.

That was my first and easiest victory. A visit to Señora Matilda de Rodríguez that afternoon proved to be less promising. I played on the fact that we could be distant cousins because of the Rodríguez connection, but her response remained distant and cold.

"Señora Casanova de Villaverde," she began imperiously, clearly enunciating each syllable in my complete name. "I couldn't possibly accept your invitation because I may be involved with another organization. I do not believe it is wise to maintain loyalty to both. Surely you, of all people, do understand."

Was this a veiled reference to my writings or to my unwavering support of independence, I wondered? Warning bells rang in my head but I could not give in to such doubts—not just yet.

Meeting with Señora Rosalía de Hourritiner the following week was much more rewarding. A short, stocky and jovial woman, Doña Rosalía's spacious home on Fifth Avenue was conveniently located for the twenty-two women who had personally given me their pledge of support. As I entered the drawing room, I saw she had already prepared a virtual feast of delightful confections, steaming hot Cuban coffee alongside a pitcher of rich warm cream.

"My dear, dear Señora de Villaverde," she said smiling broadly as she extended both of her hands to mine. "You are most welcome! And your idea for forming a woman's club precedes you, my dear! It is, by far, the talk of the town, and I would be delighted if the ladies held their meetings in my home! Please, do tell me you accept my offer!"

Over all, I counted twenty-five women who had given their word to consider joining Las Hijas. Women like Señora de Hourritiner, connected to well-known families, were critical to the success of the enterprise because their names carried instant recognition and respect. By the beginning of February, I was confident that I'd secured the commitment of a number of important ladies eager to join the association and I distributed the following circular, a reminder to attend a celebratory meeting to launch our newest venture:

CIRCULAR

Because of your patriotism it is expected that you will attend a meeting on Saturday, the 6th of February, from one to two p.m. in the afternoon, at the Hotel Saint Julien at

Washington Place to celebrate together. Please take the liberty of bringing with you a list of the names of friends and other interested individuals. May God grant you long life.

Nueva York, February 5th, 1869

E. C. de Villaverde, Secretary

When fourteen ladies joined me on that Saturday to duly constitute ourselves in association and to be known, henceforth, as La Liga de las Hijas de Cuba, I was delighted with my accomplishment. Because of my fluent bilingual skills and personal connections and because I knew the position could carry a great deal of power, I graciously designated myself as the secretary of the association.

Curiously and most unexpectedly, no sooner had I formed Las Hijas when a close friend invited me to join her in forming another women's organization. In truth, I believed there could never be too many groups raising funds for the Army of Liberation, so I accepted her invitation. The group was named "La Junta Patriótica de Cubanas en Nueva York," (The Patriotic Cuban Women's Council of New York). It constituted itself on February 26th, twenty days after Las Hijas. As you can well imagine, I was excited by the prospect of so much political activism on the part of ladies who rarely, if ever, assumed a role in public life. I looked forward to the time when we could combine our efforts into one large women's patriotic assembly, increasing our visibility, our fundraising networks and, finally, our women's voices in the decisions of the Junta government.

And yet, in spite of the hustle and bustle and my excited anticipation at beginning our women's work, I expressed misgivings to Cirilo about this arrangement. "What if, instead of solidarity, the women's groups begin to compete with one another, recklessly working against each other? What if the targeted sources for funds are not large enough to give money to so many groups?" I asked.

I may have been näive, but I convinced myself that whenever possible, we women would work in unity. "This will certainly go into the records as my contribution to bringing the ladies out of the 'dark corners of the home,' as Ana Betancourt Mora requested," I said laughing and scattered the gremlins of doubt back into the recesses of my mind.

It was not very long, a week at the most, when I began to suspect something was wrong. I knew somewhere along the way discord was bound to surface, but I did not expect it so soon. Enraged, mostly at myself for giving so selflessly of my time and energy when I had my own affairs to put in order, I controlled my emotions sufficiently to act within reason.

It began quite innocently with a jointly sponsored concert we planned to give at Steinway Hall in the names of both, Las Hijas and the Junta Patriótica. I thought that five dollars per ticket was a fair price because the wealthy could afford to pay that amount. This was, after all, an event to raise money. But the ladies of the Junta Patriótica argued the price per ticket should be one dollar, making it easier for poor Cubans to attend. I, who collected donations every day of the week to help the poor, knew that one dollar could buy their groceries for the week! I had no intentions of taking the bread out of their mouths by asking them to pay anything. "Rather than entertaining poor Cubans, weren't we pledged to help them?" I asked. By charging five dollars, I was hoping to attract a wealthier class of people who could afford to part with that sum of money and afterwards indulge in fine cuisine at an upscale dining establishment, like Delmonico's, without giving the matter a second thought.

As if to rub salt into the wound, the ladies of the Junta Patriótica revealed they did not have to agree with everything I proposed *on principle*! That comment disappointed me enormously, but I forced myself to smile and deal with the situation rationally, because I'd be working with these ladies in the future. Knowing well how caustic I could be, I resisted criticizing them and carefully pondered the situation before I sat down to write,

> To: Señoras Zayas de Castellanos, Castellanos de Castellanos and Montejo de Sherman.
> Ladies:
> After thinking over our last meeting and the systematically tenacious opposition you took to my proposal that we sell the concert tickets for five dollars, when you wanted to charge one dollar, and you agreed to my idea on the onerous condition that I sell one thousand tickets, I think you do not have the right to impose such conditions on me. Afraid that new and broader disagreements will arise in the future, I've decided to leave the organization without abandoning the concert project which I initiated.
> There were two reasons for wanting to sell the tickets at a dollar: (1) so poor Cubans could attend; and (2) that you did not have to approve everything I proposed. Clearly, I was not sponsoring the concert for people who could not afford it, and I do not expect good results from our efforts if you oppose me so passionately. I regret leaving such amiable friends but the needs of the patria come first.
> I am your most attentive servant and paisana.
> E. C. de Villaverde, Nueva York, February 20, 1869.

From that day forward I vowed to devote myself solely to the work of Las Hijas and the politics of support for Cuba Libre.

As the secretary of an active association, letters and writing and meetings and charities seemed to consume my days. It was the 10th of March when I wrote to José Morales Lémus, director of the Junta Revolucionaria, proudly informing him about the success of Las Hijas in raising $2,000 for medicines and bandages and $1,288.47 for the sick and wounded. Delighted with our accomplishment, I hoped Morales Lémus would appreciate our efforts. After all, as far as I knew at that time, he was a decent man who'd struggled to gain American support for the Cuban rebellion. In all sincerity and in the spirit of camaraderie, I wrote the following letter:

> *To: C. José Morales Lémus,*
>
> *The committee of the society, Liga de las Hijas de Cuba . . . since the 6th of February various ladies have constituted themselves in formal association under written by-laws, and elected officers to discharge the duties required of all public corporations. Subsequently, they agreed to celebrate a great concert as the most expedient manner to raise funds. In fact, said concert sponsored by the committee took place on the 9th of March with great success, and we deducted the costs which were extensive and that left $3,288.47, which we deposited in the committee's bank account. Fulfilling the objective of our mission, we have the honor to place at your disposal as representative of the free government of Cuba, $2,000 to invest in medicines, bandages, lint, and the remainder to help the sick and wounded of the liberation army. Please pick it up at your earliest opportunity.*
>
> *E. C. de Villaverde, Secretary. March, 1869.*

That July a strange, anonymous letter reached me at the Casanova Mansion from a patriot in Cuba who had refuted derogatory references to me in the pro-Spanish press. By then, of course, I knew the newspapers in Cuba had labeled me a traitor because of articles and letters I'd published supporting the rebel cause. In all honesty, I reveled in their assessment of my actions. "How simply delightful," I remember saying aloud to no one in particular as I read the patriot's letter. If the press actually took the time to discredit my reputation in print, it could only mean that I was doing good work for *Cuba Libre*. I thanked the patriot, recognizing that he, if it was a he, had risked his life by corresponding with me. Taking that issue in consideration, I carefully wrote,

Havana

To Whom It May Concern:

I've just received your letter of the 10th, which has agreeably surprised me. But your praises confuse me. Until now, I've only been doing my duty in helping our patria in the only ways I can from here, as a woman with a family. Undoubtedly, the thought that my efforts are not the only ones coming from those of my sex pleases me, and in addition, that you take the risk to write to me since your letter could have fallen into the hands of government spies. Your example gives me courage and will probably inspire others. . . .

Your humble servant,

E. C. de Villaverde, Nueva York, July 14, 1869.

From then on, my anonymous correspondent became a worthwhile ally as he or she opened my eyes to new ideas, new possibilities and venues for raising money. I lost no time in asking my anonymous friend in Havana if he or she would be willing to raise money for Las Hijas. Donations had already reached us from wealthy Cubans on the island who secretly supported the rebel cause. Why should Las Hijas not expand this network more aggressively?

Havana

To Whom It May Concern:

. . . Do you think you could sell some raffle tickets there for an allegorical painting of the Cuban revolution and for a magnificent cross encrusted with precious gems which I've received to raise funds? In case you find buyers for the raffle tickets, for each dollar I will send you a number and I'll keep a copy of it. In case there is a winner, I'll hold on to the prize for the winner . . . Don't be afraid that you bother me with your letters, far from it. I am pleased, because if it were up to

me, I'd be everywhere inspiring courage among the
disillusioned, the timid and the luke-warm.
E. C. de Villaverde, Nueva York, August 4, 1869.

Everyone in Las Hijas would do well, I reasoned, to contact old friends in Cuba for monetary support. Surely my own childhood friends, whom I counted among my loyal supporters, owned jewelry that could be sold here in New York. These friends could sell raffle tickets for us and find other means of aiding the cause.

I'd reached the point where I now used the pseudonym, "Lolita" or "Fany" in the event that my letters to Cuba were intercepted. I also cautioned my contacts to do the same. Letters left the mansion every day on their way to ladies in Latin America, in the Caribbean and in other states of the Union. Given my natural inclinations and my zealousness, I was not hesitant to contact people I knew only by reputation nor to disguise my letters to intimate friends and family. In August, for example, I wrote,

Havana
My Dear Friend,
. . . I celebrate your suggestion that we blanket the area with announcements about the raffle. My friends and others are of the opinion that the cross, being raffled along with other gems, forms a good lot that will bring the most benefits. As you will see from the manifesto of the "Liga de las Hijas de Cuba," for which I serve as secretary, when you indicated we should send raffle tickets to the wife of Juárez, we had already written to her and to many other distinguished ladies in South America . . . .

Those of us who are in exile have contributed so much that it is difficult to raise funds by subscription. So it would be convenient if you tested the waters there for subscriptions; with a small amount given by many, one could raise a great sum of money. From what we have seen, you are capable of great

sacrifices. . . . Money, money and money is the salvation. . . .
God give you courage and steadfastness to serve the patria, and
life to see her free and blessed.
    Adiós, I am your
    "Lolita," Nueva York, August 29, 1869.

I soon discovered I was not alone in my zeal as the ladies of Las
Hijas began to push the boundaries of polite society in their quest
to contact allies for our sacred mission. Frankly, I was elated with
their dedication and, yet, I felt that Las Hijas needed to feel
acknowledged and rewarded for their efforts. "Their sense of mission should be kept continuously alive," I thought, "expressed in
the broad range of activities we undertook."

In part, I believe that was one of the many motivations I felt
when I took the liberty of asking the esteemed General Giuseppe
Garibaldi for his moral support on behalf of our association.
Everyone knew about the general's triumphs and brilliant testi-
monials in support of Italian unification. In that regard, he was
not unlike our own *paisanos*. He, too, suffered life in exile when
he lived in Staten Island. He worked as a candle maker to earn a
living. On one occasion, I had the pleasure of hearing him speak
in New York. And so it was that I wrote,

Caprera
To: Señor General José Garibaldi
My Dear Sir:
    You must not think it strange that a totally unknown
person should write you these lines. You are a citizen of the
world, friend of all people, champion of liberty, and these
titles give me the right to address myself to you.
    Since the revolution began in my country, in October,
1868, I've been observing the European press expecting at
least a brave word in favor of the Cubans from the heroic
Garibaldi, who has never, in any way, refused to lend his

sword, his support or the influence of his name to any nation that has fought for its liberty. . . .

I am the secretary of an organization, the "Liga de Las Hijas de Cuba," created to raise funds and help the patriotic army. The association has asked me to write to you, not for funds or monetary aid, but because words written by you supporting the great radical Cuban movement . . . would be priceless for us.

Your most attentive admirer,

E. C. de Villaverde, Mott Haven, January 3, 1870.

Señora Emilia C. de Villaverde

My dear señora:

With all my soul I've been with you since the start of your glorious revolution. It is not only Spain who fights for liberty in her own house but wants to enslave the rest of the world outside. But I will be, all of my life, on the side of the oppressed, be the oppressors kings or nations.

Affectionately yours,

G. Garibaldi, Caprera, January 31, 1870.

Delighted at the thought of soon sharing Garibaldi's communication with the ladies of Las Hijas, I carefully tucked his letter into my satchel in preparation for our next meeting. Las Hijas, I remember thinking, was well on its way to becoming an association of importance.

Eleven

My Family Faces Danger

*"Well, let the young man die where he is." By order of General
Dulce, and against the wishes and solicitations of Mr. Casanova,
the prisoner was sent as a common felon to the hospital of the
chain-gang, which is located in the upper part of the same jail.
There, away from the care of his mother and sisters, young
Casanova went through his dreadful illness and eventually
recovered, thanks to the money freely spent by Mr. Casanova in
paying for medicines and nursing. Soon afterward, the prisoner
was remanded to his solitary cell, where he was kept for more
than three months, until he, being under age, was claimed as an
American citizen because of his father's nationality and restored
to liberty.*

"Memorandum of Inocencio Casanova,
A Naturalized Citizen of the United States."
Nueva York: Impreso por MacDonald & Palmer.
733 Broadway. 1871.

Gathered around the round mahogany table in the tastefully
furnished Fifth Avenue parlor of Señora de Hourritiner, I felt
deeply satisfied that the association's first year had been so productive. As I gazed at the ladies around the table, I thought about
how blessed I was to have such loyal friends and compatriots, the
ladies of Las Hijas. Along one wall of the formal parlor, a Cuban
liberation flag was mounted between twin windows adorned with

sheer curtain panels and yellow, silk drapery. "How appropriate," I thought. Señora de Hourritiner had made our meeting space conspicuously patriotic and welcoming to our work. I carefully reviewed my notes and prepared to read aloud a listing of our activities since the club's founding. We calculated and evaluated the fruits of our labor over the past year, but the main topic of conversation turned, as I expected, to the letter from General Garibaldi.

"Well, I am one who was truly amazed that such an important leader recognized our cause. This kind of support should be announced in all the newspapers of the city because it will attract others to join us in our fundraising efforts," remarked our president, Señora de Macías, as she accepted a dainty cup of afternoon coffee from the parlor maid. Her comment, coinciding with the aroma of freshly baked pastries and steaming coffee carried into the room on silver trays by two Irish maids, indicated the business part of our meeting had come to a close. The ladies were free to take up any issue they deemed important.

"Well, I'd praise the general less highly," retorted Señora de González y Ruiz, a haughty woman, wife of a wealthy merchant connected to Havemeyer, Townsend & Co., the largest sugar refinery in Brooklyn. "He could have been a bit more—Oh, I'm not quite sure of the word—effusive! That's it! The letter is too simply stated." At this remark, the ladies rushed in to offer their own opinions, and the afternoon threatened to become a free-for-all.

"Ladies, not intending to change the conversation," interjected Señora de Fernández, arms leaning lightly against the back of a high-backed chair, "but has anyone read the survey conducted by Morales Lémus and the Junta Revolucionaria? My husband brought home a copy, and I thought it was quite a revelation." She walked around the high-backed chair and came to sit at the table where several of the ladies had remained. "It states that more than half of all Cuban émigrés in New York are women and children. And among the women, most are homemakers, not wage earners in the factories or in shops, even though some do earn a living as seamstresses or nannies. Surely we can agree that these women are probably dependent on charity and need our help. However, I'm glad to say," she continued, "ours is not the only association responsible for their care."

"No, it is not. The Junta Patriótica is very active," I responded in faint praise as I recalled my last encounter with that group, "as is the American Ladies Club and the Hijas de la Libertad. And there are now women's clubs in Philadelphia, New Orleans, Baltimore, in Key West and in Mexico."

"There are two newly formed children's clubs that teach patriotism so that the little ones do not forget their homeland," someone volunteered from across the room.

"But before we adjourn and socialize, forgive my indiscretion, Doña Emilia, but is it true that you visited the White House with regard to your esteemed father, Don Inocencio, some time ago? That you had an emergency meeting with the President of the United States in Washington, D.C.?"

Surprised, I raised my head and locked eyes with the speaker, Señora Rosalía de Hourritiner, as she invited me to relive the most horrific experience I'd ever had in my life. To be sure, our closest friends were knowledgeable about the incident that had taken place some nine months earlier, but my father had insisted on maintaining silence about it, at least until he'd decided on his course of action.

For the briefest of moments, I had the strangest sensation that my vision seemed out of focus and the Cuban liberation flag hanging so solidly between the windows appeared to sway. While I decided just how much of my private life I wished to reveal to the ladies, I steadied my hand, carefully placed my pen next to the ledger where I'd kept the minutes of Las Hijas and took a deep breath. Leaning back comfortably into my chair, I sat up straight and folded my hands on my lap. Only then did I begin to address my *paisanas* in a low tone, noticing there was not a sound in the room except for my own voice.

"Even though it was a heart wrenching experience that still makes my heart palpitate every time I think about it, I'll tell you what happened to our family . . . why I requested an audience with the President of the United States. My story should serve to rid you, once and for all, of any doubts you might still harbor about our struggle. . .why it is that we fight so fiercely against the corrupt and abusive government that strangles the land we all love so dearly. I'll tell you what I know of the incident. This is the story as my father told it to me."

"Long in the habit of spending the winters in Cuba for reasons of health, my parents left New York in November 1868, a little more than a month after the rebellion at Yara had begun. In early December the Spanish authorities issued the first order of arrest for my father and my brothers. You should know, ladies, that my father and my brothers are American citizens, but that fact did nothing to change the circumstances. Their crime was supposedly non-payment of taxes, but the invoice for taxes on the estates had never been issued.

"Forty *voluntarios* and civil guardsmen invaded Armonía, my brother José's estate, armed to the teeth. When they discovered my brother had escaped, the guardsmen insulted my sister-in-law, committed unspeakable outrages inside of the home and did costly damage to the property. The plantation's engineer was shot dead in front of his wife and four children. As if that weren't enough, they promised to return and shoot, on sight, everyone on the estate.

"Thank the Lord the American consul came to my father's aid during those months and had the charges dismissed, but a second order of arrest was issued in late December. This game of intimidation continued without respite and my poor father, aged and in delicate health, went from one official to another trying to clear up the matter without success. All along, the American consul was there to protect him and, once again, had the order dismissed.

"But the Spanish authorities continued their harassment unabated, simply as they desired without concern for the validity of the charges. To complicate matters even further, the newspaper, *La Aurora,* printed an edict commanding José to present himself to the authorities on the charge of . . . *high treason*! My brother immediately went into hiding and, to protect my other brothers, Manuel, Pedro, Rafael and Ricardo, only my father had knowledge of his whereabouts.

"My dear ladies, this is the type of persecution that we are fighting against every day! Today, it is my family that is branded as traitors for everyone to fear; today it is my family whose reputation is ruined and businesses embargoed. Tomorrow it could be your loved ones in such a predicament. By law, traitors must forfeit all their assets to the authorities, and this is not just happening to the Casanovas. It is happening to other good Cubans, to friends and neighbors."

It felt as if the air had been sucked out of the room. Even the sounds of the dainty porcelain cups clinking against the saucers and the tinkling of the silver spoons had stopped. I picked up the story from where I'd left it.

"In early January of 1869, my youngest brother, Rafael, took advantage of a government proclamation that lifted the ban on publishing a newspaper. He began to print a small weekly sheet. To spite my father, Captain General Dulce disregarded his own liberal proclamation and ordered Rafael's paper to be shut down. Dulce promptly imprisoned Rafael and tried him for violation of the law of the press. But the magistrate who reviewed the case failed to find him guilty and assured my father that his son would soon be released."

Murmurs and gasps arose again from my audience, many of whom knew of others persecuted for the simple act of publishing a newspaper, but I dismissed their agitation and continued.

"On orders from that despicable despot, Dulce, he was not released. Instead, Rafael was left to rot in that stinking, filthy, rat-infested hole that passes for the public jail. A few days later, he contracted a severe case of smallpox and was so ill my parents did not think he would live. In spite of my father's pleas, Rafael was not allowed to be sent home. He was sent, instead, to the chain-gang hospital like a common felon, without the care of doctors or of his beloved mother and sisters. He did not die only by the grace of God and was released after three months because he was the minor son of an American citizen!"

A sigh of relief arose from some of the ladies; others invoked Divine Providence and the saints and commented on my ordeal.

"But, Ladies," I interjected rather loudly, commanding their attention once again, "what you have heard so far is only the good side of the story. Let me inform you about the rest.

"No sooner was Rafael released than my father was thrown into the public jail to suffer almost two months of insulting harassment, searing heat during the days and cold stone for his restless sleep at night. This time, help was not forthcoming because he was denied the visits of the American consul. Much of his property was confiscated, the workers killed or forced into hiding, the houses destroyed and the crops burned to a crisp.

"At that point in the ordeal, my husband and I discovered what was happening. It was April 4th, 1869, Easter Sunday. If you recall, on that day Las Hijas planned to host a special breakfast following church services for members and their families. Cirilo and I were just about to board the train at the Casanova Station to attend services at St. Patrick's with Las Hijas, when we heard the commotion of a horse and rider galloping at full speed toward the railroad station. It was Mauricio, one of our house servants. Rapidly dismounting, he ran to us obviously distraught. Without saying a word, he thrust a telegram into my hands . . . hands that trembled uncontrollably as I tore open the envelope . . . and . . . read the contents.

"'My father is being held captive in Cuba, accused of treason,' I told Cirilo breathlessly as he grabbed the telegram from my hands. If my husband had not been with me, I swear to you, dear friends, I don't know what I would have done. I only know at that moment, I felt such rage and desperation that, had I wings, I would have flown to Cuba and physically assaulted the authorities right then and there in return for their treachery.

"At the first telegraph station, we left the train and sent a telegram to Mr. Hamilton Fish, the Secretary of State, informing him of the imprisonment, stressing the fact that my father was an American citizen and property owner in this country. On Monday afternoon, we were in Washington, D.C. I met with representatives and senators, cabinet secretaries, the attorney general and anyone else I could find to inform them of my father's case and secure their help. With only the titles of señora, *cubana* and daughter of an imprisoned American to my name, doors miraculously opened for me. I was amazed that I was able to approach the most influential men in Washington. Fortunately, the name Casanova meant something. It was not unfamiliar to many of the elected and appointed officials as, in the past, my father and my brothers had had dealings with Washington and the White House. My brother José, you may recall, was once consul for the United States in Guayaquil, Ecuador.

"On Tuesday, we went to the White House at the appointed hour and entered the Great Hall reserved by the president for petitions from the general public. In spite of the multitudes waiting to meet with the president, we handed our card to the clerk and, after a very short wait, were ushered upstairs to a smaller waiting room. So distraught was I that I barely noticed the pale haze of marble dust floating in the air and lightly falling on our clothing, the result of massive construction authorized by the president and Mrs. Grant to repair and remodel the White House.

"We were told by the second-floor clerk that the president and his cabinet were in session in the Cabinet Room, adjacent to the

Executive Office. My husband and I were then ushered into an anteroom. I forced myself not to dwell on a worst case scenario and began to focus instead on the shabbily decorated anteroom. I noted faded curtains and scratched tables, most probably, I imagined, because government finances had been depleted with the Civil War.

"Soon, we were ushered into the Executive Office by a Mr. Babcock, the president's private secretary. President Grant himself greeted us and led me to the sofa, where no sooner had I sat down than I began to sob copious tears of pent-up anger and frustration. Between sobs, I told him my story. The president, a kind, portly gentleman with a ruddy whiskered face, handed me a handkerchief, which I have with me still.

"'My dear lady,' he said, 'you may leave here in peace without fear for your father's life. They will not lay a finger on him, nor will those Spaniards dare to raise the ire of this nation.'

"Cirilo caught my eye over the president's head as if to confirm my own understanding of the president's words. I believed the president was telling us that since the United States had not yet endorsed either side in the conflict, it seemed Spain was not about to lose favor over the fate of one American businessman. On the 20th of April, the very day orders from Washington reached the commodore of an American vessel engaged in maneuvers in Cuban waters, my father was set free.

"And this, my compatriots, is why the work of Las Hijas must go *beyond* fundraisers and bazaars! Our efforts must be expanded more effectively. We should be thinking big, providing money for training soldiers and buying weapons; we must never give in to anything short of independence!"

In my rush of words, I suddenly realized I might be frightening some of the women. No one spoke. The room, once again, was filled with the silence of a cathedral. Through the sheer curtain panels on the windows, I noticed a few swirls of bright snow dancing about in the falling dusk. A few words were uttered here and there, but mostly we bid each other farewell, subdued by the implications of the story. We began to gather our belongings to head for carriages that would take us to our homes before the snow began to cover the ground in earnest. I remember thinking how glad I was that I'd be returning to the mansion instead of our New York townhouse. The mansion had, in recent years, become my stone-hewed refuge from the world.

Homeward bound, I sat in the train compartment snug in my woolen cloak, attempting without success to hold my fur collar close to my neck against the draft that seeped in through the cracks in the window frame. Staring out into the darkness, I barely noticed the intermittent flicker of lights coming from sparsely spaced houses that dotted the landscape. My mind was back in time, back to that warm spring day in 1869 at the end of a lilac-laden April when my parents had escaped the clutches of the despot and arrived safely at our front portal.

I heard the horses' hoof beats and ran to the front porch just in time to see my husband gently helping mother climb down from the carriage. I gasped and could do nothing to hold back my tears at the sight of my poor father. Once a robust, energetic figure, he was now a slight, bent man, broken in body and spirit. Where was the father of the fabled *Canarias*? The protective riding companion of my youth? As soon as he saw me, he held out his slender arms to enfold me. I ran into his arms, noting his sad, watery eyes.

Locked in the circle of his embrace, he whispered to me in a raspy voice, "Thank God you are safe! I was so worried about you; the scoundrels threatened me with harming you, kept reminding me that I was the father of that traitor, Emilia Casanova!"

I stared at him in utter disbelief! *My safety?* But he was the one who had suffered imprisonment unjustly. It was then that I understood that the bloom of the Cuban sun was no longer on his cheeks; his loyalty to the Spanish government had been forever severed. He was my father once again, the protector of our family against injustice.

That very night, my family sat at the long, polished table in the dining room. My parents, sisters, nieces and nephews, we all gave thanks that we were alive and together again. The warm glow reflected on the table surface from lighted candles in silver candelabras filled the room. All of us were bathed in dream-like illumination, enveloped, as it were, in a golden, protective cocoon surrounding the Casanovas and the Villaverdes.

Deep in conversation at one end of the table, their gray heads close together, father and my husband exchanged information about the progress of the rebellion, plotting a strategy for using our dock and storage caves to advance the cause. In spite of his frailty, my father's eyes gleamed with an intensity, a hatred I'd never seen before. His illusions about Cuban reform had been crushed. The bloom of Cuba had left him . . . Surrounded by her grandchildren, mother seemed tired but content as the children jostled, one against the other, to sit closest to her. When my sister, Cecilia, began to shepherd the little ones to bed, I retired to my own chambers, intending to rid my soul of the raw, black anger that had invaded it. Taking my pen in hand, I wrote the letter I'd been composing in my mind all night.

> *Your Excellency and Captain General (of the Western Sector)*
> *of the island of Cuba,*
> *D. Domingo Dulce.*
> *Havana*
>
> *They tell me that only because he is my brother, Your*
> *Excellency denied after conceding permission to transfer the*
> *young man, Don Rafael Casanova, from the military hospital*
> *to a private home where he could recover from smallpox with*
> *the nurturing of some of his family members. Being so cruel,*
> *that information seems incredible to me. And it seems*

incredible to me because what I do or don't do so many miles away has nothing to do with my brother. This seems incredible to me . . . Is the persecution and trampling of my father, elderly, sickly, moderate and removed from political ideology and agitation, sanctioned by your laws? . . . My brother's youth and my father's reputation absolve them of any wrong doing.

Your Excellency, you should make amends, because for twelve years I have been married to a declared enemy of the state and in all that time I have not depended on my father, nor have we shared similar political opinions. I am certain my father has not plotted against the government, and anyone who knows him would know he is not capable of defying the authorities. I, on the contrary, do not hide the fact that I detest your government and will do anything I can to derail it.

Therefore, for your own good, for the honor and dignity of the nation you represent in Cuba, you should not openly advertise to the world the scandal of punishing a father and brother for the acts of a daughter and sister.

Your attentive servant,

E. C. de Villaverde, Nueva York, April 22, 1869.

His Excellency, Captain General Domingo Dulce, did not answer my letter. Instead, the inappropriately named despot, who in his actions showed not a drop of sweetness, sanctioned the vilification of my name in the government-protected newspapers. By December, the situation had gotten so far out of hand that reports reached my ears of my symbolic burning in effigy in my beloved, native city of Cárdenas. I admit, those affronts were painful to acknowledge, and even more so for my family, who feared for my safety, but as I'd done throughout my life when confronted by adversity, I intensified my commitment to the cause.

*Your Excellency and Captain General (of the Western Sector)
of the island of Cuba,
D. Domingo Dulce.
Havana*

Granted, it is unusual for Cuban women to address captain generals, but since I've long emancipated myself of colonial tutelage, I think I can exercise the right of all free people who have reason to complain to you about your vassals. At the risk of distracting you from more important matters with the indifference practiced over there, I inform you that the conduct of the press in Havana regarding Cuban women, especially the one who directs these lines to you, is now beyond scandalous and touches upon affront. Not because I'm preoccupied, nor have such poor taste as to waste my time in reading dailies consigned to the defense of the most brutal despotism over that land, but because some of the editors took the liberty of sending me the newspapers, I've discovered something of what the Spanish press vomits against me and my female compatriots.

Undoubtedly, this may seem strong language coming from a woman, but it is dictated by indignation upon hearing that in Cuba the government is moral and just when the authorities, omnipotent for everyone, are neither moral nor just enough to punish the abuses of the press.

As far as I'm concerned, don't think, your excellency, that the attacks in the press do me harm. My paisanos know me well and that's enough for me. I will continue on my path, I will despise the meanness of spirit of my enemies, lament the misfortunes of my paisanas, although they are condemned to suffer them, and will do everything in my power to help destroy the government which is the abomination of my land and the dishonor of the civilized world. When it has collapsed, when there is no sign left of the ominous domination, if I am still alive, I'll go to my country to *celebrate your erasure from the face of America. That's what I think, and thanks to Divine Providence, that is what the immense majority of my people think.*

With all due consideration,

E. C. de V., Nueva York, December 28, 1869.

Twelve

No Good Deed Goes Unpunished

During the month of January 1870, I discovered a children's choir in St. Bernard's Church in New York. . . . It inspired me to present the children in a fundraising event . . . to aid the many paisanos who, in the majority, are poor and in misery. . . . I promised to cover all the costs. . . .

I endured many disillusionments; few were the Cubans who purchased tickets from me. The person you would least expect would comment "for what reason did these poor come to this country; why didn't they go to Mexico instead." Not a few would say that their money was for the war and not for the poor, etc. I passed countless uncomfortable moments, a thousand embarrassments begging for favors, gave out innumerable free tickets, exhausted myself and worked without rest, almost always alone and sometimes accompanied by Mrs. Keeler.

Emilia Casanova de Villaverde,
"Los Niños del Coro de San Bernardo." January, 1870.

Without exaggeration, I remember not a day went by that some poor soul did not ask me for charity. Refugees came to me for warm clothes, employment, donations, lodging and even their daily bread. The city could not provide for the fast growing population of workers and immigrants because its own finances were said to be near ruin. Almshouses and some of the hospitals did offer shelter and food. Most of the needy were foreign-born, but the Spanish-speaking refugees came to us for help, their *paisanos* in the community. When I look back, I recall fleeting images: a slender girl whose small frame belied her ten years, enamored of the red woolen cloak I'd given her; a grateful grandfather thanking me for an iron bed frame because he'd no longer have to share his bed with his grandson; images like that. I kept accounts that I gladly paid for with my own money in several thrift stores just for the purpose of helping our poor *paisanos*. You can understand, then, why I began to search for new venues for my charitable work. Unfortunately, the new fundraising projects that I envisioned also began to open my eyes to unexpected divisions in the expatriate community.

A concert by American children in St. Bernard's choir was one such project and it played over and over in my mind like a repetitious melody. This was not a fundraiser sponsored by Las Hijas, so I could not count on any of the ladies to help organize the event. Instead, the principal of the parish school, Mrs. Keeler, a lovely and quite personable American woman, assisted me in organizing the concert.

Almost no funds were donated by my own community of Cuban expatriates, even though many of them were well-to-do. In fact, many of them expressed negative feelings toward the refugees, articulating resentment for their having come to New York in the first place. It was Mrs. Keeler who gently suggested we approach Americans for money, arguing that if they gave generously, that might encourage the wealthier Cubans to also give.

One cold, wintry day with our list of donors in hand, Mrs. Keeler and I visited the offices of the Junta at 71 Broadway, where we conversed with Señor José Manuel Mestre, a member of the Junta's new executive board. I'd met Mestre on other occasions. He was a lawyer and abolitionist, and we'd met at social and political gatherings. I recalled that he had co-authored a popular translation of *Uncle Tom's Cabin* into Spanish. In October, I'd attended a lecture he gave wherein he praised the noble flag of Free Cuba and wondered if he had in mind one of the many I'd sent to the generals on the battle front. In short, I expected his generous support on the matter of the children's concert.

"How awkward it would appear," Mrs. Keeler cajoled and I supported her opinion, "if Americans supported a fundraiser for destitute refugees, but well-to-do Cubans in the city did not." We emphatically stressed the benefits that would accrue from the Junta's support, not to mention good will and recognition. But after lengthy evasion of the subject by Señor Mestre and aggressive arguments by us, we were forced to leave the offices empty handed. Needless to say, I felt deeply embarrassed in front of Mrs. Keeler.

As it happened, our beautiful concert was a resounding success, but that was due in great measure to the energetic commitment of dozens of people, many of whom were Americans I'd not met before. In appreciation, I penned a letter to the editor of *La Revolución* mentioning all those worthy individuals who were to be commended for their role in mounting the event, while sarcastically insinuating that the Cuban expatriate community should be ashamed of its lack of participation. I sat at my desk and tactfully wrote,

> *To: Director of* La Revolución
> *My dear Sir:*
>
> *In response to your offer of February 16th, I'm sending a draft of the announcement I wish to publish in* La Revolución *and thank you for the favor of doing so.*
>
> *In similar appreciation I wish to thank Mr. Covel, 544 Broadway, for the magnificent piano he lent us for our use the night of the function; Herr Klein, corner of Houston and Bowery, for the scenery and decorations; Mr. Wallack of the Wallack Theater, for the curtains and "bambalinas" and for a flag of Free Cuba of substantial dimensions; Father Healy, St. Bernard's Church, for facilitating the performance of the children's choir; the Rector of the Lassalle Institute for the*

orchestra of forty children; Mr. White for volunteering to accompany the choir on the piano, and Mr. Cooper, owner of the facility, for heading the list of donors with a donation of five dollars, which allowed us to rent the hall.

What is left for La Revolución *to do, relying on its popularity among Cubans, is to make giving fashionable among those people with resources, and I will then see my efforts celebrated as a brilliant success.*

Sincerely yours,

E. C. de V., Mott Haven, February 25, 1870.

"Why," I'd ask myself over and over, "should this incident weigh so heavily on my mind?" By all accounts, it *was* a success, yet something was nagging at me. When I reviewed what had transpired in the course of our actions, I likened the experience to the purchase of an artfully crocheted tapestry with an ugly tear on one of its corners that you tried to ignore, thinking that by doing so all who saw it would note only its beauty. But you couldn't ignore it. The rigidity in my shoulders and neck, I feared, signaled the start of another headache.

The money was not raised for *me*, I reasoned, nor did I hunger for a place in the limelight! I became aware of that unpleasant tightening at the back of my neck every time I thought of it. I told myself, the Casanovas were comfortable enough to allow me and my family to live very well with sufficient means to advance the causes about which we were passionate. Our children would receive good educations or apprenticeships that would encourage them to accomplish something useful with their lives.

The point was, I knew the concerts were a wonderful vehicle for helping the city's poor Cubans. But after several such experiences, regardless of the depths of my charitable nature and the enormity of the growing misery of my *paisanos*, it had just become too painful for me to organize another one. And that, I finally conceded, was at the core of my dissatisfaction!

After all the obligations one assumed, the embarrassments one endured convincing people to purchase tickets, the guilt one felt for neglecting home and family . . . in the end, one was left to suffer the whispers, innuendoes and downright mean spiritedness of one's own people. "No," I thought, "this was no longer for me." I could not subject my family nor myself to the hardship it had placed on all of us. There would be other means to alleviate the misery of the refugees. I only needed to find them.

I suddenly paused in amusement and smiled. Just the notion of devising new ventures, facing new challenges, elevated my mood and stamina considerably. I felt as if I could actually move mountains! And that was the usual way I'd resolve my problems.

In the spring of 1870, Las Hijas and I devised a unique plan to help the refugees that essentially replaced organizing and promoting concerts. We proposed to transport Cuban refugee families from New York City to South America. Astonishing? I'd be the first to admit it was far-fetched and would require diligent promotion at the highest levels. But the notion of relocating people was not unknown in a country that sought to relocate indigenous peoples and former slaves who hoped to be repatriated to Africa. Representing Las Hijas, I embarked on a second trip to Washington, D.C., this time to convince President Grant and Admiral Porter to designate a naval vessel for that purpose. This visit, with my husband at my side, gave me an opportunity to strengthen my friendship with influential individuals and others who in the future might be of service to our cause of *Cuba Libre*.

As before, following a short wait in the Great Hall I was ushered upstairs and encountered the president's private secretary, Mr. Babcock, who graciously directed me to wait in the anteroom. The chamber looked lovely, richly decorated with comfortable seating, not at all the way it had been on my first visit. With renovations apparently completed, there was no sign of construction in evidence. Before long, President Grant himself appeared at the door to the Executive Office and welcomed me like a long lost friend.

"Madame Villaverde," he bellowed jovially. "It is a pleasure to see you again under happier circumstances."

I remembered with a hint of embarrassment how I had cried unabashedly in his presence the last time we met. I smiled at him as if in apology for my past actions.

"It is, of course, my pleasure as well, Mr. President," I answered, feeling awed by the presence of the President of the United States. "Thank you so much for meeting with me.

"Today, I am here on a mission of mercy," I began, settling myself in ladylike fashion on the edge of the chair he offered me directly opposite his own massive desk. A burly man, he settled comfortably into an oversized, upholstered captain's chair, as he had done, no doubt, multitude of times with other visitors. The president pressed his fingertips together in church steeple fashion, his elbows anchored solidly on the desk, and waited for me to speak.

"As you are no doubt aware," I said, entering into my prepared speech and wondering just how aware he really was about the drastic conditions among the poor in New York City, "among a growing population of immigrants from the Caribbean and European countries, there are hundreds upon hundreds of Cuban refugee families living in misery in New York. These, Mr. President, are the unseen casualties of the war in Cuba, and they are indeed war casualties," I emphasized a bit too dramatically, "as surely as if they had taken up weapons and fired them in combat.

"As you doubtless know, Mr. President, the financial straits of many expatriate Cubans and also Puerto Ricans living in the city hover on sheer poverty. The economy is not good, jobs are hard to find and many live in squalor. Disease afflicts the downtrodden in their poor neighborhoods. I've personally seen how difficult it has been for the refugees, so many of them women or widows with young children, or the aged, to adjust to a declining social and economic status. They are not at all doing well, in spite of the fact that they come here to escape a war and find a better life."

I felt his rapt attention. His eyes had not strayed to other matters as he listened to me very carefully. Perhaps I did not sound like an overzealous missionary, after all.

At that point, he rose from his seat and stepped over to a small, exquisitely lacquered, red table of Japanese origin, set beside the windows framed by lavishly styled draperies. He studied me, his piercing blue eyes unblinking, when he thought I was not looking. I hoped that he knew me to be an intelligent woman, a revolutionary in spirit and a representative of a bonafide organization. His allies in Congress, with whom I'd engaged in debate over the status of Cuba on a previous occasion, may have warned him against me. As one congressman had said to Cirilo, who'd also accompanied me on that visit, "this little lady should not be taken for granted. She is well-informed, speaks her mind and is not afraid to look you straight in the eye as she shreds your arguments to pieces." I remember how, on our journey back to New York, we laughed at their reactions to my well-informed, impassioned defense of the rebellion.

I continued to observe the president and decided he was just deep in thought as he reached for a cigar from an intricately carved humidor on top of the lacquered table. Oh! I said to myself as he removed the band. It is a Cuban cigar, a product, according to its signature band, from the famed Yvallero estate near Havana. I recognized the artwork and for no apparent reason, felt pleased with the connection to the homeland, insignificant as it was. Grant returned to his place behind his desk, looked at the cigar in his hand but did not light it.

"Madame Villaverde, you seem to have a strong following in the press."

For the briefest of moments, I froze in my seat wondering to which articles, in particular, he referred. Was he informed about the essays that argued for U.S. support of the rebel forces . . . or my unabashed condemnation of the Spanish colonial government? Much of my writing was in Spanish. Had someone translated my essays for him . . . and was that someone friend or foe of the rebellion?

"Allow me, Madame Villaverde, to commend you," he continued, a slight smile visible at the corners of his mouth, "as you are obviously well-prepared, having had a broad education. I say this because so few young women are as conversant in history and government as you seem to be. And please allow me to commend you, as well, on your mastery of the English language."

"Thank you, Mr. President," I smiled, lowering my eyes at his effusive compliments. Silently, I thanked my English *aya* and my husband for a job well-done. I proceeded to lay out the plan to move refugee families.

"Mr. President, I am the secretary of an organization, La Liga de Las Hijas de Cuba, dedicated to supporting the liberation movement. We are petitioning the government of the United States to designate a naval ship to transport refugee families to South America where, because of familiarity with the Spanish language and culture, they might find a better life."

President Grant did not immediately react to my proposal. Sensing surprise and hesitation, I prepared to rapidly jump in to fill the void with more details.

But the president took his time, perhaps mentally calculating the value of the lucrative trade in sugar and cigars between both countries, or the consequences of taking sides with either the Spanish or the rebels. In the end all he did was promise to seriously consider my proposal.

As he walked with me to the door, I noticed the Cuban cigar was in the smoking position between his index finger and his thumb. We took leave of one another but not before I caught sight of an object out of the corner of my eye that sent cold chills down my spine. There, for all the world to see, leaning against the lower left corner of the humidor, was the unmistakable calling card of the abominable Captain General Don Domingo Dulce. Were the cigars from Havana a gift from the captain general?

Weeks passed before I received any word from the White House. When the president's message finally arrived, it was gratifying. The telegram informed Las Hijas that the United States government agreed to place a ship at our disposal. Our refugee families would be transported to South America with all due haste. But to our dismay, once we publicized the plan among the refugees, it could not be executed because the numbers of families willing to make the move were not sufficiently large enough to offset the costs of the transport.

I could not help asking myself what really went wrong? Why weren't enough families eager to move out of their miserable squalor? Had the shifting political ideas of our Junta leaders influenced them in some way? Perhaps they imagined their stay in this city to be so temporary that they could afford to wait out the war and return to a country they knew and loved, once a peace treaty was signed. I never did find out the reasons why this venture did not succeed, but in the remote recesses of my mind, I'd always wonder if, in some way, the captain general had intervened. What I do recall is a sense of disappointment and isolation. . . .

Cirilo was the first to notice my depression. The Casanova household continued to run smoothly, my work with Las Hijas and the American ladies group continued to bear fruit, but he realized something was not quite right. I thought that by deliberate concentration on trivial details, fresh flowers on the dining room table, the children's studies, my own writing, I could hide my melancholy indefinitely. But, as always, when it came to issues about me, Cirilo was the first to notice.

One evening, the Casanova household was unusually still. Muffled children's laughter drifted down from the third floor, but silence followed on its heels almost immediately. I sat lost in thought in the overstuffed green velvet armchair next to my desk, a knitted throw covering my lap to ward off a chill in the early spring air. On my lap, the opened book should have signaled to anyone in sight that I was not to be disturbed, but in truth, I had re-read the same passages again and again.

Suddenly, the door flew open and Cirilo darted into the room without knocking, supposedly in search of an old copy of *La Revolución*, which, when found, absorbed his attention so completely that he took possession of the chaise. He was uncharacteristically agitated while reading, grunting and arguing as if the editors were present in our chambers. Yet, every so often, he looked over at me as if his agitation was deliberately staged to get my attention.

"*¡Será posible!*—Is it really possible?" he shouted, adjusting the spectacles that sat precariously on the tip of his nose. He pointed to a passage from a speech given by the intellectual, Eugenio María de Hostos, to a congregation of Puerto Rican expatriates.

"Hostos says," quoted my husband, "'But on this very day, at this very moment when we engage in fraternal discussion, the Committee on International Finance, which in the U.S. Senate, decides the relationship between the States and other countries of the world, adopts in principle, the right of belligerence.'

"What do you think of that, Emilia! . . . Emilia?" He repeated my name a second time. "What's wrong?" He asked the question in a compassionate tone and confided, "I've asked you a question several times, and you seem to be a thousand miles away. . . . I've wanted to ask you for days if anything was wrong, thought you would be excited about this article, but I now notice you are again despondent. Is it something I've done? Are you not well, my love?"

His voice startled me with questions I could not understand at first, so engrossed was I in my own negative thoughts. But then, like a river raging free to break its banks, my words rushed out helter-skelter forming thoughts that had burrowed themselves in my head for several days.

"Why is it," I closed the book on my lap and turned to face my husband, "that people won't lift a finger to help their fellow countrymen? These same people rarely take the lead in anything that causes them a smidgen of personal discomfort. They'd never say, 'count on me,' when faced with humanitarian needs. Yet, they snicker and become so envious, so jealous, that they'd willingly neglect the well-being of their own parents rather than see others receive accolades and attention for their charitable work? Why do I feel that there is constant opposition to the things I try to accomplish, either in my own right, or in the name of Las Hijas?"

Cirilo let out a long sigh and softly said, "Emilia, when in our lifetime, my dear wife, has the plight of the poor and the oppressed been a cause for the well-to-do? Our expatriates act here as they've always behaved at home. This should not surprise you."

I rose from my chair feeling less discouraged for having voiced my concerns to my husband and began to arrange the stack of neglected notes and letters spread out on the green felt cover of my writing table.

"I know I'm not the only person committed to the ideals of a free Cuba," I said as one of the letters slipped from the pile and fluttered onto the Persian carpet. "There are hundreds of people just like me in this city who sacrifice comfortable domestic lives to perform charitable work for the poor, calling attention to the struggles of our people in the homeland. So . . . why should I sense a lack of unity, a disconnect in our efforts?

"Cirilo, you know me better than anyone." I proceeded without letup, bending to pick up the letter from the floor. "And you know it is not often that I allow myself the luxury of reflection, but I find myself in an uncomfortable situation. You, above all others, know I expend precious energy in fighting the slanders of the authorities in Cuba and, now, I find mixed support from my own community in New York? It's just not right."

As was his custom, Cirilo mulled over my remarks for a moment or two before responding. "What you may be feeling, my dear," he slipped a marker into the newspaper to hold his place before he folded it, "in all probability has nothing to to do with you personally. I can assure you of that . . . but you may be caught in the divisive political wrangles within our own expatriate community, especially between those who now promote self-government or autonomy within the monarchic structure of Spain and those Cubans who refuse to accept anything short of independence. Here are Don Eugenio's remarks. Study them carefully. If he is right, Emilia, the liberation struggle has already won a powerful ally in the U.S. Senate."

He leaned over and enfolded me in a supportive embrace before leaving the room. While I was left less disheartened, I was not altogether convinced that he was right. The page from *La Revolución* with Don Eugenio's remarks rested conspicuously on the green floral hammock beside my chair, waiting for me to pick it up and read it.

Despite the rumblings of political discord among Cuban expatriates, a few days later I was delighted to learn about the creation of a new group, "El Club de Nueva York," a Cuban-Puerto Rican association that might succeed as a forum for hammering out a unity platform. My brother, Manuel, had become a member and highly endorsed it. But, then again, every time a new group was organized, and we now had hundreds of such groups working for the war effort on three continents, I thought the same thing: This might be the one to bring about unity. "Once and for all . . . " my words escaped from thoughts and, spoken aloud, sounded amusing even to my ears. Here I was talking to myself. Best to put it down on paper so that I could share my ideas with the ladies of Las Hijas.

We need to lay aside our ideological differences, I wrote, and concentrate all our efforts on one thing: independence. "Our heroic compatriots on the battlefield do not fight for split ideologies. When a Spanish bullet pierces their hearts, they are not thinking, 'I'm shedding my blood, or giving my life for the cause of a compromised position!' They are fighting for one thing and one thing only: independence. A Free Cuba—*Cuba Libre*."

We needed, also, to create more organizations promoting independence. If Rights of Belligerence were indeed declared for the rebels of Free Cuba, then our cause would attract serious support from other nations as well. Our insurgency would finally receive the legitimacy that we deserved.

In the months that followed, I confronted the work of Las Hijas with added vigor. I felt a sense of urgency that I couldn't explain, except to say that by promoting those projects that strengthened the independence faction, I believed we would be able to halt the spread of propaganda that favored compromise. One way to do this was to encourage the founding of new organizations. And so, I wrote . . .

> *Señoritas Filomena y Caridad Callejas*
> *Charleston, S. C.*
> *My dear Compatriots:*
>   *By way of our friend, Castillo, I received a box of lint that you sent with the objective of dispatching it to our brothers, today fighting for the liberty and independence of our homeland. I had the satisfaction of putting the box in the hands of General Quesada, who, in his name and that of our citizens thanks you profusely, telling me that I should encourage you on this beneficial road, no less dignified but honorable for all patriots.*
>   *I am pleased to learn that you are truly Cubanas, and from here I salute and embrace you as sisters and enthusiastic*

companions. *Do not shy away, but do proceed to find other Cubanas willing to lend their services to Cuba in any way they can for their own satisfaction and to encourage others.*

I'd like to publish your names, but Castillo told me that you request anonymity and I respect your wishes. But without revealing your names, there are other ways that you can lend your services to the patria . . . .

I am the secretary of a society of artisans named "Liga de las Hijas de Cuba," whose objective is to provide resources of all kinds to aid our brothers over there and in the immigrant communities. Could you not form a subsidiary of our society? It would be a worthy effort if you would try like others are already doing in Key West and New Orleans. As soon as your by-laws are in place, I'll send you samples so that you can determine your arrangements.

Whether or not you decide to do this, I'll take great pleasure in corresponding with you in the same gallant manner in which you've written to me, and in choosing me as your vehicle to send your offerings to the patria.

I extend my arms to you in friendship and grateful companionship, your humble servant,

E. C. de V., Mott Haven, August 28, 1870.

And now, I was prepared to move on to the matter of the sword.

Thirteen

A Sword for General Quesada
and Other Decisions

To: C. Emilia C. de Villaverde

I've seen, with appreciation, that you head a list of donors with the objective of gifting me with a Sword of Honor, and I dare to beg you, with the best intentions, to retire said list for many reasons.

In the first place, I don't think I yet deserve distinction so notably given that there is much left to do in the grand opus that we have undertaken to hurl the Spanish despot from our soil.

In the second place, the government of Cuba in its solemn constitution in Guaimaro entrusted me with the modest sword I carry and I've sworn to present it, victorious, to the archives of the capital.

Finally, a collection initiated in this city to present a sword of Honor and Valor . . . to my distinguished friend and companion in arms, General Thomas Jordan, could cause the enemies of Cuban liberty . . . to divulge that honoring me opens the road to rivalry and ambition that so far has been closed to those who defend our independence.

For these reasons, I beg you respectfully to suspend the collection.

M. Quesada. New York, May 16, 1870.

If the pen is mightier than the sword, perhaps Las Hijas should have stuck with the pen, for even the simple act of honoring one of our own with a gift of a sword became problematic. I clearly remember the incident because it was tied in with the matter of the jewelry and the disturbance at the Casanova Mansion. It all began on the day Las Hijas met on the matter of General Quesada's gift.

I remember the Hansom cab giving a sharp jolt as it plodded its route along Broadway on its way to Fifth Avenue, weaving expertly in and around the city's congested traffic lanes. Seated in the relative comfort of the sheltered carriage on my way to the appointed meeting, I was beset by personal concerns. Unable to fully concentrate on anything, I attempted to find amusement in the haggling of peddlers and other cab drivers I saw from the window. But I kept coming back to Cirilo's observations about the ruptures within our expatriate community. My husband believed I was innocently caught in the cross hairs of conflicting political positions, but I was certain it was deliberate.

I had made dangerous enemies, especially in the pro-Spanish press. Since my women's organization became active, the first of its kind, I set an example of the potential power that women could wield. And here I was, a very visible, outspoken individual who publicly denounced injustice, called for the abolition of slavery and for independence, challenged the men who seemingly headed the Junta and spread my gospel far and wide through my writings and perceived militant acts. I was, for all intents and purposes, not acting like a lady! They thought we should be like children, seen and not heard. When a woman, such as I, dared to exert control, there would be consequences.

Such realizations angered instead of helping me to consider conciliatory modes of behavior. I wanted to force those contrary factions to unmask themselves, to come out of hiding and show the people who they really were. I'd make it my personal crusade to confront every accusation against me and Las Hijas, using all available means of exposing the truth. I'd invest my energy in selling the jewelry donated by the women in Cuba and Latin America to finance expeditions and pay for the sword of honor. And any monies that we raised, I'd give directly to the Mambí generals. I would, God help me, bypass the authority of the Junta! And the awarding of that honorary sword to General Quesada was to be our opening salvo, whether he accepted it or not!

Much sooner than I'd expected, the Hansom cab stopped at 309 Fifth Avenue, directly in front of the impressive, four-story brick and brownstone townhouse that was Señora de Fernández's residence. Plans to convert Fifth Avenue into a wide boulevard had not yet displaced its magnificent natural setting, one that suggested leisurely pastimes, parasols and sun bonnets, lazy days reading books in wicker chairs somewhere in the seclusion of a corner garden. Beautiful thoughts but not for me.

Ordinarily, this bucolic scenario would have enthralled me. That day, I hardly noticed lush plants and flowering fruit trees. My focus, instead, was on the issues at hand and how best to convey the importance of the sword to the group.

The driver opened the small window just above my head and I paid him forty cents for the ride. As I stepped down from the carriage, adjusting the veiled hat that matched my emerald green day dress, I quickened my steps, narrowly missing a puddle, a remnant of yesterday's spring showers.

It was absolutely absurd, I said to myself, lifting my ruffled apron skirts to avoid another puddle, that the Junta planned to award an honorary sword to a Confederate officer, General Thomas Jordan, who temporarily became the Mambí Army of Liberation's chief of staff. Our very own General Quesada, brother-in-law to the Cuban provisional president, was not an occasional warrior; he had been connected with the rebellion from the start. Rumor had it that Jordan could no longer tolerate the rebel form of guerrilla warfare and resigned his command, intending never to return to Cuba. Was that the kind of valor we were meant to honor? I should say not! And I did not hold back from expressing my views to everyone. It was a foul mood that consumed me and that I brought into the meeting.

"Señoras y señoritas, please, *please* attend to business. Let us concentrate on the agenda before us for which I need your undivided attention."

I clapped my hands lightly, reminded of my old governess' habit, to signal the end of social chatter and the beginning of the secretary's reports. The ladies wore the fashionable pastel colors of the season and, against artistically arranged floral decorations in the home, it was as if we were sitting in a garden. That setting alone should have soothed my temperament, but it did not. "How absurd!" I thought, "This is beginning to resemble a ladies' tea party, despite the seriousness of the business at hand!"

"Señora de Fernández has already informed us of the upcoming events for which we will need to take a vote following my discussion of the honorary sword," I said.

Fourteen women took seats around the table, three remained at the sideboard indulging, to one extent or another, in a second round of tea or coffee, dainty sandwiches and sugared treats. Two young ladies, not much older than Narciso, continued to share idle gossip in whispered exchange. This event had all the earmarks of a non-productive meeting, I thought as I teetered on the brink of losing my patience.

"As you know," I began with renewed vigor, "we've received a letter from General Quesada asking that we *not* honor him with a special sword, because this might be construed among some in our community as divisive. The good general cautions that our noble gesture might ignite feelings of jealousy or envy, or worse, perhaps division among the high ranking military officers who serve our cause."

"Who could possibly doubt our motives?" declared one of the young women previously engaged in gossip.

Señora de Fernández interrupted in her capacity as president. "Please keep your comments to yourselves until we open for discussion." She nevertheless quickly added, ignoring her own appeal, "The general is related to the president of *Cuba Libre*. Who would indeed question our actions?"

Affirming control over the meeting one more time, I continued to deliver the report. "I've written to the general, not specifically addressing his concerns about divisiveness, but stressing the fact that it is just too late to change the course of our actions. Too many people have contributed to the effort, and the sword has already been commissioned from a well-known foundry in New York. I've secured Irving Hall for the event for the evening of July 29th. That will give us ample time to publicize the event, print and send invitations and attract the attention of the press."

There were, surprisingly, no questions or comments about the honorary sword, which pleased me immensely, because the major reason for honoring Quesada was to demonstrate Las Hijas' undivided loyalty to a meritorious Cuban hero. This gentleman, who distinguished himself in battle and in diplomacy, had recently garnered concessions from Washington to create a Cuban rebel naval and military center to aid the cause. We were certainly not about to support the Junta's honoree, while their own executive council was said to harbor mixed feelings about the revolution. Las Hijas were positioned, therefore, to make a strong statement.

"Our next order of business is my report on the course of the war," I announced.

As if opening a flood gate, I remembered in a flash the distressed informant who had pounded at our door the previous evening, before the foyer clock had struck the eleventh hour. He was a handsome young man, a law student from San Carlos in Havana. Wearing nondescript clothing, he looked to be barely out of his teen years. A native of Oriente Province, the scene of some of the heaviest fighting, it was clear to us he had made a difficult journey and that he was deeply troubled. As he recounted his story, he became more and more agitated. Unable to control his nerves, he almost choked on his tears as he anxiously apprised us of his ordeal.

His wife and mother, he reported, had been captured by the Spanish army's henchmen, the *voluntarios*. Anyone who had ever encountered the *voluntarios*, as my father and brothers had, could confirm the brutality and ruthlessness of this civilian volunteer branch. Newly elevated to positions of authority, they were besotted with power they'd never known before the war.

"They invaded my home and assaulted my wife and mother, Don Cirilo. They harassed and pushed them with the butts of their rifles and carted them off to a concentration camp! I don't know where. . . . They want to exterminate the Cubans, don't they, Don Cirilo?! That's what they plan to do, those wretched animals!"

All of this, he conveyed in a series of spurts and pauses. He ran his shaky fingers through the strands of his coal black hair and I could easily see the tremors had not yet subsided. Cirilo soothed him as much as possible, offering him a generous glass of brandy to quiet his nerves.

Even after sipping the brandy, the young man continued in the same vein. "They passed new laws, Don Cirilo, did you know that?" His voice became subdued as if the very walls of the room could betray his whereabouts. "They're much harsher than ever before. Anyone found on the roads after curfew will be shot immediately; anyone caught in collusion with the 'enemy' will be summarily executed and his property confiscated; anyone suspected of conference with the enemy will have their property embargoed."

He sipped the brandy again and finally began showing the first signs of relaxation.

"After June 1st," he continued, "anyone over the age of fifteen found loitering outside towns occupied by the Spanish military will be treated like enemies. And those of us who manage to stay alive are rounded up and hauled into the camps."

I shivered uncontrollably. I wondered if my friends in Cuba, loyal to the rebel forces, were also in jeopardy, if their connection with me and my agent to funnel their assets out of the country had been discovered. I prayed for, not just my childhood friends and family, but the *Mambí* women who were in the thick of battle: those who spied, carried information, nursed the wounded, foraged for food and prepared the meals, washed the clothes, and when necessary, picked up a weapon to kill the oppressors right on the battlefield, on a road or in their own homes.

I suddenly became aware of the restless stir of one or two of the ladies at the meeting. Someone coughed politely, bringing me back to the task at hand.

"I'm sorry . . . I . . . the beginning of the spring campaign has not gone well for our patriots," I said, awkwardly resuming my report to Las Hijas. "Not because the Mambíes lose courage and determination on the battlefield but because they lack arms, munitions, equipment and supplies. Much of the fighting is confined to the eastern provinces. And the western provinces, rich in land and resources, have not been penetrated. It's been difficult, in so short a time, I'm told, to discipline the Mambíes to follow a conventional style of combat. Many of the soldiers, be they Negro or white, come from the lower classes, not familiar with military conduct. The Spaniards count on the efforts of 13,000 well-disciplined soldiers and expect reinforcements. That is what the peninsular generals have in their favor.

"But our patriots use subterfuge. Well trained by the general from the Dominican Republic, Máximo Gómez, they've perfected the art of the ambush, cut and run, or rather, they engage in guerrilla engagements that force the Spaniards to fight the enemy in all directions at once. And that is to the Mambí advantage. Unfortunately, the columns have had to abandon their women, the children and the elderly so they can move rapidly to evade discovery. What our patriots do have in their favor is their intimate knowledge of the terrain and the profound love they hold for the *patria*."

My pulse quickened as I dwelled on the courageous examples set by women in the battle zones, like the *mulata* patriot, Mariana Grajales, who, when her husband gave his life in battle, sent out her sons—the valiant Antonio Maceo among them—to take his place. And I wondered, could I have sent my Narciso or my young Enrique into battle? That was as difficult a question for me to answer as I suspected it would be for everyone else in this room.

"My compatriots," I continued, surveying the comfortable but untested *paisanas* who surrounded me. "It seems to me . . . actually . . . there is no doubt in my mind . . . that we must increase our shipments of supplies and munitions. If the donated jewelry brings in the money I think it will, we are ready to launch more expeditions and to fund the training of a battalion. And my dear friends," I smiled, wondering to myself just how many women gathered here today were true revolutionaries and how many considered Las Hijas a mere social pastime, "it is time to look in our own jewelry cases for those precious little gems we rarely wear anymore and consider sacrificing them for the cause. I've already gathered my share and look forward to a substantial collection from you."

I couldn't help noticing that several among my own dearest friends raised their hands protectively to their throats and caressed the bejeweled accessories encircling their necks.

Señora Concepción C. de López
Matamoros
Dear Friend,

    In these moments that I write, positively nothing is known about the expedition that left here on the 14th. There were 300 men, most of them Cubans, with a good array of weapons. The ship was the "George B. Upton," which I'm assured would arm itself after the cargo and expeditionaries disembarked. I'm very concerned about the whereabouts of those lost because there was no military officer to guide them.

> *On Broadway they are forging a magnificent sword that*
> *the Cubanas are going to give General Quesada to take to*
> *Cuba, where he is expected to return soon. Here, there are two*
> *factions: one for Jordan, the other for Quesada. With the*
> *latter we are the enthusiasts, the real Cuban people. With the*
> *other, the conservatives who expect to resolve the revolution*
> *through negotiations with Spain . . . Quesada's main enemies*
> *are Morales Lémus, Aldama, Cisneros (Hilario) and their*
> *numerous supporters who, in the majority, live off the crumbs*
> *that fall from the table of the first two; they don't think with*
> *their heads nor work out of pure patriotism.*
>
> *Of the five newspapers now published by Cubans, only La*
> *Voz del Pueblo is fair with Quesada; the rest make war*
> *against him shamelessly. The Diario Cubano is the most*
> *indecent and is sustained by Morales Lémus. La Estrella de*
> *Cuba, directed by Juan Manuel Macías and La Revolución,*
> *edited by E. Piñeiro, make war more underhandedly; but one*
> *or the other is encouraged by Morales Lémus, who in spite of*
> *being sick in Brooklyn . . . congratulates them for their attacks*
> *on Quesada. For that reason, he remains here plenipotentiary.*
> *With regards,*
> *E. C. de V., Mott Haven, May 27, 1870.*

One magical evening, the presentation of the sword of honor was
a complete success! I glowed with pride to realize that Las Hijas
and our mission had gained deserved recognition and the good
will of the general public. Irving Hall, usually the venue for concerts and recitals of classical music, held an impressive audience
of celebrities that night. So many people gathered around us,
wanting to talk and congratulate us, that I lost sight of my husband in the crowd. Up until then, he had been by my side,
engaged in conversation with Don Eugenio María de Hostos.

"What a pity General Quesada left so soon after the ceremony," I said loudly to the Señoras de Fernández and de Hourritiner, trying to be heard above the din of the crowd.

"Oh, yes," they responded equally as loud.

"But his closing remarks, 'the *vivas* for President Céspedes,' and how he, General Quesada, would use the sword to defend justice and the law, were just priceless," interjected Señora de Fernández. "I'm glad I was able to clarify for the audience that the sword we presented to him was not *the* Sword of Victory that will be placed in the archives once we win the war . . . and that our sword would be considered nothing more than an expression of our gratitude for the services that he has already rendered, and as proof of the high esteem and appreciation we hold for his undying commitment to independence."

Overhearing our conversation, Señorita García expressed her delight at the words of the man who served as master of ceremonies of the event, who pointed out, to his amazement, that he was witnessing the "fair sex" taking the lead in *public*! We all laughed, recalling the precise moment when he had uttered those words.

"Wait," I giggled, my cheeks flushed with excitement, "He is in for more surprises if he thinks we don't have a role to play in public life."

"And you, my dear Doña Emilia," interjected Don Eugenio, who had suddenly materialized by my side along with my husband, "were commended for your leadership in bringing this event to successful fruition."

I smiled and bowed my head in gratitude to this eminent leader who in his closing remarks to the evening's event reminded the audience of the importance of our two homelands of Cuba and Puerto Rico that awaited us, and had given us the strength and fortitude we needed.

Much later, when our carriage had almost crossed the hydraulic iron gates that led to the Casanova Mansion, I collapsed.

Other than what I learned from my loved ones, who, it appears, never left my side, I remembered little of the eight weeks I had spent confined to my bed. Attacked by a particularly virulent strain of influenza, family, friends and foes filtered in and out of my fever-laden, restless sleep. My daughter's spirit was a constant companion, as was my mother who, I realized, was very much alive because I welcomed the soothing, cool compresses she laid on my fevered brow.

Cirilo told me I spoke a lot with him about death, that I said I would welcome it except for the children who still needed me. I also told him that I'd place my trust in God and an afterlife in which I was sure I'd be with Emilita once again.

The children were not allowed to see me for fear of contagion, so when I heard Enrique weeping, I thought I was dreaming. I remember opening my eyes and there he was, his three-year-old self looking more like a doll than a real boy. From that moment on, he became my personal savior. He gave me the incentive to get well because he still needed his mother beside him.

Slowly, I recuperated. On warm sunny days, I was allowed to recline on a garden chaise and enjoy the salty sea breezes, damp earth smells and sounds of nature. I watched the children at play and marveled at how lovingly my nieces and nephews took care of young Enrique. Gradually, I began to concentrate on my work, but not without a great deal of physical effort.

Of all the tasks awaiting my return to routine, the issue of the jewels was foremost. When I received a letter in August from my sister, Cecilia, asking why I had not acknowledged receipt of a box of jewelry, I realized how serious the situation had become . . . and just how long I'd been incapacitated. Before I could respond to Cecilia, I carefully reviewed an old copy of the letter I had sent to the editor of the *New York Democrat,* an accounting for my disposal of the donated jewelry. At this point in my life there had circulated an unspoken assumption among my enemies that I had used the proceeds from the jewels for my own benefit. If the constant fighting against such accusations delayed efforts to sell the jewelry, it also alerted me to maintain meticulous accounts of all my transactions.

Mr. Director of the New York Democrat:

. . . In this affair of the jewels, like in all those I've participated in, I've proceeded with openness . . . not doing anything in hiding, nor anything that at any time could embarrass me, or changed my mind upon receiving jewels from Havana with the instructions of what I should do with them, . . . my first step is to publish a manifesto signed and dated from my home address. This declaration could have been published in "La Revolución" had the editor in chief honored his promise to do so last August. . . .

There have been several reasons for my working independently until now. First of all, to dispose of the jewelry the way that I do, I follow the instructions of the ladies who are targeted by the ferocious voluntarios but nevertheless dare to send them to me, confident of my patriotism and my past political history. In serving my homeland, I don't have to follow a well-worn path; being from a well-known Cuban family gives me the same right as others and every member of the Junta Central Republicana de Cuba y Puerto Rico; I need not bow down to others regarding patriotism and honor; everyone should be measured with the same ruler. I must have learned something in the sixteen years since my emancipation from colonial tutelage. Finally, in carrying out this enterprise, with rare exceptions I've only asked for help from those who know me and care for me as a Cuban woman. Be it noted that the Junta has conveniently created a raffle for jewelry, appealing to the same people I have.

I was surprised to hear that some of my own people, who have never wielded the sword against our common enemy,

wield the pen against one of the Cubanas who has the honor
of meriting the hatred of the voluntarios. *I've said all I have*
to say about the business of the jewels. . . . . I'll remit copies of
this declaration to all my agents in Latin America to be
published where last year's declaration appeared.
       Your attentive servant,
       E. C. de V., Mott Haven, June 4, 1870.

Then, I wrote to my dear Cecilia.

My dear friend and companion,
       I am convalescing from a grave illness. . . . . I've received
nothing even though I wanted it and anxiously waited for it.
. . . I will investigate the route of the package. . . . I strongly
suspect it ended up in Aldama's hands. If so, it's the same as if
the box had fallen into a pit. . . . God knows that for want of
the jewels, nothing big has been done here. Answer me as
soon as you receive this. I've written to you many times.
Adiós, courage, valor and onward.
       Your sister,
       Lolita, New York, August 24, 1870.

As I remember, we never did find out what happened to the box
of jewels. To this very day whenever I recall this incident in my
life, the memory of Cecilia and her eleven-year-old daughter, sentenced to six years in prison in 1871 by the *vouluntarios*, for supposedly burning letters received from me, is forever seared into
my conscience.

If indeed the Junta had appropriated our avenues for selling the
donated jewelry, the time to confront the "Aldamistas" was fast
approaching. But not for a moment did I imagine it would happen
so soon or in so complicated a fashion.

Part IV

New York City

(1871–1882)

Fourteen
The Aldama Affair

To: Señoritas Filomena y Caridad Callejas, Charleston, S.C.
. . . The truth that Aldama and his associates have not wanted
nor want the revolution to triumph is proven by the fact that
right now they are in secret talks in this city with Azcárate, a
Spanish commissioner, to see if the patriots would lay down their
arms and return to the yoke of a modern Spain, which I do not
know if it is less oppressive than the old one. . . . I swear to you,
my sisters, that they will not get away with this and that sooner
or later they will get what they deserve.
E. C. de V., Mott Haven, October 12, 1870.

There they were! I sighed as one does in reconnecting with old friends who've shared memories best forgotten. My carefully handwritten papers were spread out on my writing table and looked as fresh as if they had been written yesterday. Names leapt out from the pages: Aldama! Zenea! Azcárate! Mestre! Echeverría! Next to each name was the boldly penned word TRAITOR!

The Aldama affair signaled a turning point in my life. It was the catalyst for some of my grandest triumphs in support of *Cuba Libre* and some of my most calamitous disasters. Absorbed in reviewing the letters I'd written more than twenty years ago, I wonder how such a simple and apparent series of events could cause so much havoc.

As I remember it, the New York Junta people were considering a compromise between Cuba and Spain to end the war. Toward
this end, they had sent one of their own, Juan Clemente Zenea,
protected by safe-conduct letters from the Spanish Consulate in
Washington, to make contact with the provisional Cuban Revolutionary President Carlos Manuel Céspedes. To me, these actions
spelled treason against the rebel army from the start, against President Céspedes and against the expatriates in exile in New York
who stood firmly on the side of independence.

The ladies of Las Hijas chose to call an extraordinary session
of the group on the 4th of February to discuss Zenea's voyage to
Cuba on the Junta's behalf. An amiable fellow, Zenea was considered one of the foremost poets of our generation. He had been
born in Cuba, but grew up in Madrid following the death of his
mother. As a young man, he moved to New Orleans in pursuit of
an American actress with whom he had fallen madly in love—at
least that is the story that the gossips circulated about the man.
Later, disillusioned by the affair, he came to New York and
immersed himself in the political objectives of the Junta.

As I recall, right from the moment of what I came to label as
"the Aldama affair," I was not the only one who felt uneasy when
that Cuban lawyer, Nicolás Azcárate, arrived in the city from
Madrid in 1869. It was an open secret that he brought with him a
confidential memorandum written by two important Spanish lib-
erals who sought to democratize the monarchy. The two were
Prime Minister Francisco Serrano and the reformist, General Juan
Prim. Apparently, Azcárate's clamor for Cuban-Spanish unity fit
well into the Spaniards' reform plans.

Within New York's expatriate community, even a suspicion of
compromise caused great consternation. Rumors regarding
Azcárate's visit and the true nature of a so-called "secret" proposal
ran rampant. Always wary of Spanish ploys, the Cuban community sounded warning bells while letting imaginations run wild.

Many believed the proposal laid out the blueprints for a cease-fire; others insisted it was a compromise, commanding the patriots to lay down their arms and accept autonomy along the same lines that Spain had proposed for Puerto Rico. No one was gullible enough to think that independence was even mentioned in the proposed plan.

For months, the clubs, social groups and the city's Spanish-language newspapers hinted at some sort of conspiracy between the Junta and Spanish officials. What was known, however, was that the Junta's executive officers, José Manuel Mestre, the lawyer who refused to donate to the children's choir, and Miguel Aldama, director of the Junta, wined and dined Azcárate. When questioned, they openly denied knowing anything about plans or proposals. Yet, despite their denials, everyone knew the Junta facilitated the voyage of a courier to Cuba, the unfortunate Juan Clemente Zenea, and endorsed him as an emissary to the provisional President Céspedes and others of high rank in the Mambí Army of Liberation!

Not until Zenea was caught and imprisoned by the Spaniards in Cuba, *but not executed on the spot*, did the plot become crystal clear, at least, to me. The Spanish military and its *voluntarios* seldom hesitated to assassinate Cuban sympathizers upon apprehension. In fact, it was written into their codes to do so. Well, as an emissary from the Junta, Zenea was a prized capture, but he was not garroted to death.

Not one to speculate in silence, I told anyone and everyone who would listen to me that Zenea was a double agent, working for both Spain and the Junta, but few people believed me. For months, I hounded the clubs with that information but, alas, I was treated like the fabled Cassandra of Greek legends, whose curse was to tell the truth but no one would ever believe her.

Soon afterwards, I discovered with certainty that I had been right. The wife of President Céspedes, who traveled with Zenea under his protection when he was captured, told me so. As it was later divulged, Zenea did hold safe-conduct documents from the Spanish consulate in Washington. It now became clear that this double agent had intended to deceive the Mambíes by pretending he was one with the cause, while all the while he sought compromise with the enemy. And that was the crux of the matter as I laid it out for all to read in my letters.

Since I was a girl of eighteen, I've never wavered in my solemn oath to fight for and defend a Free Cuba. That commitment I've honored as sacredly as my own marriage vows. Now I faced a moral dilemma. I felt it was my duty to expose those who had failed as Cuba's caretakers. If need be, it would fall upon my shoulders to publicly denounce the traitors for placing the *patria* in imminent danger. And if I failed to accomplish that, I might as well have joined the ranks of the betrayers.

So it was that at the special meeting of Las Hijas on a quiet Saturday afternoon in February, I presented my evidence to the ladies like an experienced lawyer would. We were gathered at the Fifth Avenue home of our incoming president, Señora Angela Q. de Embil, comfortably seated in the drawing room. I sat at a small desk where I could take notes and read out loud any resolutions we would compose. There was a sense of purpose and solemnity within the room. As if we were in a court of law, I carefully recorded the actions of Las Hijas so that, in the future, no one could possibly misinterpret our reasoning.

The first item on the agenda was the triennial elections. Señora Angela Q. de Embil officially became the new president and the other executive slots were filled by loyal supporters of Free Cuba, several of whom happened to be related to the Quesada family. I proposed to the membership and the newly elected executive council that our organization take on the responsibility of caring for the family members of General Quesada while they lived in refuge in the city. I stated that this was a proper and humane activity for our organization to assume. The proposition passed unanimously.

As it happened, Señora de Céspedes, wife of the provisional president of Free Cuba, attended this meeting as a guest. Invited to address Las Hijas, she humbly described to us the long, sad history of suffering, scarcities, punishments and difficulties of the patriots, not the least of which was the difficult work to change inadequate and unhealthy conditions in the rural camps for women and children. Moved by her emotional appeal, Las Hijas selected three of our members to raise funds. Their charge was to call upon the charity of the American people to specifically alleviate our compatriots' hardship. It was a minor issue but I remembered how outgoing Americans had been in support of St. Bernard's Church concert in the past.

The required business completed, we finally came to the pressing issue of the day: the stated resolutions. As secretary, I read them aloud. After the briefest of discussions the resolutions were approved . . . I was excited and apprehensive at the same time as I recorded . . .

La Liga de las Hijas de Cuba
in extraordinary session considered:
In as much as Don Juan Clemente Zenea, prisoner in the Castillo de Cabaña in Havana, as has been plainly proven, went to the island of Cuba with patriots commissioned by the Spanish agent, Don Nicolás Azcárate, with safe conduct from the Ultramar Ministry or of the Spanish Ministry in Washington and ample letters of recommendation from C. Miguel de Aldama, general representative of our republic, and from its diplomatic envoy, C. José Manuel Mestre, with the negative intention of deceiving President Carlos Manuel de Céspedes, disheartening the patriots and discrediting those patriots over here, including the women, with the goal of

desisting from the pledge to liberate the island by force of arms and to reduce us . . . to compromise with Spain:

Resolved: That this organization views the conduct of Don Juan Clemente Zenea in his recent visit to Cuba as high treason and expects all Cubans of strong heart and true patriotism to condemn the name of the traitor in infamous perpetuity and general abomination.

Resolved: That the Citizens Aldama and Mestre are to be considered principle accomplices in the underhanded treason of Zenea for having provided the letters of recommendation with which he was able to reach the presence of the president and for villainously deceiving him by passing as their messenger to convey oral information; and as such accomplices, they do not deserve the confidence of the Cuban patriots.

Resolved: That our president, Carlos Manuel de Céspedes, has not lost the love and respect of his people. As ignorant as he was of the true character of the traitor, Zenea, he declared that whatever the outcome of the struggle, he would not compromise with Spain.

Resolved: That at the cost of the organization, copious copies of these resolutions will be circulated so that they will be known by all Cubans and interested parties, so that the traitors will be punished and justice be done for a people who almost unprotected and completely alone has continued to struggle for their freedom and independence.

A version of the minutes and resolutions were sent to the Associated Press and to the French and Italian newspapers of this city. Other copies were mailed to newspapers in Madrid and Germany. By Monday, our information appeared in various newspapers. On Sunday it was extensively covered in the pages of *El Demócrata.* Copies were mailed to newspapers in Madrid and Germany.

We terminated our session in a less stressful manner, raffling off an allegorical painting of the revolution in Cuba and, for posterity, signing our names to the minutes: Angela Q. de Embil, María Josefa de Moya, Francisca Fernández, Ana Q. de Céspedes, C. Quesada, Caridad Quesada, Concepción de Orta and Emilia C. de Villaverde.

I found it hard to believe. The far reaching repercussions and unintended consequences of our joint actions were vastly unexpected. Within days, the ladies of the Liga de las Hijas de Cuba and, in particular, the group's secretary, yours truly, were buried under the praises or admonition of the press. I was stunned by the mean-spiritedness and hatred we received from so many of our assumed allies in the political arena, but felt gratefully vindicated when others showed an outpouring of support.

Publicly humiliated, the traitors Aldama and Mestre rushed to defend themselves, but all of the business of the Junta, from raising money to provisioning the army, came to a complete halt. It meant our patriots on the field of battle were virtually bereft of critical resources, and for that I felt I was to blame.

Frankly, I believed we women of the Liga de Las Hijas de Cuba were performing our patriotic and civic duty on the day we endorsed the resolutions. Because of his highly vulnerable position in the Junta, Aldama incurred the greatest injury to his reputation. The Spanish newspapers printed an insulting and abusive letter, addressed to provisional President Céspedes, denouncing the damage done to Aldama's reputation as a patriot and the defamation of his position as director of the Junta.

As for our side, the offensive and negative newspaper accounts where the Aldamistas (Aldama's followers) published vile attacks about Las Hijas, forced us to bring before the public even more damning evidence against the traitors. Regrettably, we lost the support of some people who thought we rubbed far too much salt into open wounds.

In the minutes of our sixth meeting, I'd prepared additional resolutions on the Aldama affair for Las Hijas. The ad hoc secretary,
Señora C. C. de Orta, wrote,

> *Acta Sexta. New York City. February 23, 1871*
>
> *The ladies, whose names appear below met in the home
> of the president, who called this meeting to deal with the
> statements of the commissioners and the director of the Junta,
> inserted in the pages of* La Revolución *on the 14th of this
> month.*
>
> *Las Hijas read the newspaper with deep sorrow because
> they fear the publicity brought upon them by the director and
> his representatives . . . will bring repercussions against the
> government of the republic or some degree of discredit to the
> Cuban people.*
>
> *Regrettably, Las Hijas have resolved to summon their
> deliberations anew before their compatriots, not to retaliate
> for the gratuitous faults heaped upon them, but to amplify,
> motivate and ratify the resolutions adopted in the session on
> the 4th of the current month.*

The minutes were brought to me at my home by messenger
and awaited my approval. I read over the opening pages, anxious
to see if the new incriminating evidence against the Junta would
appear strong enough.

> *These gentlemen say that "the revolution has elevated the
> slime to the surface of Cuban society, evil abominations full
> of rage, etc., etc., and given impeccable credibility to their
> slanders . . . to make the wounds more painful, has placed the
> dagger in the hands of the women, who for no other reason
> than to amuse themselves by meddling in political affairs
> have lent themselves to become instruments of unscrupulous
> manipulation . . . have compromised the reputation of
> President Céspedes' wife . . . have ruthlessly insulted the
> truth, the honor and the patria as personified by the three*

gentlemen and have plunged the blade into the hearts of said gentlemen, making them suffer worse sorrows than exile and more despicable than Spanish despotism."

La Liga has stated that Citizens Aldama and Mestre should be considered accomplices in the treason of Zenea. Upon hearing such a "discourteous insult," Citizens Aldama and Mestre became frightened and such was their indignation that their blood ran cold in their veins.

It may all be here, I'd thought, not yet allowing myself to breathe a sigh of relief. The intensity expressed in the language seemed to leap from the page as I read through the minutes so faithfully recorded by Señora de Orta. But had she disclosed *everything,* all the relevant facts? *El Demócrata's* article of January 1869 announcing Azcárate's arrival in New York with the proposal for the Cuban Junta? The protest against Azcárate's political writings by the Society of Cuban Artesans in August of that same year? And the warnings against any proposed plan in the pages of *El Demócrata* in September?

Why had not anyone taken note, when the Mambíes responded to rumors of a supposed compromise plan? Their own newspaper, *La Revolución,* railed against Azcárate's mission and any consideration of compromise! The paper attacked Aldama directly as head of the Junta. Because of that, he was forced to deny any involvement in the issue. That was on the 20th of September of 1870! The traitorous emissary, Zenea, was sent to Cuba in November. Did she remember to include all that?

. . . and considering the responsibility that the other commissioner, Echeverría, has assumed by voluntarily placing his signature at the bottom of the declaration:

It is Resolved by the Liga de las Hijas de Cuba:

1st—That the Citizens Aldama, Mestre and Echeverría do not possess the necessary qualifications to perform the duties of Free Cuba,

*2nd—That the interference of those three gentlemen in
the public affairs of Cuba is disastrous for the cause of liberty
and more disastrous for those serving in that cause,*

*3rd—That the resolutions adopted by this organization
on the 4th of February, 1871, stand ratified.*

"Good! Señora de Orta had covered it all. She discredited their
so-called proof and re-inforced the evidence on which we based
our resolutions," I whispered under my breath, careful to maintain
my composure as I continued to read the document.

*Signatories: Angela Q. de Embil, C. C. de Orta, I. G. de
Valdés, M. de Izquierdo representing M. J. de Moya, Ana de
Castillo de Callejas, the Señora Concepción de Orta.*
*Señora Emilia C. de Villaverde has received and approved a
copy of this agreement.*

Convinced that the minutes were sufficiently comprehensive,
I proudly placed my pen to paper and confirmed my acceptance
by writing, "*This is a faithful copy of the minutes of the session celebrated the 23rd day of the month of February. E. C. de V., New York.
February 27, 1871.*"

But these actions, I realized with a slight sense of foreboding,
now sat upon our shoulders like a great weight. It was going to be
up to us, Las Hijas—the so-called "fair and gentle sex"—to maintain the strength of the Mambí Army and to see to it that our
patria won independence. From that point on, our work intensified and I entered a mad whirlwind of revolutionary activity, convinced it was my personal duty to win the war.

To: Señora Angela Q. de Embil
Nueva York
Dear Angelita,
After I left you today, I thought I should not lose any more
time in forming the Battalion de la Cruz for which I've named

Ensign Beraza as Captain because he is knowledgeable about tactics, so that he can recruit and organize them before long, it being very convenient that they learn at least how to handle arms and to train and drill.

As soon as I arrive in the city, I'll find an armory where the recruits can drill. I've told Beraza that at the very least he should recruit one hundred men and I've promised him that we will equip and arm them.

We will submit this project to La Liga de Las Hijas de Cuba for consideration at the first meeting, if you approve it and think it convenient.

Adiós! Your compañera, E. C. de V., March 31, 1871.

To: Señoritas Filomena y Caridad Callejas
Charleston, S. C.
Dear Co-Citizens,
. . . You should know that we are recruiting the Cubans who will form the Battalion de la Cruz. I want them to drill and become skilled in the use of arms because this will be what decides the issue and it is important that they do honor to the Liga de las Hijas de Cuba. . . . I can't write to you as often as I would like, although I value you like sisters in the same way I value all the good patriots; but you have no idea of my duties. I lack the time for my domestic obligations, everything has been abandoned because I've dedicated myself to Cuba.

E. C. de V., Mott Haven. April 1, 1871.

To: C. Coronel Manuel Suárez
Cuba Libre
Valued Friend,
. . . the flag borne by the Battalion de la Cruz has been stitched by my own hand. I hope it is better defended than the

one I had the pleasure of presenting to the Rifleros de la Libertad. This Battalion has been armed and equipped by the Liga de la Hijas de Cuba, for which I serve as secretary. We've taken the first steps, and I promise you that we will not rest until you tell us that you don't need weapons to finish off the enemy.

I recommend again the young man, Porraspita, and with regards from Villaverde, I declare myself,
Your humble servant,
E. C. de V., Mott Haven, May 12, 1871.

On the thirteenth of May, I finally overcame my hesitation long enough to write a detailed letter to President Céspedes explaining my involvement in the Aldama affair, lest he blame me for the entire loss of resources and revenue that resulted from the unfortunate incident. In truth, I'd continued to feel remorse over the army's loss of weapons, medical aid and munitions. Thus, I had thrown myself, body and soul, into making amends, committed to save the movement in every way I possibly could. As you no doubt imagine, with organizations such as ours, all failures and grievances fall at the feet of the leaders.

I wrote, " . . . *If you rush to judge the Liga de las Hijas de Cuba, from this moment I appeal to the conscience of my compatriots and to the judgment of history. . . . If the Liga, instead of praise, receives the reproval of the government of the republic, I should be the only one chastised because as author of the resolutions, I'm prepared to accept the responsibility. . . ."*
President Céspedes did not answer.

The heat was unbearable on that Friday in mid-July when I was summoned to the city for the business of the rifles. My parents had already left for Saint Catharine's, a small town on the Canadian side of the border south of Toronto and close to Lake Ontario, where we would join them within ten days. I had dismissed most of the household staff early, owing to the weather. I would much have preferred not to leave my home at all, to spend time instead with the boys doing nothing more than playing games or relaxing in the cool gardens of the Casanova Mansion. But that morning I received a telegram informing me that the rifles were ready for inspection and if I waited any longer, they would not be ready for transport on the next ship leaving for Cuba.

For some time, I'd been in the habit of sending Winchester rifles engraved "To the bravest," with my name etched underneath. I wanted to recognize the valor of our soldiers by honoring those who most distinguished themselves for some heroic act and awarding them a Winchester rifle. Because I planned to be away, I wished to make sure the rifles left for Cuba without further delay.

The city was, as one might expect, more frenetic than usual. Added to the overwhelming heat, humidity, crowds and traffic was a strong police presence. The visibility of law officers surprised me at first. But I soon remembered that two days earlier there had been violent conflict between Irish Catholics and Irish Protestants. It was a march or a parade commemorating the Orange ascendancy of Protestant Ireland. Dozens of people were injured. Distrust seemed to hover over everything. I passed disgruntled people huddled in small groups, whispering among themselves and menacingly appraising passersby as they came into view. It was as if the riots had escalated from fisticuffs into conspiracy.

On Fulton and Nassau streets the newsboys hawked papers in high, squeaky voices, shouting about the latest development in an investigation of corruption at the highest levels of city government. That too added to the excitement in the air. Tammany Hall politician, William Tweed, a dubious character known for doling out patronage to the newly arrived Irish immigrants, was accused of lining his own pockets with profit made at the expense of the city. But I heard nothing about Cuban affairs from the newsboys. That, to me, was a welcome respite.

As it turned out, it took longer to approve the engraving on the rifles than I had anticipated, and late afternoon traffic was so congested that I returned to the mansion much later than I should have. Except for the rapid clicking of Negri's nails against the marble floors once he heard me enter the foyer and his furiously wagging tail as he greeted me, the house was unusually quiet. I patted the dog and stood in front of the mirror to remove my hat and gloves. "The boys must be in their rooms," I thought, then remembered they had already left for St. Catherine's with their grandparents. I went to look for my husband.

As I expected, he was in the conservatory enjoying his last cup of coffee of the day. Cirilo did not turn to look at me as I entered the room, but continued to focus intently on the views that surrounded the glass-enclosed room. The western sky slashed with breathtaking streaks of dark purples and orange-reds, residues of a setting sun, filled the room from multiple perspectives, and you could see the dark silhouette of the shrubs and trees contrasted against the brilliance. Before I could greet him and begin to tell him about my grueling day, he spoke.

"Señora," he said in a voice as cold as steel. "Do you purposefully intend to make orphans of your sons, and me a lonely widower? Or is your obsessive behavior begging for a relapse of the illness that invaded your body less than a year ago?"

Silence hung like an oppressive shroud in the room. I was completely unprepared for Cirilo's outrage.

"You, Señora, seem to have lost sight of your priorities . . . you do not consent to live a life of moderation. You do not consider your health. You are, Emilia, in a word, obsessed!"

His sarcasm, usually reserved for his writing, had never before been directed against me. But he was right about my illness: under the stress of recent months I had begun to experience extreme tiredness and shortness of breath. It was the anger in his voice, however, that cut through me like a razor. How dare he, of all people, say such things to me when he was equally dedicated to the cause!

I stood before him, cold as a statue chiseled from a slab of marble, but did not respond. After a minute or so of heavy silence, I turned briskly on my heel, my head held high, and left the room, struggling to control my tongue and my hot, angry tears from spilling over. The last thing I heard was faithful Negri's nails clicking on the foyer's marble floor as he followed at my heels.

Fifteen

Failed Expectations and Other Setbacks

Well, then, if the Spaniard kills every man that falls into his power while the neutral Christian nations stand still, mere lookers on at the fight, do you think that the Cuban should fold his arms and let himself be killed, so that you, civilized people, may not be scandalized? . . .

We Cubans, allow me to state once more, having failed to obtain from Spain every sort of concession, even the autonomy England has readily granted you long ago, are fighting for dear liberty for ourselves and for thousands of poor African slaves, as well as for complete independence.

This we will achieve sooner or later, aided or unaided by foreigners, or perish we must in the noble attempt.

"A Cuban Lady." *Daily Telegraph*.
Saint Catharine, Canada. July 25, 1871.

Until the day the article appeared in the *Daily Telegraph*, there had been no war in Saint Catharine, not even between myself and my husband, for we had reconciled our differences by promising moderation, as married couples often do. There had been no failed expeditions in Saint Catharine that doomed honest Cuban volunteers to watery graves, no lost jewelry, no newspaper scandals, no fundraisers and certainly no desperate situations that tore you from the bosom of your family at all hours of the day or night. The small Canadian town of Saint Catharine was our summer refuge in the same way it had been a welcoming beacon for African American slaves as the final station on the Underground Railroad.

For a few weeks during the year, the Villaverdes, the Casanovas and dozens of expatriate Cuban families, who longed to luxuriate in the healthful benefits of cool breezes and sparkling lakes, could leave the worries of the world to others. But when the *Daily Telegraph* intruded into our sanctuary, bringing the war into our cottage by printing its questionable version of the Cuban insurrection, I, the responsible "Cuban Lady" that I was, felt obliged, indeed compelled, to write to the editor and set the record straight.

> *Editor: "Daily Telegraph" The Cuban Struggle*
> *Dear Sir:*
>
> *You write in your issue this morning that "the revolution going on in Cuba is one of the most disgraceful events in the annals of civilization." I neither intend to contradict you or assert that the patriot "has the best cause;" but allow me to say that it appears you are not altogether acquainted with the real facts in the case . . . .*
>
> *A Cuban Lady*
> *Saint Catharine, Canada. July 25, 1871.*

It may have been the relaxing pastoral setting of my surroundings or my usual compulsive nature, but I'd written a full two-page letter to the editor detailing the oppressive colonial history of Cuba. This I accomplished in secrecy without the knowledge of any one else in the family, for we made it a strict rule not to bring either our business or our political passions to Saint Catharine.

Mother spent her time embroidering table cloths and writing letters and picture postcards to her grandchildren, lest they forget their *abuelita* in the few short weeks we were away. Father worked, unsuccessfully I might say, at limiting the numbers of cigars he could smoke in any given day, losing himself instead to

endless games of dominoes with old friends, after which he celebrated with a drink in one hand and a cigar in the other.

My little family had too much togetherness to please Narciso,
who at thirteen hovered between engaging in the pleasures of a
child at one moment and those of an adolescent at another. To his
parents, nothing was more hilarious than our afternoon outings,
when we all piled into a small carriage: two boys, two parents, one
nanny and one dog. And then we added the parasols, picnic basket, blankets, butterfly nets, fishing poles, current reading materials and a change of clothing for Enrique who, at four, still managed to fall into a lake or a mud puddle or to scrape his knees.

Mother awaited our return from those excursions with tall
glasses of lemonade for everyone. I'd report on the boys' latest
escapades and, no matter what, she always thought the children
were most clever.

"Mamá," I told her once, "Enrique is incorrigible. Today he
tried to drown a frog holding the poor animal in the water for five
minutes!" To which she quickly responded, "But, dear, he was
only trying to make the frog feel comfortable."

On the day before we were to return to New York, the family
sat together for the evening meal somewhat reluctant to leave the
peace and tranquility of their surroundings. At one point, Cirilo
turned a casual, yet conspiratorial, glance toward me and spoke in
a quiet, light-hearted manner, as if he were seeking my opinion
about the fine points of tea in China.

"That was an informative letter you sent to the *Daily Telegraph*, my dear. Canadians must be grateful now that they fully
understand the complete genesis of the Cuban revolution."

I responded with a smile, "My dear. I just wish I knew who the
'Cuban Lady' was and why she would do us all such a grand favor.
I would extend to her my deepest appreciation." We both chuckled under our breaths and realized that when politics began to
seep into our days of leisure, it was time to head for home.

Where would I have been without my letters? Now, more than ever, the correspondence became my lifeline to the rest of the world. After a month of relaxation in Saint Catharine's, I returned to consider the many disappointments that had lately entered my life. The lost jewelry, disappointing losses of expeditions and munitions, an unrelenting smear campaign against me in the pro-Spanish press and, recently, the unexpected absence of my companions at our meetings of Las Hijas.

During the voyage home on the New York Central railway, I distanced myself from family conversations, wrapped as I was in my own private musings. I was not displeased with myself for having written to the *Daily Telegraph*, correcting erroneous impressions of our struggle for liberation because I was again convinced that the struggle to change opinions and gain support could be accomplished through writing. It was my best weapon. And to think, four years ago I was prepared to forfeit my letters for the sake of an organization. My correspondence to scores of ladies and gentlemen throughout Central and South America, from Caracas, Venezuela, to Montevideo, Uruguay and to Buenos Aires, Argentina; to supporters in the Caribbean and in the United States; to generals and world leaders like Giuseppi Garibaldi in Caprera and esteemed writers like Victor Hugo in Guernesey; had all left my hand intended to raise sympathy and support for the cause of *Cuba Libre*. To reach their hearts and gain their trust, I'd had to bare mine, exposing my inner thoughts. Where others would shield themselves in impersonal objectivity, I'd reveal my dedication and principles as honestly as I could. In so many ways, I was confident that the power of my words was far more effective than taking up the sword. Writing is regenerative, I realized. It changes opinion from person to person and promotes life to spread the seeds of change, but the sword ends life without the promise of changing anything.

Belligerence, however, was the topic on everyone's mind. After almost four years of bloodshed, civic groups and organizations had called for the United States government to declare support for the rebel faction. Until then, the U.S. Congress would not do so, arguing that American citizens would suffer, lose the right to claim damages and loss of property if the rebellion turned into an outright war. And declaring Rights of Belligerence would do just that, label it a war between two opposing factions. But to gain support for belligerence or any movement for that matter, the pressure of a unified group was also important. With that sobering thought, I recalled nothing of the remainder of the trip until I awoke in New York City.

My own father had been a victim; he had lost assets and property in Cuba. Upon our arrival from Saint Catharine, several long-awaited letters stacked neatly on the marble-topped table in the vestibule shared space with a dozen or so calling cards from people who'd visited in our absence. More energetically than expected after our lengthy voyage, father tore open one of the envelopes and read its contents.

"Finally," he remarked, a tiny tremor in his voice, "the wheels of justice are in motion. The American government in Washington has filed a claim on my behalf against the government of Spain for *'personal indignity and injury done to him by causeless arrest and imprisonment; and for the value of his said estates which he is not allowed to superintend or to sell; and for the obstruction of his business.'* We're asking for an award of $3,500,000. And that is less than half of the value of the entire property."

He fumbled through the rest of the correspondence without enthusiasm. I could tell the news was more distressing than comforting to him. After a while he spoke again in a soft tone, his eyes lowered, pretending he was engrossed in other matters.

"This news should be welcome, but I fear the chances of receiving any compensation from Spain are slim. More than that," he sighed in resignation, "I feel that I have lost my home in Cuba forever."

But the news that hit all of us like a bolt out of the blue a few months later was not at all welcomed, confirming father's assessment of Spanish vindictiveness! Eight first-year medical students had been executed in Havana on November 27th for desecrating a Spanish tombstone, and thirty-six others were sentenced to prison for aiding in the desecration! By all accounts, it was a careless student prank, writing slogans on a tombstone. When news of this senseless slaughter reached our ears, I sprang into action without wasting any time: we needed to find a way to free the incarcerated students before they were all arbitrarily murdered by the *voluntarios*. They ranged in age from just sixteen to twenty. I wanted to scream to the heavens. "Why these students were mere children! Whatever were the demonic Spaniards thinking? How far will they go to eradicate our people?"

Controlling my impulse to lash out at the enemy in print, I disclosed the full story to the six remaining active members of Las Hijas in order to formulate a plan of action.

"Apparently the first sentence called for leniency," I remembered telling them. "But a rage-filled mob of *voluntarios* who waited outside the prison walls protested the first sentence, threatening violence against the soldiers and the students. They called for blood, and fearing the crowd would become uncontrollable, Captain General Crespo ordered the eight students to be executed before a firing squad. I have no idea how he selected the victims, but at least two of them were only sixteen years old."

Eager to save the lives of the imprisoned students, on December 17, 1871—I recall the date because I feared our demands would come too late for the remaining prisoners—Cirilo and I, accompanied by several courageous ladies of Las Hijas, arrived in Washington, D.C. We intended to petition Secretary of State Hamilton Fish, along with the Congress of the United States, to intervene immediately in this tragedy. As I remember, the issue took several meetings before it was resolved. Our earnest contingent met with President Grant once and attended three meetings with Mr. Fish.

"What is it that you wish my government to do for these young students, Madame Villaverde?" Mr. Fish asked me, obviously frustrated by the lack of an acceptable solution.

"Our goal is simple, Mr. Secretary. You can ask the Spaniards to rescind, or at the very least, reduce the sentences passed on the thirty-six students. But I grant you there is a better solution. You can have the U.S. government bring the students to this country immediately!"

Back and forth we argued the benefits of various proposals. By the third meeting, we'd reached an agreement. The United States government, in partnership with Great Britain, would ask the Spanish government to rescind the sentences and let the students complete their medical studies in Spain. And that is how the matter was resolved. I was not totally pleased that the students would go to Spain, but at least it removed them from the wrath of the military and the *voluntarios* in Cuba. Historians would write about this tragedy as one of the most horrific events of the war. How could they not?

Neither the renewed calls for support of the rebel army nor our success in removing the medical students to the peninsula succeeded in saving La Liga de las Hijas de Cuba! Some blamed it on the economic depression; others said that four years of a losing war without external support simply sapped the strength of our already demoralized expatriates. I only knew that toward the end of 1871 I could no longer rely on my compatriots and closest companions to attend meetings or engage in fundraisers. They no longer cared to fulfill the organization's mission.

I stood by silently and watched as, one by one, the ladies of Las Hijas abandoned their commitment to our cause and to me. I sorrowfully watched them organize a series of vapid little clubs that had less investment in *Cuba Libre* and more to do with enhancing their own social connections. Meeting after meeting, I found myself taking on additional responsibility and expenses while pretending to believe that the low attendance was due to one unavoidable family matter or another.

"They're just tired of a struggle that has yielded so few victories," I whispered to myself as I helped young Enrique sound out the words in a book of children's verses. That afternoon, I snuggled with my child on a cushioned chaise in the conservatory, surrounded by the last vestiges of autumn colors as the grays of winter advanced. Suddenly, we heard a flock of Canadian geese honking as they flew overhead in tight formation. Mesmerized by the beauty of the birds in flight, we stopped our reading and watched until the last one could no longer be seen. I marveled at the precision of their graceful squadron, focused on the majestic leader on whom the rest relied to reach their destination. I wondered if I was still a strong enough leader to reach mine.

I attempted to hide my disappointment from Cirilo and the rest of the family. I downplayed the desertion of the ladies. "A few of them continue to work with the organization, of course, promising to complete several projects on our agenda," I explained. "The others are just very busy with their own families, but I'm certain they will participate in fundraisers."

Inside, my heart ached, one moment siding with the ladies, silently praising them for their good work, and another condemning each and every one of them to damnation for their ungratefulness. After all my time and energy, I fumed and, yes, all the money spent from my own pocket to ensure favorable outcomes of our work! But for all my anger at the ladies, I was grateful to have had the support of courageous women in a decidedly man's world and lamented their absence.

"Of course, I'll continue to work under the banner of La Liga de la Hijas de Cuba. After all, I founded the group, and everyone recognizes our organization. With the few women who remain loyal to the association, we will accomplish our goals, which have always been to support the rebel patriots. We mustn't lose sight of our priorities."

My husband stared at me in support, but not quite sure just what to make of my manic ramblings. He, nonetheless, committed himself to help in whatever way he could. In this regard, he did not have very long to wait. The first test of the effectiveness of the pared down organization under my leadership loomed right around the corner.

In the name of La Liga de las Hijas de Cuba, I presented a petition to the U.S. Congress the following February requesting Rights of Belligerence for Cuban revolutionaries. Washington, D.C. was a whirlwind of partisan activity and I sorely missed Cirilo's company and wisdom on this trip—at the last minute he could not accompany me. With only young Enrique at my side, I prepared for the encounter. Narciso stayed in New York, but was very interested in everything that had to do with Cuban and American politics. He begged me, just before I left, to remember every detail of my experience so that I could share it with him upon my return. On the day before my congressional appearance in Marble Hall, I wrote him about my views on Washington society and hastily appended a note for his father.

Mi Querido Hijo, My dear son, I wrote . . .

> *There are ladies here who beg to be with me where entry is forbidden to the common public. I don't doubt that being Americans they are surprised, like that lady in Montreal when we went to see Victoria Bridge, by the easy way doors are opened for me. People offer me their respect. They smother me so much it suffocates me instead of giving me pride. I don't need formal entry to the wives of senators, ministers and other persons in Washington. In this, Enrique plays a big role, especially in the hotel. Well, he is so adorable*

and lively he attracts attention and people come to me to caress him and hear him speak English and Spanish so well.

People are anxious to serve me, bring me the paper, especially when there is news of Cuba. This is all great praise, but for someone else: not me. I wouldn't change my little home, not even for Mrs. Grant's Blue Room in the White House. No, not even my dining room, which is more dear than all the dining rooms in the palaces of Washington. One cup of coffee there tastes better than the dozens of exquisite and costly plates I'm served in Arlington.

I have to edit the talk I'm giving Congress in the name of Las Hijas. . . . Assure your father I want nothing more than this . . . a recognition of belligerency and slavery abolished . . . and basta! It's late and my eyes and arms hurt me. ¡Adiós, querido hijo de mis entrañas! Don't forget my advice to be loved and respected by all.

Recibe el cariño y bendición de tu madre, Emilia.
Washington, February 2, 1872.

The following day, after enduring a long, heated debate on my proposal, the petition was denied because a similar proposal had recently been presented in Congress. Nonetheless, convinced that few Americans really understood what was taking place in Cuba, I felt I had enlightened those well-intentioned, but misinformed, gentlemen on issues about which they may not have had full knowledge. The rest was in God's hands.

I circulated the speech I had given in Congress, entitled "Memorial Presented to the Congress of the United States Petitioning for Rights of Belligerence for Cubans," in the name of the Liga de Las Hijas de Cuba. Looking back, I wonder how I maintained such a demanding schedule. I probably wrote more than anyone needed to know in that lengthy document, but in truth I believed an overview of the history of liberation and the abolition of slavery throughout the world was needed.

I mostly focused on Cuba's attempts to gain independence over some fifty years, from 1818 to our current struggles that saw the light of day in 1868. I mentioned the founding fathers of the Latin American republics in the first third of the century and the abolitionist papers written by Cubans in New York during the 1850s. But above all, I invoked America's own struggles for independence and abolition of slavery during our own times to remind the Congress of the United States that Cubans had as much right to fight for complete separation as did they in 1776.

In September, another memorandum appeared on the Rights of Belligerence. This one came from the Minister of Foreign Relations of Colombia, South America, addressed to Secretary of State, Hamilton Fish. The document proposed joint action between his country and the United States on the issue of belligerency.

"Cubans," he said, "after having proclaimed to the world their determination to be free and independent, are now, and have been for the last four years, engaged in a daily struggle with their mother country, seeking to accomplish the work of liberation."

I shared the piece with Cirilo, delighted with its succinct argument. But the proposal from Colombia was flatly rejected by Congress.

Yet another group composed of prominent African American leaders in New York explored the long history of slavery in Cuba at their December meeting at Cooper Institute. Their arguments and support, in favor of both abolition and belligerency, appeared in the pages of the *New York Herald.* I read Cirilo their poignant words, " . . . *the voice of this Cooper Institute meeting is the voice of all our citizens of African descent, including especially those four millions lately released from the shackles of slavery* . . . ", which coincided with the emancipation theme in his own novel, *Cecilia Valdés,* that he was in the midst of re-writing.

With reinvigorated interest from several quarters on the matter of Rights of Belligerence, and with a favorable report father received at the Casanova Mansion from the ship, the *Virginius*, I began to feel more optimistic about our efforts, inspiring us all to stay the course. Word was that the *Virginius* had successfully completed its second expedition to Cuba, bringing badly needed weapons and munitions to the resource-starved Mambíes in the eastern provinces. Originally christened the "Virgin," the ship had been purchased in August for $9,800 by an American supporter of Free Cuba named John F. Patterson, so that it could be registered as an American steamship flying American colors. But the actual owner was our own General Quesada, with the backing of the Junta and Casanova funding. A fast blockade runner, the steamship was commissioned by the Confederate States of America in 1864 and designed to carry soldiers and supplies along coastal waters. In the service of the Cuban rebels, the *Virginius* was particularly welcomed at ports of call that were sympathetic to the Cuban cause, but she was known to change her colors as was warranted, sometimes flying the Stars and Stripes and at other times hoisting the flag of *Cuba Libre*.

Elated by the news, I clearly recalled the ship's first voyage on October 4th, 1871, when it left from the Casanova docks on Long Island Sound. "Had it not been for that first successful voyage," I told my father, "the Mambí Army of Liberation would have been permanently crippled for lack of resources! And now, to think, that after all the failed expeditions we've sent to Cuba, the loss of so many young lives, the enrichment of the Spanish military at our expense, we finally, *finally*, have a vessel that can outrun their naval man-o-wars."

I recalled the unfortunate expeditions of the *Fanny* and other ships that had been intercepted by the Spanish, their Cuban passengers executed. And I'll always remember the volunteers of the Battalion de la Cruz who perished, many of whom I'd personally known or recruited.

But with the *Virginius'* first success, I have to confess, I held my breath expecting to hear the worst: the ship's capture or sinking. . . . I playfully grabbed the telegram from father's hand to read it for myself, my mind racing to envision the next fundraising strategies I'd work on to support the ship's upcoming missions.

Those were days of mixed blessings. I'd lost the support of Las Hijas, but we did manage to save the lives of the students. And the *Virginius* proved to be a successful gamble. Yet, despite my exuberance, I was uneasy. I dared not admit it to myself, but locked away in a tiny recess of my soul I dreaded that my jubilation could bring forth disaster at the blink of an eye. "Best to be grateful in humility," I cautioned myself, "than to tempt the furies with happiness."

In retrospect, I should have found satisfaction in all of our accomplishments, but I did not. A few weeks earlier, father had informed me that the new Spanish Minister to Washington, a man named Polo de Bernabé, had implored him to please keep me out of politics. Laughing, I told my father, "That's a major cause for celebration. I must be doing something right, if the Spanish authorities are that upset with me!" But there was a sense of foreboding I could not describe. There was nothing I could do but wait, and wait I did.

Sixteen

The Virginius
An International Incident

. . . Mme. Villaverde was next called upon at her residence on Twenty-fourth street. It was she who equipped 100 of the patriots for the expedition. There were several of the prominent leaders in the Cuban cause at her place discussing the matter. It was the opinion that the present state of affairs would result in the United States and British governments taking some action. . . .

"The Virginius."
The New York Times, November 8, 1873.

At first, I screamed! By all the saints in heaven, there was nothing else I could do but scream. My father, my husband and I had just finished taking mid-morning coffee in the library, bringing one another up to date on personal and family matters. Each of us was prepared to go about our business as we usually did on most mornings, when the butler discreetly entered the room and handed the unmistakable pale yellow envelope of a telegram to me on a silver tray. I vaguely remember standing up, my hands automatically smoothing the front of my skirts. I opened the envelope, glanced at its contents and suddenly doubled over, holding onto my stomach to protect myself from what seemed to be a sharp, painful blow. . . . Far off in the distance, I heard someone moaning, "No . . . no . . . no . . . " over and over again in a hauntingly mournful tone. The moaning, I soon realized, was coming from the innermost depths of my own anguish.

It all happened so quickly it was difficult to breathe, to follow the sequence of events. I must have stumbled, because the next thing I remember was Cirilo calling my name, cradling me gently in his arms. In a blur, I remember my father leaving his armchair and scooping up the telegram that had slipped from between my trembling fingers. As the clock in the foyer struck the quarter hour, my father solemnly declared, "The *Virginius* has met its ruin within site of Guantánamo Bay!"

No one really understood the extent of my emotional investment in this ship that was to be the instrument for bringing victory to the patriots and an end to five years of warfare. As difficult as it was for me to revisit, indeed, to reconstruct what had actually happened to the ship, my side of the story has never been told to anyone outside of my family, even though the affair virtually crushed all my hopes and dreams for a free Cuba.

As you already know, the Casanova Mansion contained subterranean caverns that we used to store weapons and ammunition, along with other munitions that we either purchased or collected for the rebel cause. Early on, I'd convinced my father to build a tunnel leading to the waters of Long Island Sound, where yachts and steamers could dock and load equipment heading for Cuba. Dozens of vessels steamed from our shores carrying medicine, bandages, lint, clothing, shoes, weapons, uniforms and whatever else we could commission to sustain the Mambíes. But the images most indelibly and vividly seared into my memory were the ones of the young men we recruited for the expeditions, among whom there was always one earnest recruit that I'd entrusted to carry the banner of *Cuba Libre* which I'd sown with my own hands.

In the final phase of their training, they often stayed with us at the mansion until the time was right for sailing. I can still hear their expressions of excitement . . . can still remember the anxiety on the faces of the young recruits, members of the numerous battalions I'd outfitted as they boarded the ships for Cuba. As it was with the Battalion of La Cruz and the Guardia de la Bembeta, it was I who personally funded, organized and outfitted the expeditions.

But luck was not always on our side. So many of the ships we equipped and sent from our dock either met with misfortune or failed to outrun the Spanish blockade. Attacked on the high seas, their cargoes were confiscated and the passengers killed or taken prisoner. Each time I received distressing news of another failed expedition, I suffered for the loss of so many young lives, as if they had been my own flesh and blood. Above everyone else, I carried the responsibility and guilt for their demise.

But the *Virginius* was different. She had succeeded for *three* years in carrying out extraordinary missions, and no one will ever convince me that our efforts did not make a difference. They did. Soon after she made her first run, the rebel forces began to rally, to win more victories and the tide turned—it *turned* in our favor.

I cannot remember how many months it took before I could actually speak coherently about "The *Virginius* Incident," as it was christened in the press. For a while, it helped me to piece together, to retrace the chain of events that led to the taking of the ship. I read every account, sought minute bits of information from seasoned seamen and waited anxiously for official reports from Washington. Looking back, I think I tried to convince myself that its demise was inevitable in the way that chance lays fallow the best made plans.

Except for the *Virginius'* urgent need to overhaul her engines that June, the ship's final voyage began as usual. But when she dropped anchor at the port of Aspinwall in Colombia to make repairs, a Spanish ship, the *Bazán*, lurked close by and attempted to intercept her. As luck would have it, another ship, the American *USS Kansas*, interceded on behalf of the *Virginius* because she was flying the Stars and Stripes. Once the *Virginius* became aware of the Spanish threat, she was forced to leave the safety of the Colombian harbor.

While the *Virginius'* drama unfolded on the high seas, I received an inquiry from an anonymous donor wishing to buy thirty to forty thousand pesos worth of Cuban bonds. Such substantial funds could be used to buy munitions and equip volunteers, I reasoned. I wrote immediately to Carlos del Castillo, the Junta agent in charge of finances. That was on July 1st.

Dear Friend:

I've received word of an individual looking to buy Cuban bonds in the amount of thirty to forty thousand pesos in cash. Since I must give him an answer by tonight, I need to know if you have bonds available and at what price. It would be my great pleasure if, through my efforts, your agency would be the beneficiary of this impressive sum of money.

Your attentive servant and ally,

E. C. De V. Nueva York, Julio 1, 1873.

Once Castillo received payment for the bonds, I personally negotiated the purchase of arms and munitions from the firm of Remington and Sons, on behalf of the Cuban republic. By September 11th, I was finally able to write to General Quesada in Cuba about the arrangements I'd made to ship the armaments, and assured him that I was also arranging the transportation of several volunteers who would board the *Virginius* in Jamaica.

In early July, the *Virginius* had pulled into the port city of Kingston, Jamaica, where she would remain until mid-October, awaiting the transfer of munitions and volunteers. Determined to complete all that was required on my part for that mission, I'd organized and equipped the Guardia de Bembeta, a battalion of twenty-six youths whose well-being I'd entrusted to General Quesada. The young men eagerly jumped at the opportunity to do their duty as loyal Cubans, and I felt so sure that placed under the command of an experienced general, they would bring days of glory to the *patria*. In so doing, *God help me*, they might perhaps honor the woman who made it possible and sincerely regretted not being able to share the dangers of the campaign with them.

From communications with the commander of the *Virginius'* expedition, the respected Bernabé Varona, I knew him to be a cautious man. My hopes for another successful run were pinned on General Varona, known by everyone for his astute leadership. There were, nonetheless, some setbacks in the planning, but these were never enough to derail the mission. One such incident, I clearly recall, occurred when the shipping company that was to take the volunteers to Jamaica failed to meet its obligation. At the last minute, it refused to make port in Jamaica, offering to take our group to Port-au-Prince instead. I feared they would not arrive in time to make a connection with the *Virginius* and argued fiercely with the steamship company, to no avail. My letter to General Varona informed him that

> *Following your instructions, I presented myself at the agency of the steamship "Atlas," and experienced a monumental battle with the agents. Regardless of all my efforts, I could not get them to make a stop in Kingston to leave your passengers. The most I could do was to arrange for forty to disembark in Port-au-Prince for a $1,600 note, $800 in cash and the rest to be paid within thirty days in the names of Quesada and Castillo, as you yourself instructed me. I could send one or two more at no cost and, if necessary, take one or two in hiding.*
>
> *I'm sending you twenty-five dollars ($25), which I grabbed from Mr. Garrison to help with the passages.*
>
> *At your disposal,*
>
> *E. C. de V., Nueva York, September 12, 1873.*

Once it appeared the new arrangements for transporting the passengers were securely in place, I then turned my attention to the maintenance and armament of the Guardia de Bembeta. By the middle of September, my composure was truly at the breaking point. I feared my packages containing the arms and clothing would be confiscated by the enemy, that General Varona would not pay careful attention to my instructions nor care for my volunteers. My frustration and anxiety at not being personally in control of the situation weighed heavily on my mind. The letter to General Varona, dated September 17, once again, detailed the numbers of revolvers, carbines, holsters, ammunition, machetes and clothing for my recruits. Please . . . please, I remember sending silent prayers to the heavens, do not let my volunteers and their equipment fall into enemy hands. But to General Varona, I wrote,

> *The bearer will deliver a package containing seventeen leather holsters for the Remington revolvers that you received without the holsters in the box delivered to General Quesada on the 6th of September.*
>
> *I don't know if Quesada told you that I armed and completely equipped not only the twenty-six men that I offered for your battalion, but four more who approached me at the eleventh hour.*
>
> *Their armament and equipment consists of Remington carbines with their straps, revolvers of the same manufacturer with their holsters, machetes with their sheaths and belts, munitions, 1300 bullets for the revolvers, 500 for the carbines, 76 yards of denim for jackets and thirty changes of clothing. . . . I expect all of this was shipped on time and that you will reclaim it as your own when the time comes . . . the packages are six and bear the initial V, inside of which you will find the corresponding number.*
>
> *Pardon my minuscule details, but I want you to know everything as I want these effects in which I have invested so much care to reach you and not fall into the hands of others, but only to the hands of the young men that make up the Guardia de Bembeta.*

Porras Pita and Rubiero will give you a list of their names
so that you will know who they are, and do not abandon them
because I intend to support them from here on out.
Yours,
E. C. de V., Nueva York, September 17, 1873.

By late October, the Virginius had left Jamaican waters carrying British and American passengers, Cuban rebels, weapons and munitions. She set sail for Port-au-Prince, Haiti, where on October 25th, the crew loaded several more boxes containing 300 Remington rifles, 300,000 cartridges, 800 machetes, shoes, clothing and gunpowder. As I carefully laid out my actions to coincide with those of the ship's trajectory, I was astounded to realize my own state of nervous anxiety. How meticulous I was in relaying every detail even to the smallest degree, as if I too prepared for combat!

Among the passengers of the Virginius was the commander of the expedition, the aforementioned General Bernabé Varona. William Ryan and Joseph Fry were the captains of the ship. Jesús de Sol, Agustín Santa Rosa and Pedro de Céspedes, brother of the provisional president, were among the passengers. I name these men in particular, not just for being loyal Cubans, but because they all held American citizenship.

Well, to continue, anyone can cite for you chapter and verse of the rest of the story because the tragedy was exploited by pacifists and warhawks alike in all the newspapers. Because the Virginius was thought to be an American ship, it became an international incident. For that reason, the United States hovered on the brink of declaring war against Spain during the first weeks of November of 1873.

The tragedy actually began on the 30th day of October. Intercepted by the Spanish ship, the Tornado following an eight-hour sea chase, the Virginius was boarded and hauled into Santiago, Cuba, where the Spanish commander, a particularly cruel man named Burriel, immediately arranged for a military tribunal.

The trials, of course, were shams and the accused, mere pawns in the hands of a prejudiced court. Within five days, Ryan, Varona, de Sol and Céspedes forfeited their lives before a firing squad. Two days later, Fry and thirty-six British and American passengers met the same fate, among them, most of the eager, patriotic young men belonging to my own Guardia de Bembeta.

Those mad days of retribution became virtual killing frenzies, as if a contagious hysteria had taken hold of the Spanish military. The bodies of the slaughtered were mutilated; the assassinations numbered some 150 individuals. It finally came to an end but only by happenstance. A British warship, the *HMS Niobe*, arrived in Santiago. Apprised of the situation, the British captain demanded an immediate halt to the executions, threatening to bombard the city of Santiago to smithereens.

When I first heard the complete story, my mind reeled, refused to acknowledge the reality of what had taken place. The press hounded us for weeks, once the true ownership of the ship was discovered. Cirilo and I stayed in our New York townhouse, which became the gathering place for members of the Junta, politicians, writers and representatives from the various organizations devoted to *Cuba Libre*. Everyone had something to say but no one knew what to do next.

No longer able to delude myself, I feared I'd lose my mind if I continued to think or talk about the war. And so I buried the incident, erased it from my consciousness. Under an encompassing dark cloud of sorrow, I grieved instead for the families of the young men who had so prematurely given their lives to the cause. Unfortunately, I felt helpless to offer them anything but my condolences, empty words at tragic moments like this. If I'd had the chance to defy convention and thrown myself at their feet seeking forgiveness, I would have done so.

How surprising are the memories one retains following a shock to the system like the *Virginius* incident. A few days after we had received the news about the executions, a young Spaniard appeared at our door asking for help in finding a job and getting settled in New York. He was in debt and feared losing his current lodging in a local *pensión*.

It was unfortunate that it was I who answered the door because, I'm ashamed to say, I directed all my anger and frustration at him. I remember being indignant and berating this innocent man, who was not at all connected with the war in Cuba, about his lack of sensitivity.

"Is it possible," I ranted, "that you, a Spaniard, asks for my charity when the blood of my friends and *paisanos* is still warm, shed indiscriminately by you Spaniards in Santiago, Cuba? Is this your idea of a cruel joke? Did you intend to insult me under these most grievous circumstances of my life?"

Bewildered, the man stammered and swore he knew nothing about what had happened in Cuba. He begged my forgiveness and lamented that he had only come to see me because of my reputation as a charitable woman. My kindness and helping hand was known throughout the city. Sad and dejected, he turned around and left our home as if rejected from his final recourse.

I remember this boy so clearly. To this day, I think of him as a boy, because he was not much older than the scores of young men I had sent to Cuba. Almost immediately, my heart reached out to him. "Please, don't despair," I begged him in a low tone. "At this very moment it is not possible for me to do anything for you. But later on, when my spirit is less anguished, if you have not found the solutions to your problems, and present yourself again at my door, I'll do anything I can to help you."

Was it possible that this stranger who appeared out of nowhere, a young Spaniard at that, was meant to sow the first seeds of redemption in my soul?

Seventeen
Prior Debts and New Directions

No, I will not be silenced! I'll clamor against their failed procedures. I'll denounce to the world their autonomous plans, and if no one hears me, nor gives me justice, I will remain, always, with the consolation of having met my most sacred obligations as a citizen and a patriot.
Emilia Casanova de Villaverde, Mott Haven, May 6, 1876.

Some people believe that time heals all wounds. While I certainly do not subscribe to that trite bit of wisdom, having experienced losses that will forever remain sealed in my heart, I can say the passage of time was good for Cirilo and me. I began to feel at peace with the troubles of the past and looked forward to the future once again. Cirilo was editing a commercial newspaper, *El Espejo*, a printed sheet or two of trade information that advertised a wide assortment of American goods for export. We found ourselves spending more time in our New York residence, a comfortable townhouse efficiently cared for by a housemaid, a cook and a butler. The change in lifestyle gave me less responsibility with household matters than I'd had at the mansion and more time for writing.

On one of those rare afternoons at home, when the luxury of domestic matters absorbed my attention, I started a conversation with Cirilo regarding the current state of political affairs among the expatriates.

"It was not so much that I disliked them as individuals," I said, trying to explain my point of view. "It was more that their failures as the so-called *anointed* representatives of Free Cuba in exile did more good for the Spanish forces than for our own people in the trenches. Seriously, Cirilo, I deeply, *deeply* resent their ineptitude. The men of the Junta should have been replaced long ago, or is it that the Cuban people do not truly desire independence at all? Aldama may be replaced by that fellow named Machado as the new director of the New York Junta, but really, leopards don't change their spots so easily."

I laughed as I rearranged the placement of two delicate porcelain vases on the marble mantel of the fireplace. The fireplace was the central focal point of our newly decorated drawing room, and I was intent on making the space comfortable and inviting for the entire family. I'd wondered if the vases interfered with the serene composition of clock and candlesticks that now occupied pride of place on the mantel and meant to ask my husband's opinion. But when I turned away from the mantel and the vases I'd lovingly arranged, I found Cirilo had long since left the room. I'd been talking to myself! Cirilo's mind was clearly not on my ideas. He must have been drawn to the printed pages he had intended to proofread that morning in preparation for the next edition of his newspaper.

El Espejo was a welcomed addition in our lives, particularly in mine, because it allowed me the opportunity to write again. In addition to publishing commercial information, *El Espejo* also published interpretative essays. The paper became our newest vehicle to launch an intensive separatist campaign. On the matter of liberation, our *paisanos* had reached a crossroad; given the choice of either compromise or separation, most opted for the former. Firmly on the side of separation, Cirilo and I, old radicals that we were, still hoped to sway opinions, even though we both had to admit that this would probably be the last opportunity we had to make a difference. The war in Cuba, as we well knew, was sadly on the wane.

Putting aside my regrets over past failures and failed expeditions, I worked tirelessly on my essays and continued to damn the factions courting compromise. An experienced agitator, I discovered all sorts of resources and old documents at the New York Historical Society on 2nd Avenue. I widely distributed my articles to be read in the cigar factories and to be dispatched to contacts in Chile, Peru, Jamaica and beyond.

Some readers believed my essays were inflammatory. Well, if inflammatory articles were needed to inspire a renaissance of fervor and unity among the expatriate community, then I was prepared to set the world on fire. I chose specifically to criticize the alarming disunity among my fellow Cubans in an effort to awaken them, to shake them from their lethargic passivity. By their lack of moral support, I argued in my essays and letters, they shared the blame for the assassination of President Carlos Manuel de Céspedes as surely as the actual assassins who had murdered him.

For all intents and purposes, we could say the war was over by 1876. Oh, to be sure, battles continued to be fought and won in the eastern provinces under the tenacious leadership of the Generals Máximo Gómez and Antonio Maceo, neither of whom ever succumbed to the notion of a compromised peace. But when General Vicente García crippled the movement by calling for an assembly of the disgruntled, and then as provisional president was willing to entertain peace terms, well, the war was virtually over. After eight long years of devastation, isolated pockets of combat lingered only because the truly committed among the Mambíes held sacred the ideals of liberation, despite disunity among the larger rebel forces and a virulent distrust directed against Maceo because of his African race.

"Was he planning to turn Cuba into a Black Republic," the white generals whispered behind his back as he won victory after victory. Even the Spaniards themselves addressed him with respect, calling him *señor*. Idolized by his followers, both black and white, Maceo's daring deeds fueled the legends surrounding his exploits, but that also made him the target of envy and of numerous assassination attempts. The man walked a fine line with a double price on his head; one placed there by the Spaniards, the other by the Cubans.

Among the expatriates, I'd say that except for those brave hearts like ourselves committed to unconditional independence, the struggles were essentially dismissed while talk of compromise loomed large on every street corner, in the factories, organizations and meeting halls. And to my personal irritation, the Junta, touting compromise from the very beginning of the movement, remained convinced that it represented the wishes of all in the expatriate community. At least that was the common misconception, for they were far from representing mine. And that was exactly what I wrote in a letter to General Máximo Gómez in 1876.

> . . . I've written to you on several occasions but I have not received an answer, probably because the agency [the Junta] has seen to it that you know nothing about us nor we about you.
>
> Nonetheless, recently I've seen published two letters from you to your "friend" Aldama in which you complain that we've abandoned you and the Junta. How is it that you do not, for a moment, wonder that if that individual has been abandoned by the émigré community, it is his own fault? Is it because he is burying the patria? Open your eyes and install another individual in his place who will help you give us what we do not have and which we desire: patria!
>
> I've just learned that the patriots, Simoni, Castillo, etc., have reached Cuba Libre, and although I am happy for their safe arrival, it hurts me to know that they only carry correspondence from Aldama, which has to be a glorification of himself and a defamation of all of us good patriots. . . .

The final blow to independence arrived rather anti-climactically with the Treaty of Zanjón in early February of 1878. Spain emerged victorious, but sparks of combat continued, credited especially to the courageous heroism of Gómez and Maceo. I remember it as if it were yesterday: the where, when and how I learned about Maceo's fearless rejection of the Spanish peace treaty.

Looking back, it was on a quiet Saturday afternoon, the 6th of April, that the rebellion had taken an unexpected turn. I remember it was during the weekend because it had long been our custom to spend that part of the week with family, and we'd made a conscious effort to let political issues rest. But Narciso was a follower of the New York Mutuals, a baseball team that once included Esteban Bellán among its players. Along with friends from St. Joseph's College, Narciso planned to attend the game on that Saturday afternoon. And Cirilo, preoccupied more than usual with writing an article about the post-war status of slavery in Cuba, was pressed to hold a meeting of our compatriots about the issue.

As was our custom, we met at noontime in the *pensión* of Madame Griffou. A beautifully fashioned Victorian hotel, number 21 West 9th Street, Madame Griffou's had become the unofficial headquarters for Cuban political meetings. And Madame Marie Griffou, an attractive, effervescent French woman known to employ freed slaves from Cuba to manage the *pensión*, was undoubtedly the essence of discretion.

Her meeting rooms, each tastefully accented with expensive Anglo-Japanese pieces, antiques and dark mahogany paneled walls, offered complete privacy. Thus, it was not unusual for two rivals, be they organizations or individuals, to meet at the same time without awareness of one another's presence on the premises.

"The problem remains the lack of universal freedom, and that must be addressed," I remember Cirilo railing to the group, almost spilling the contents of the coffee cup he held in his hand. "The Treaty of Zanjón freed all the slaves who fought in the rebellion, but what about the rest? Those, my friends, who remained loyal to their masters, who did not fight in the rebellion, remain slaves!"

There were ten of us sitting around the damask-covered walnut table in the "rose room," so called because an array of pink satin roses delicately positioned on climbing trellises and other floral arrangements in standing ceramic vases filled the room. I was the only woman. Several of the men in our party edited a number of the local newspapers. Others were writers or journalists. While plans were underway to attack the issue of slave non-combatants in the press, a soft knock drew our attention to the French doors. Madame Griffou entered the room carrying a bundle of newspapers. She smiled and lit up the room with a twinkle in her blue eyes as she said, "I think, *mes amis, madame,* that you will wish to read this." And so it was that I read for the first time Antonio Maceo's declaration, "Protest of Baraguá."

As I read the paper aloud to our *paisanos,* my head reeled in the excitement of the moment, as if I'd consumed too many cups of champagne. The opening sentence—I wanted to laugh out loud when I read it—offered a vindication of my every action. I sought Cirilo's eyes across the table as if to alert him, "Listen . . . *listen* to what Maceo has written. . . ." I read aloud to the group controlling the breathlessness I could feel rising in my throat.

"We shall not enter into the peace agreement. Our policy is to free the slaves, because the era of the whip and of Spanish cynicism has come to an end, and we ought to form a new Republic assimilated with our sisters Santo Domingo and Haiti."

Everyone in that room observed a moment of silence in respect for the esteemed leader and because they agreed with his sentiments.

The Protest of Baraguá, named for the place where it was declared, was issued on March 23rd, 1878, just a week or so after General Maceo had met with General Martínez Campos and other Spaniards in truce talks. *La Verdad* newspaper praised Maceo to the heavens, calling him a hero . . . "and it appears it is up to him to raise Cuba again to the pinnacle of its glory." At that moment,

I too believed a hero had been sent by God to save the *patria* at the eleventh hour.

It became known as *la guerra chiquita* or *la guerra chica* (the tiny war), this year-long refusal to accept the peace treaty. Cirilo and I were steeped in the politics of the moment from the tops of our heads to the tips of our toes. José Martí, the gifted writer, sought refuge in New York that bitter January during the freeze of 1880. The son of a Spanish father, Martí had paid for his opposition to the Spaniards with seventeen months of forced labor in Cuba. A slim man of delicate features, one could not help but notice the smoldering intensity and intelligence in his dark eyes, but he was still a shadow of the revolutionary or visionary he would become. At that point, he was a writer and a journalist. He wrote in English for several American newspapers and in Spanish for others in the United States and Latin America.

Cirilo and Martí were thick as thieves. They reminded me of an elder statesman guiding his young protégé. I'd observe them sometimes from my window when they left our house for a meeting, traversing and sliding over mounds of snow that had not been cleared away for months. That year, the city suffered the onslaught of numerous winter snowstorms, one piled on top of the other and, difficult as it was, walking became the safest and fastest way to get places. Cirilo and Martí, and I must include myself as well, met frequently at Madame Griffou's to discuss and plan rebellion through the printed manifestos. You could feel the excitement in the air and, for a brief period, you would have thought we were back in time, back in the thick of battle.

In the headiness of the *guerra chica*, our maturity peeled away from us like a serpent sheds its skin. Clearly, rebellion rejuvenated us, fired up our political passions again! It gave me new life, helping to wipe away so many of my past disillusionments. When Gómez and Maceo called a meeting of patriots in New York City to organize a new invasion, I was beside myself with anticipation,

eager to meet the heroes of the Protest of Baraguá and to personally proclaim my loyalty to them once again as a citizen and a
patriot.

My first impressions upon meeting them, I remember, were
mixed. I thought that the short, cropped white hair, white beard
and moustache he sported made General Gómez appear fatherly.
With his round glasses and wiry build, it was difficult for me to
think of him as a fighter. But the mulatto, Antonio Maceo, taller
and younger, seemed every bit a man of action. He wore a military
style uniform with a wide-brimmed, buff colored hat that brought
out the warmth of his brown eyes; he spoke to us in an engaging
and forthright manner. His second in command, the boyish Puerto Rican general, Juan Rius Rivera, did not address the audience
but was embraced and applauded by his compatriots. Enthralled,
I observed the three leaders and marveled at the unspoken promise of a Pan-Caribbean unity so aptly represented by these men.

"¡Compañeros!" I called out when I finally had the opportunity to speak to them alone. "Allow me to be your representative
here in New York! I'll bring the faithful into the fold and expose
any conspiracies in opposition to your plans!" I stated this in
spontaneity, offering my services to the exalted generals in all sincerity. Politely, they informed me that they had chosen to wait
before making any decisions, that it was imperative to have everyone's support on the matter of unifying the expatriate community.
Something in their demeanor raised nagging thoughts, and I could
not shake the feeling that my solid stand in opposition to the
Junta, my unwavering refusal to consider compromise in any
form, or perhaps that I was a woman, was the true reason they did
not accept my offer.

How interesting, I later reflected in the privacy of my home,
my *paisanos* had always considered me a valiant, strong woman,
intelligent, shrewd and well-spoken. I received the same accolades
after my speeches as Maceo and Martí. I was admired and praised
for my political essays, given standing ovations for my speeches.

I'd done and had given more to this revolution throughout my entire life than dozens of men who dawdled on the margins of *Cuba Libre*, living on the crumbs of recognition from our leaders. Yet, my sex appeared to render me incapable in the eyes of our leaders.

But soon, the failure of the *guerra chica* left little doubt in anyone's mind that the war was finally over. Whatever issues had emerged over my competence as a woman were laid to rest. I faced the harsh reality that Cuba would forever belong to Spain. My sacrifices, my loyalty, my love of *patria*, I feared may have ignited more animosity among my *paisanos* than gratitude.

How did I accept defeat, you ask? At first, I remember feeling nothing . . . nothing at all. No joy or sorrow, no love, resentment or anger. As I commended Cuba into God's hands, I was devoid of emotions. And the hollow puppet I'd become longed to draw the curtains of my life against the raw reality of fate, longed to nestle in the warmth and shelter of my home. Who would ever know, I wondered, or care to remember the Cuba I knew before the scourge of war?

"*Ay, por favor,* Cirilo, please! listen to me," I laughed uncontrollably in spite of myself. Since the end of the *guerra chica*, I remember quarreling incessantly with my husband over the direction his book was taking. He had finally found the time to devote himself exclusively to finishing *Cecilia Valdés or the Angel's Hill* and worked on the manuscript for hours on end. Indeed, every Sunday, a day of rest for everyone but Cirilo, he was sprawled out in the library, pen in hand or hovering over our splendid workhorse of a desk, notes and papers strewn over every inch of it. This was, to be sure, Cirilo's labor of love, his love song to a Cuba as he still remembered her.

I read every chapter, helping to correct, edit or revise, and mostly to discuss with him the ideas he expressed in the book. It was my job to find cohesion among the many scenes and chapters, to unify, cut and modify. And, as a voluntary responsibility, I took it upon myself to make certain the characters were believable. Thus, the major source of our quarrels!

You might say that life had interfered with the completion of this novel. In 1858 he'd made an earnest attempt, but we were forced to leave Havana with our young son because of government threats and harassment. Once back in New York, by necessity, Cirilo devoted his time to teaching and the responsibility of administrating the school he founded to support the family. Then came the rebellion, and with the war all semblance of creativity flew out the window replaced by political tracts and incendiary journalism, meetings, organizations, plots and expeditions.

"The pen and the word," as he was fond of saying, "became instruments at least as virulent in the United States as the rifle and the machete in Cuba."

As in all things my husband pursued, there was a higher purpose for writing *Cecilia Valdés* and this he clarified to his readers in the preface. His generation bore witness to realities in the *patria* at a specific point in history. Had not colonialism influenced the nation's development, it could have evolved very differently. Cirilo felt compelled to capture in print that moment in time, to record Cuba's physical features, social and moral characteristics "before her death as a nation or her elevation to the life of a free entity." Either way, at the end of the ten-year rebellion, Cuba would forever be a changed country.

Of the many discussions and disagreements we had, perhaps our differences regarding the role of women during the 1830s, the time period for the story, was the most striking. Oh, to be sure, my husband was an excellent writer and storyteller. His characters, especially that of the exquisite, young Cecilia, were painted in truth and decorum. He gave action and thoughts to those groups on society's margins in ways that had seldom been explored in other, less realistic, novels. Exposed for all to read, the inhumanity of slavery and cruel nature of those parasites whose lives flourished because of the institution, would undoubtedly create ardent abolitionists among all his readers. But on the portrayal of the true nature of women of privilege, none held more authority than I.

"Women did indeed shape their own experiences!" I recall saying. "There is no argument about that. They were not simpletons, sitting still on the sidelines like lifeless dolls and playing out a role dictated by society. Look at me! I am not unique. Did I not ride my horses everywhere, arrange competitions with children of all classes and color despite what people said? Did I not council Papá about his businesses and oversee his estates here *and* in Cuba?"

"I understand what you are saying, Emilia, but although you don't want to admit it, you were probably an exception, and a big one at that. Even you must recognize that women in early nineteenth-century Cuba lived circumscribed lives," responded my exasperated husband in a particularly argumentative tone, simply because I had deigned to criticize one of the characters in his latest chapter. "They married partners chosen for them by their parents because that holy union was intended to enhance power and wealth, or they entered convents. *¡Punto final!* End of discussion."

He clasped together the papers I'd been reading, a look of unbending stoicism across his face, and continued, "Unlike the lower classes, however, where women could, or indeed, often had to work for a living, the privileged classes held certain consistent expectations for their women regarding their actions and demeanor."

"Oh, do tell!" I mocked gently. "Is that the reason we married some twenty-three years ago? Was ours a marriage of power and wealth?"

Softening my tone, I explained, "My dear Cirilo. Think of what a great contribution you will make to future generations who will surely flock to your novel in droves, like flies to opened jars of honey on a summer's day. If you could, my dear, convey to them the image of a strong, yet humble, woman who would epitomize lofty ideals but at the same time be smart and capable. Why, such a woman could indeed oversee a plantation. She could be actively involved in the pleasures of life and, for want of a better description, she could be her own woman, not a pawn subject to the designs of the men or the social customs of her times. Cirilo . . . just because she lived long ago, please don't deny her courage and intelligence. What a formidable gift you will be able to give your female readers! That to me is the true essence of your character, Isabel."

Cirilo completed in two years what had taken him forty years to contemplate. I remember my reading final chapters as bittersweet because the journey was coming to an end. As with all things one grows to love, and characters in a novel are no exception, I felt a sense of loss, an end of a road never more to be traveled.

"Well," said Cirilo, quietly sighing like a man who had concluded a long but difficult journey. He sat back in his chair in silence, arms folded across his chest for several minutes. "It is done," he finally said. "Tomorrow I'll gather the manuscript and take it to Narciso so that he can get the compositor to begin setting the type."

Our son, Narciso, was now the editor and owner of *El Espejo*. After much deliberation, Cirilo had decided that his novel would see the light of day on the pages of this newspaper. It was expected that the novel would be serialized before appearing in book form.

My husband rose from his chair and walked across the room to the sofa where I sat holding the final chapters on my lap. I gazed up at him, still absorbed in the fortunes of Cecilia, Isabel, Adela and Leonardo. His eyes softly studied me, a shy, almost expectant look upon his face. I noticed how tired and old he appeared as he caringly handed me another page, as if he were offering me a long-stemmed red rose.

"Emilia, my dear, I'd like you to read one more page for me." He smiled timidly.

At first, I held the page at arm's length, not having the immediate use of my spectacles, which rested on the side table next to the sofa. I reached for them and smiled up at him. "Of course," I remember saying. The single page contained the dedication of the book. I read . . .

To the Women of Cuba

Far from Cuba, and with no hope of ever seeing its sun,

its flowers, or its palms again, to whom, save to you,

dear country-women, the reflection of the most

beautiful side of our homeland, could I more

rightfully dedicate these sad pages?

The Author

Part V

New York City

(1892–1894)

Eighteen
Organizing "Mercedes Varona"

*Cuba and Puerto Rico are the two wings of one bird. They receive
flowers and bullets in the same heart.*
Lola Rodríguez de Tió. *Mi Libro de Cuba.* 1893.

Doña Inocencia Figueroa had followed her heart in forming
the club, Mercedes Varona. "Lately, she had not looked at all
well," I thought. Her lovely green eyes were frequently swollen as
if she had spent the night crying, or perhaps it was just the lack of
sleep. Emilita, my own daughter, *que en paz descanse,* may she rest
in peace, would have been about her age, and I sometimes found
myself thinking of Doña Inocencia as if she too, were my daughter. And I suppose, in some ways she was as close to being a fos-
ter daughter as anyone could be. I had offered her my support, my
council and my many years of experience in drafting bylaws and
procedures when she created Mercedes Varona.

The monthly meetings of Club Mercedes Varona were held at
the home of the Figueroas, No. 57 West 25th Street, not far from
Imprenta America, Sotero Figueroa's publishing house. Both Doña
Inocencia and Don Sotero moved in José Martí's inner circles and
were seen as leaders in the expatriate community.

Patria, the official newspaper of the Cuban Revolutionary
Party was published at Imprenta America, Don Sotero being its
editor-in-chief. Oftentimes, when I dropped in unexpectedly at

the press, Doña Inocencia would be working beside her husband. She would set type, edit and proofread printed pages while their children, two small girls and a toddler, played quietly in a nearby corner. In my opinion, it was not a good environment to raise healthy children, but I never commented about that to her because it was apparently the best they could do.

As founder and president of Club Mercedes Varona, Doña Inocencia presided over our meetings. I remember the April meeting, in particular, because it ended with a startling revelation. Before getting to the business at hand, Doña Inocencia proceeded to explain the history of the club and its structure, excusing the repetition for those members who had heard it before. "The Club Mercedes Varona is one of the three initial organizations that came together to found the Cuban Revolutionary Party," remarked Doña Inocencia. "The organization was named in honor of a young woman who gave her life in the conflict during the war of the ten years.

"The head of the Cuban Revolutionary Party is, of course, José Martí," she softly explained before two-year-old Julia wandered into the room and demanded her mother's attention. Weepy and irritable, the child suffered from a springtime cold and was obviously miserable. Julia's small head of dark blond curls was damp with perspiration and one did not have to place a hand against her forehead to know she was feverish. At this unexpected turn of events, Doña Laudelina Sosa, the club's vice president, took it upon herself to continue the narrative.

"Martí is the Delegate, the title he chose because he is one with and of the people. We, the people, have elected him to take the lead. He was elected, as were the secretary and treasurer, by an advisory council made up of the presidents of all the organizations, from Florida to New York, that agreed to participate within the party structure." All of this, she reported with great enthusiasm. This is all spelled out in *Patria* every week.

"The local councils of presidents represent geographic regions. Mercedes Varona belongs to the New York Council. The membership of each individual club elects its own club officers and sometimes a representative to the regional council. We are happy to say that in this year of 1893, we already have *eleven* women's clubs within the party structure.

"The primary function of the clubs we must not forget is, of course, to raise funds," I interjected for the benefit of the new members whom I did not know well. "All members pay dues according to what they can afford. You must understand, *señoras*, what a privilege it is to belong to such an organization. It is a very civilized way of structuring the Cuban Revolutionary Party.

"In the past, when I was involved in creating La Liga de las Hijas de Cuba and other groups, the associations were often at odds with one another. Women became competitive. Our clubs worked independently from one another, and the women had absolutely no voice in electing officers of the Junta or deciding on any other matter. In fact, neither the public vote nor our opinions were permitted to us."

I ended my discourse with a slight upturned tilt of my head, held high, as if to let the members of Club Mercedes Varona know that some of us are old hands at this business of organizing.

Doña Inocencia had deposited Julia in the bedroom and I could hear her speaking in a low tone to her cousin, a girl not more than twelve or thirteen years of age, who lived with the Figueroa family. "Please see to it, Anita, that the baby and Alejandrina are fed," she said. Her daughters attended to, she clumsily made her way back to her makeshift podium, and my heart almost sank with concern for her in her eighth month of pregnancy; it was clear that she needed loving care and rest.

At that point in the meeting, two members of Mercedes Varona entered the room and, once again, the business at hand was disrupted due to their late arrival. Genial, enthusiastic welcomes aside, the first, Doña Lola Rodríguez de Tió, noted poet and advocate for women's education, seemed to fill the room with positive energy and spontaneity. A jovial, rather corpulent woman, her laughter and high spirits contagiously filled the air, a much needed diversion because the small room was beginning to feel crowded on this warm spring day.

The other was Doña Carmen Miyares de Mantilla, a lovely woman with striking black hair pulled back into a bun away from her face, who was commonly regarded as the love of Martí's life. Both newcomers commanded respect, but Doña Lola's reputation as a leader for Puerto Rican independence was revered. Her revolutionary lyrics of *La Borinqueña* anthem, sang by one and all, bore testimony to the arduous struggle for liberation and a life lived in continuous exile.

When we finally addressed the agenda, the "business at hand" struck us all like a bolt out of the blue. Doña Inocencia wished to resign from the presidency of the club! She, who was its architect and nurturer since the club opened its doors in 1892; she, who steered this formidable entity into history, for it was the first political affiliation that allowed women to vote in this country; she, who gathered members like moths to a flame, whose leadership was vital to the club's existence, wished to leave Mercedes Varona! I glanced at Doña Lola and saw she was as surprised as I, but Doña Carmen, intimate friend of the Figueroas, sat grim-faced, lips pressed together, eyes staring into space, as if she could read on the somewhat distressed, rude walls the true motivation for Doña Inocencia's decision.

So much had happened since Doña Inocencia appeared unexpectedly in my home on that frigid morning in January. In the quiet solitude of my chambers, I mused over the rapidly evolving changes in my life since I'd met her and carefully lifted the lid off a large rectangular box marked R.H. Macy & Company that rested on my bed. Under protective layers of soft paper and muslin, my new plum, taffeta ensemble with the tiniest of cream-colored stripes running lengthwise, awaited inspection. Just looking at the outfit brought a smile to my face. A modest, but fashionable, three-piece dress, it had a long pleated bustled skirt, tight fitting bodice and a puff-sleeved, ruffle-necked jacket that extended over the hips. It would do, I thought, for any number of social functions.

I stood before the mirror and held the jacket against my face to see how it looked. Surprised, I stared at myself, startled to discover how very gaunt and matronly I had become. When had I begun to resemble my mother, I wondered, chuckling softly under my breath. The plum colored patina of the material emphasized an abundance of new silver strands in my hair, more than I cared to see, but after years of wearing black crepe mourning dresses, my unusual appearance was somewhat refreshing. I gazed at my image in the mirror a while longer, remembering the days when I had seamstresses design and make my gowns instead of buying ready-to-wear outfits on the Ladies Mile. Well, now was not the time to dwell on the fortunes or misfortunes of the past. There was much to do in preparation for this evening.

Destiny had a curious way of playing tricks, I suppose. That particular morning Doña Inocencia had come to ask a favor. She wanted my support to organize a woman's club that would form part of a broader, more ambitious, entity called the Cuban Revolutionary Party—*El Partido Revolucionario Cubano-Puertorriqueño.* The name had a familiar ring to it, but was simple and to the point.

It was the vision of José Martí, but a multitude of Cubans and Puerto Ricans from as far away as Key West, Florida, and as near as Philadelphia, Pennsylvania, had a say in its formation. In March, I had read about its objectives on the front page of *Patria.* "Now that was a historic moment, a day to remember," I thought. The first goal of the revolutionary party was to unite the efforts of all Cubans and Puerto Ricans, regardless of race or class, in an effort to secure the absolute independence of Cuba and to promote and aid that of Puerto Rico. "With all and for the good of all," Martí had written.

"Cubans and Puerto Ricans, together again in a liberation movement to sever the Spanish colonial yoke once and for all," Doña Inocencia had told me. "But this time it would be different."

And for so many reasons, this time, I'd wanted so much to believe she was right.

Martí was the person to make it happen. He had a special . . . I would say, a singularly impressive ability for bringing people together in common cause. He made it known, in all sincerity, that he valued the worth of all people, viewing women and workers, the poor, the rich, blacks and whites as equal players in the enterprise. And every week in *Patria's* four columned, four pages, along with news of the organizations, he praised groups and individuals, mourned their passing, announced their achievements, never once letting people forget just how important they were to the movement. One had to admit that in the few short years leading up to the formation of the Cuban Revolutionary Party he had created solidarity where divisiveness had reigned before. And because I believed in the ideas he expressed in a talk he gave at Hardman Hall in February, I had the utmost faith in him as a leader. And that is precisely what I told him in my congratulatory note.

I think back to that long, eventful January day, remember again the unforgettable look of determination etched across Doña Inocencia's youthful face. We talked all day. She shared with me her experiences, and I confided my own. At the end of our visit, I came to realize that although she sought my help in her passionate quest, it was I who would find a richer, fuller life because of her. Her dedication raised the hopes in me I had laid to rest after the failure of our own struggle. Reminiscing about that day, I felt a tranquility, a sense of peace I'd not felt in a long while. But from the corner of my eye I glimpsed once more the black, crepe dress draped across the bed. The insufferable black veil mockingly lay beside the dress, and I could hardly wait to feel the first twinges of freedom from its heavy weight of hat and netting upon my head.

It seemed I'd been in mourning forever. First to honor and remember my sainted mother who died in 1886. Then, for my dear father who followed her into paradise in less than six months. Of the two, he had been the less hardy and, fearing illness and an early grave, he had long since put his affairs in order.

He had sold our beloved Casanova Mansion in 1880. I shed tears for the past when he did. It had, for so long, been the comfort and safety of the Casanovas and the Villaverdes, the familial hearth around which we all forged our strength. The mansion's sale meant the definitive moment to make the move had arrived. We knew my parents' lives had come full circle, and I began to mourn their absence even before they returned to Havana.

When we received the news from Havana informing us of mother's failing health, Cirilo and Narciso rushed to Nassau Street to apply for passports. As a minor, Enrique's name appeared on his father's passport where I, as his wife, also appeared. Enrique took leave of his studies, and in a frenzy of activity we closed our home and sailed for Cuba. How were we to know it would be months and months before we returned again to New York? And all that time I spent in Cuba, I detested the fact, perhaps more than anyone else, that I was forced to remain in a country still subject to Spanish shackles. It irritated me like an uncontrollable itch under my skin that I could neither scratch nor tolerate and I swore, to all the saints above and any living person who would listen, never to set foot on the island again until it was a free country.

Perhaps I prayed to the wrong saints, because no sooner had we returned from laying my mother to her final rest when word arrived informing us that my father had taken a turn for the worst. I imagined that our enslaved nation had sought vengeance against me; extending and tightening its wretched reach, it was becoming more and more difficult for me to break free.

As I neatly placed the folded cloth sheets back into the box and spread the new dress across the chaise for the evening's affair, I felt a slight shiver run down my spine. Well, I thought it is best not to dwell on such premonitions. Best to avoid bringing unpleasantness into the evening.

"Mary," I called, just as the housemaid happened to appear at the door of my room. Our dear Mary McDonald had been with the family for twelve years, from the time we lived in the townhouse on W. 24th Street to our multiple dwelling French Flat at The Rockerham on Broadway. In that time, she had become more like a member of the family than a servant. She knew and accepted our habits, our likes and dislikes, but that factor did not seem to stop her from trying to mend what she considered our errant ways.

"I'll need you to call for a carriage. And please let my husband and my son know that I'll be ready to leave for the recital within the hour. They are aware, I trust, that it is a black tie and waist-coat event."

"Yes, Madame," she responded in a lyrical Irish brogue, sounding as if she had set foot in America the day before yester-day. As she deftly removed the mourning dress and veil from the bed, she said, "If I may ask, Madame, is Mr. Villaverde well enough to go out this evening? He was doing poorly, not at all well, last night."

Comfortably accommodated in the Hansom cab, the carriage clipped along Broadway at a steady pace toward the music hall for the evening's recital. The Sociedad Literaria, the Literary Society, an association presided by Martí, was the proud sponsor of the evening's program. They scored a coup in their estimation because the internationally acclaimed pianist, Ana Otero, was to debut a special composition. So beloved was she in her native Puerto Rico that a large audience of Cubans and Puerto Ricans would surely be in attendance.

Fresh from a highly successful tour of European capitals, Señorita Otero had conquered adoring audiences from Berlin to Barcelona. Her gift to our community was to be a repeat performance of her own interpretation of *La Borinqueña*. A lovely, nostalgic homage to the absent homeland, this revered Puerto Rican *danza* was also a patriotic salute to the Lares uprising.

Before our carriage reached the corner of W. 56th Street and Broadway, Narciso remarked, "If there is to be another social function this week, you will have to count me out. I do believe, mother, that my brother and his wife have been spared from social obligations far too long since they moved to New Jersey."

My Enrique had married Louise Horton in 1889, and visits with the family had become fewer and fewer since they had made the move. I glanced at my husband in time to see a frown appear upon his face at the mention of Enrique's name. Cirilo believed our impulsive son had married much too young.

But Narciso, a young bachelor making a name for himself in commerce, was absolutely correct. There were far too many social demands. Our expatriate community had grown enormously over the past years and increases in the numbers of cultural, religious or political associations, lodges, mutual aid societies, literary clubs and institutions related to the performing arts reflected that growth. There were, consequently, an inordinate number of social obligations.

"My dear Narciso," I responded in a familiar motherly fashion, "supporting the associations is our *duty* for the well-being of the *entire* community. Thirty years ago, New York was a very different place for Hispanic èmigrès. We didn't have the large population we have today; nor did we enjoy such a wide array of cultural events . . . literary societies or concerts or operas."

We rode in silence for a while, enjoying the pleasant summer breezes of early June. As we came close to the Madison Square

Park area, I eagerly awaited my first glimpse of the brilliant light display throughout the park. I'd never lost my fascination over electrification and I marveled at the radiance of the street lights, remembering when illumination solely depended on the subdued flickering of gaslight.

"As you can imagine, Narciso, even mutual aid groups were lacking," I continued. "Collecting donations for charity was left to individuals, like us, and the churches. Today, we're fortunate to have mutual aid groups like La Liga Antillana, or La Sociedad de Beneficencia Hispano Americana that dedicate themselves to helping the poor, the working class and just about anyone else who needs it."

I could hardly control my impulse to pontificate, aware that I'd become overbearing. "We didn't have any groups like that back then. The beauty of it for me today, what should really be appreciated, is the mixing of the classes and the races at such events, something we rarely witnessed in the past."

Cirilo, who until now had avoided interrupting my monologue, turned to me and wisely changed the subject. "Speaking of organizations, my dear, did you know that the musician, Emilio Agramonte, plans to open a school for opera and oratorio? I'd say that with Estrada Palma's school for boys and girls, and the one run by the Quesada sisters just for girls, our young people have a promising educational future before them."

"And that too," I trumpet triumphantly, "is another reason for supporting the growth of our community!"

Allowing his obstinate mother the final word, my handsome Narciso nonchalantly turned away, trying to hide the smile playing on the corners of his mouth.

A month or so after the meeting of Mercedes Varona, I surprised Cirilo during our dinner one evening with my observations. "I think there are marital problems between Doña Inocencia and her husband, and that is why she wants to resign from the presidency."

I'd been thinking about the situation for some time, trying to find ways to alleviate Doña Inocencia's problems and keep her from resigning. That evening, I had much to share with my husband. We had decided against the formality of the dining room and took a light supper in the library. The windows overlooking the courtyard garden were opened, welcoming the scent of damp earth mingled with that of freshly blooming lilacs drifting up from the street below. It was to be the two of us again this evening, as the spontaneous social visits of friends and guests had subsided years ago. As was our custom, we still delighted in discussing with one another the affairs of the day.

Mary had set a tureen of cold tomato soup, a *gazpacho* she took pride in making, on the library table along with a variety of little sandwiches and cold drinks. She had not forgotten Cirilo's favorite Cuban coffee. He ritually drank his black coffee in small sips after every evening meal. It was a habit Mary tried to break, without success, because she believed he would acquire untold benefits from the curative powers of good strong Irish tea. But Cirilo snubbed the very notion of tea, associating it with medicinal treatments for illnesses he had suffered throughout his life. To him, tea was merely a cup of slightly tinted boiled water.

"Well, as I was saying, Cirilo, Doña Inocencia is much stronger than she appears. She doesn't bow down to another's demands. Didn't she marry Don Sotero against her parent's wishes?"

Cirilo did not know her story and expressed surprise when I confided to him that Doña Inocencia's parents had frowned upon the marriage for a number of irrational reasons: Figueroa was much older than she, had been married before and had fathered four sons.

"But what I truly believe was at the crux of the matter, although she never told me, was that her parents objected to his race and lower social class. Perhaps that is why they came to New York so soon after their marriage in 1889 . . . that and the fact that Martí had invited him."

Cirilo adjusted the pillows to his comfort on the sofa and began to sip his coffee. I sat opposite him in my faded, oversized green velvet armchair and placed my empty tea cup on the small table. "You understand," I said, "Don Sotero was a respected journalist, a man who enjoyed a solid reputation for his intellectual writings in Puerto Rico. Other than the repressive political situation, there was little reason to leave the island and, yet, they arrived with his printing press and his books and opened Imprenta America. Before long, he was calling meetings of the Puerto Rican expatriate community, and he and Martí began to organize the clubs."

"Emilia, you must be cautious in what you say about their personal situation. After all, there may be plenty of other reasons for her decision. Her children are sickly, as you've often said, and she is expecting another child. The woman presides over the organization's fundraising and oftentimes helps in the print shop."

"Yes, Cirilo, I will be sure to be careful about Doña Inocencia's delicate situation." I paused for a moment, recollecting the chain of events that had taken place at the meeting of Mercedes Varona. "But you would agree with me about Doña Inocencia, had you seen the look on Doña Carmen's face. She sat stone-faced at that meeting, the only one not surprised when Doña Inocencia announced her decision to leave the presidency.

"That poor woman, Doña Carmen, herself, has suffered the innuendoes of malicious gossip and public ostracism because of her personal relationship to Martí. She is no stranger to suffering. Doña Carmen recognized that something was very wrong. You know, their enemies, those who oppose the political vision of the party, say her youngest child, Luisa María, was fathered by Martí. But in truth, he acts like a father to all her children, encouraging each and every one of them, including the girls, to attend to their studies.

"You are his friend, Cirilo. Has he ever spoken to you about Doña Carmen?"

"Emilia, Martí is in a very precarious position. He now leads a powerful international organization that is preparing for an invasion of Cuba. His brilliance is not enough, Emilia. Under no circumstance can he be perceived as an immoral man . . . a hero with feet of clay. And no, the answer to your question is he does not speak to me about personal matters."

We sat in comfortable silence, feeling the presence of one another. "Cirilo," I said after a while, "I'm convinced, the more I ponder the dreaded issue, that something awful is happening to Don Sotero and Doña Inocencia. *Pobrecita*. Poor girl!" I believe it was at that point that I decided to offer my services to the club and relieve her of obligations until she was able to resume the presidency once again.

Cirilo sighed in agreement to my proposal, but continued to read his book. And I turned my attention to answering correspondence. Saddened by my dear friend's complicated situation, I ignored hints of guilt as I cherished the sense of warmth and safety permeating our small library.

Nineteen
Final Passage

. . . He died peacefully beside the bookcase that held the books he wrote, with his loving companion by his side, who never rejected the land he loved, and with the ineffable joy of not having on his conscience, at the hour of his death, the remorse of having helped to perpetuate, in word or deed, the inextinguishable regime that choked and degraded him in his country.

José Martí. *Patria*. October 30, 1894.

They came in groups or by themselves, joining the never-ending line of mourners that seemed to swell and subside like the endless waves of ocean that washed over the pebbly shores of the Long Island Sound. They came in spite of the rain, the blustery wind, upturned umbrellas, wet scarves and wind-blown hats. They came to our flat at 1730 Broadway, where the oversized black wreath that hung upon the formal entrance door announced to the world that Cirilo Villaverde was dead.

Until the time for praying the rosary, they mingled in small clusters in the drawing room, the dining room and the library. Mary moved among them, red-rimmed eyes surveying the needs and wants of all the mourners. She replenished the tea, the coffee, the hot chocolate, the cheeses and breads, focused intently on keeping order and doing the routine chores, as if the world were not slipping right out from under her, like the sands of our beloved Casanova beach.

Here and there the whispers undulated, buzzing like a hundred bees circling their hives on a summer day. Other sounds alternated with soft sobbing and occasional laughter as someone recalled a bittersweet moment. I embraced, held hands, comforted, smiled, laughed and cried with our dearest friends and with the others who came to honor, to pay respects to the old grizzled soldier, the man of letters, who personified for them the last vestige of a heroic bygone generation.

There was Martí, looking as though he has lost his best friend . . . and the Figueroas. . . . poor Doña Inocencia, my dear friend, rekindling anew her grief for the loss of her three little girls. She looked at me soulfully, and I knew she understood. We had become kindred spirits once again. The men of the old Junta paid their respects as bygones were bygones. Estrada Palma brought them over to where I sat. And Doña Lola . . . dear, dear Doña Lola! She opened her arms wide and enfolded me in her ample embrace, the wounded bird that I'd become, newly fallen from my perch. Her affection moved me to fly. I imagined myself sitting on the soft grassy hillock, my back to the mansion, where I bathed in the spiritual solace of the seascape.

I sat, I walked, I held Doña Inocencia's little boy in my arms, I stood beside my Enrique as he and his wife welcomed newcomers or bid farewell to departing mourners. I watched and worried about my Narciso, a study in deepest sorrow, as he stared through the bay window at nothing, determined to contain the tears that threatened to overflow his vision. I saw myself from afar looking like a ghost of my former self, as my reflection joined Narciso's in the same window. And then I hear the words that utterly shatter my composure, bringing me back to earth: *Dios te salve, María, llena de gracia, el Señor es contigo . . . Hail Mary, full of grace, the Lord is with thee . . .* And I know in the deepest recesses of my sensibilities, my Cirilo is dead.

Was it only a week ago that I sent Mary to fetch Dr. Egbert Gaumsly at his Fifth Avenue home, begged him to come right away because Cirilo's cold had worsened? Yes, I remember. October 18 it was. Cirilo could not breath, could not sleep, restrained by a hacking dry cough that left him gasping for air. The doctor prescribed laudanum to bring him relief. At first, he seemed to rally, but the cough intensified, a vengeful fury painfully tightening the muscles in his chest.

"Acute bronchitis," the doctor announced.

Surprisingly, the night of the 22nd my husband appeared peaceful. I sat beside his bed throughout the night, napping for short spells in the armchair.

"Emilia," he rasped quietly, startling me out of my nap, "remember that you promised to take me back to Cuba."

I froze, but responded softly, "Yes, Cirilo. I remember."

And on the morning of October 23, 1894, at eleven a.m., my husband quietly took his leave of this world.

Two weeks and three days later, my sons and I accompany his body on board a ship bound for Havana. My husband is to be interred in the Casanova pantheon number 193 on G Street of the Colón Cemetery.

I gaze toward the far off horizon, a sense of peace filling my soul like the warmth of the Caribbean sun. The black hat and netting feel heavy upon my head, but I dismiss the discomfort, intent on watching two large white and gray seagulls perch their spindly legs on the ship's railing. They squawk at one another, contesting ownership of a tasty morsel of breakfast bread someone has dropped on the deck. I turn to feel the full sun on my face. Then I smile at the incongruity of life and whisper to the ever-present presence that is Cirilo at my side, "Yes, love. I will join you in eternal rest when Cuba is finally free. I promise."

Epilogue
Cuba, 1944

The Cuban patriots of this city were truly surprised to hear of the unexpected death of Señora Emilia Casanova, widow of Cirilo Villaverde. This lady, distinguished years ago by her personal labor in support of the Cuban Revolution and the meritorious achievements of her husband, the great Cuban novelist, Cirilo Villaverde, lived in relative retirement, although she was always addicted to the cause of her Patria. . . . Not long ago she co-founded the new ladies' club, José María Aguirre. We offer our heartfelt sympathy to her distinguished family and her many friends.

Patria. March 5, 1897.

Clearly, it was difficult for the old man to be there. He fidgeted as he sat almost in a squatting position in his white starched *guayabera* and neatly pressed black pants, braving the heat of the day. Protected only by his old straw hat, Don Narciso wore dark sunglasses, which he removed often to mop his face with a rather large linen handkerchief.

Sitting on the sharp edge of the rectangular stone tomb, a faded number 193 on the obelisk behind him, his obvious discomfort came not so much because it was an uncomfortable slab of concrete on which to sit, but because the area lacked any semblance of decent shade. And so he tried to grab the little vestiges of shade that hovered overhead from a flimsy nondescript tree. But even that simple act was clumsily executed because the slab left less than a foot of space to maneuver one's self. It was surrounded by a low iron railing held in place along its periphery by several cement posts. One could easily step *onto* the slab with the obelisk but not sit beside it with any degree of comfort. Surely this city of the dead was not intended for the comfort of the living.

Suddenly, raucous laughter startled him. It was a group of university students, probably engineering majors if one were to judge from the slide rules they carried along with their books. They joked and jostled against one another as they sauntered along G Street, seeking a short cut to their destination. Engrossed in their own merriment, they did not notice the old man, but he looked up at the students and intuitively recognized in them the promise of the future. Then, because he was here for the past and not the present, he looked down the road again for the black hearse carrying his mother's mortal remains, exhumed after forty-seven years for burial in Havana.

The Colón Cemetery was so vast it was hard to believe one was still within the city limits of Havana, and he wondered if the funeral hearse had been delayed by heavy traffic or another procession blocking the road. Whatever the reason for the delay, he hoped it would not be too much longer for the wait in the brilliant, cloudless afternoon was already taking its toll on his stamina. Although he was a sturdy octogenarian, he regretted dismissing the driver of the public car so soon after arriving at this destination.

At that moment, a black car slowly wound its way from the Malecón toward Zapata and past the Central Chapel. The old man followed its trajectory from afar. Anticipating the first sighting of the funeral director's car, he assumed it was the hearse and relaxed his stance, relieved that the second burial could finally begin. But it was not the hearse, as he expected. It was a black car, probably a 1930s vintage Ford sedan, driven by a woman. She parked a short distance from where he stood, and he strained to see if he recognized the driver.

The woman carefully stepped out of the car and walked toward Don Narciso. Her bobbed, hennaed-hair shone in the sunlight, curls outlining her face like a halo. Of medium height, she wore a stylish summer suit, a short-sleeved jacket and matching wide-legged pants that made her appear younger than her actual age: eight years the man's junior. Standing directly in front of the old man, she lowered her sunglasses, squinting sea green eyes to better peer into Don Narciso's face as if to locate the young man she once knew during the heady and turbulent times she had lived in New York. Gratitude engulfed the old man's heart: there was no mistaking the identity of this woman.

"Doña Inocencia! I can't believe . . . is it really you!"

He reached toward her with his outstretched arms as she also extended hers to him. The two old friends held each other's hands tightly, caressing one another's face with their eyes, recalling in that instant more than four decades of past sorrows and joys.

"You look so much like your father without the beard," she said smiling. "When I learned that you were coming to Cuba to lay Doña Emilia in her final resting place next to your father, I knew I needed to be here with you. Mario, my son, was to drive me but was unable to leave the office, so I drove myself. I hope you don't mind my being here."

"*Ay*, Doña Inocencia, *por favor*. It is my honor to have you by my side. My mother cared for you very much. I know she thought of you like a second daughter." He paused, recalling his mother's impressions of this woman. "When she became president of Mercedes Varona, she said the club was yours but placed in her hands for safekeeping until you returned." He continued smiling at the memory of his obstinate mother. "She thought the world of you, Doña Inocencia!"

The woman led the old man to a nearby bench, partly secluded by the lush greenery of an almond tree, assuring him that they would still be able to see the hearse from that location.

"I think of her so often . . . I think of her achievements as a woman ahead of her time and, really, as a feminist, although we didn't use that word back then. You can't imagine how it saddens me that she never received the credit she was due.

"That obituary they wrote of her in *Patria*—do you remember it? Those short-sighted men placed her in your father's shadow! Didn't they realize that *every* expedition, even those after 1895, bound for Cuba with recruits and munitions bore her stamp, either because she personally paid for equipment or recruited and trained the volunteers for combat at her own expense? And every ship carried a banner embroidered by her own hand. If that weren't enough to garner some respect, think of the network of letters and articles she spread throughout the world expressing her strong support for liberation!"

"I know," responded the old man, nodding his white haired head vigorously in agreement with Doña Inocencia. "Even after my father died, she continued to support the insurgency of 1895 under Martí. I don't know if you were aware that my mother was living on limited resources at that point. My brother and I quietly helped out—you know how proud she was—by replenishing her funds to the extent we could. We often joked about how the Casanova wealth disappeared into my mother's efforts to liberate Cuba."

The old friends sat quietly side by side, each recalling the force of nature that was Emilia Casanova.

Laughing softly, Doña Inocencia turned her head to Don Narciso and said, "I'm remembering how she intimidated the members of the clubs. Do you remember? She ran the clubs like a general, and the members of both groups, Mercedes Varona and the Aguirre Club, followed, no . . . more than that, they truly admired her leadership! That is why she was so successful in bringing in the funds used for the war. I'm sure it was the same with Las Hijas."

"No," he responded joining her in laughter, "it was much worse! She was tougher with Las Hijas; she was much younger then, but look at what they managed to accomplish!" And the two smiled at one another, reliving the memory of Doña Emilia's leadership.

Doña Inocencia leaned forward and folded her hands in her lap. "I'm sorry I didn't attend her funeral services at St. Raymond's Cemetery," she said, recalling in the blink of an eye the painful services for her own little girls less than four years before Doña Emilia's. "I should have been there . . . but I couldn't . . . I just should have made more of an effort."

"You needn't apologize. I just wish I had been able to bring her to Cuba much earlier," confided Don Narciso. "But life has a way of . . . you know, of interfering. There was the Great War and now this one. And I know she would not have wanted to be in Cuba as long as the island was under Spain. . . ."

The friends remained quiet, once more, savoring the words unspoken, each lost in private thoughts and past regrets.

"When you think about it," he continued after a while, summoning memories of the mother of his youth, "she did more than anyone else to ensure that the flag of liberation she saw from her window when she was a girl became the official emblem of this country."

"That reminds me, Don Narciso. There is one favor I need to ask of you. I guess I came here today to do what I should have done in 1897. In my heart, I know it is the right thing to do for Doña Emilia."

At that point, Doña Inocencia reached into her oversized straw satchel emblazoned with a cartoon image of a multi-colored green and red parrot. She pulled out a package wrapped in ordinary brown paper, a brown string of twine holding it together, and began to undo the knots.

As the content began to reveal itself, what the old man saw brought tears to his eyes. It was a satin banner that bore a lone white star embedded in a triangular field of crimson from which three broad cobalt and two white stripes alternated to the flag's border. He recognized his mother's stitching.

"If it is all right with you," she said gently, "I'd like to place this over your mother's coffin."

Don Narciso gave a slight nod of his head and gently squeezed Doña Inocencia's hand. Together, hand in hand, they sat and waited for Doña Emilia to arrive and, finally, after forty-seven years, claim the flag she had long wanted to unfurl in a free Cuba.

Author's Notes

This story is based on the life of Emilia Casanova de Villaverde, a Cuban patriot who lived most of her adult life, from 1855 to 1897, in New York City. An important, complex figure in American Latino/a history, Casanova de Villaverde was a woman ahead of her times, a modern-day feminist living in the nineteenth century.

She married Cirilo Villaverde, a distinguished, well-known writer who shared his wife's devotion to Cuba's independence and the abolition of slavery. In New York, she raised a family and created the first women's political organization dedicated to support the Mambí Army of Liberation during Cuba's Ten Years' War (1868-1878). Through an extensive network of correspondence, Casanova de Villaverde provided a detailed personal perspective of the period and the historical figures she encountered.

Much of what is known about Casanova de Villaverde is written in Spanish. In writing this book, my goals are to introduce her story to audiences more adept at reading in English and to convey a historical glimpse into the experiences of women of Caribbean and Latin American heritage who also happened to live full lives in the United States. That became my overarching motivation for exploring the world of Casanova de Villaverde based on the historical record and then imagining the woman she might have been.

The basic elements of her life story are known to historians and other scholars who research this period. Based on a limited archival record, she is sometimes mentioned in their work, but it is usually in a cursory fashion as an example of women's involvement in the Ten Years' War. For the general public, Casanova de Villaverde resides in the dustbin of the past, or at best, in the shadows of her husband's fame. And while she is rightfully held aloft in her country of origin as a significant figure in the struggle for Cuba's liberation during the nineteenth century, the deeds for which she is best remembered were carried out in New York City. It was there under the protective banner of American constitutional freedoms and it was there within the cradle of a robust, expatriate Cuban and Puerto Rican transnational community that she found fertile grounding for her life's work.

What was it like, I wondered as I set out in my quest for the imagined Emilia, for Casanova de Villaverde to be raised and educated within the bosom of an elite slave-holding family and then pursue an abolitionist cause? What was the catalyst for her abolitionist sentiments and resolute dedication to liberation? And how was that captured for the historical record? How did she relate to her more conservative parents, a political dissident husband and American-born children? And why did she come to confer with the president and the Congress of the United States and what were the results? How did she convince upper-class Cuban women, steeped in traditional roles as wives and mothers, to join her radical cause? Did she shape a legacy for future generations of Caribbean activist women?

The answers to these questions begin to emerge in Cirilo Villaverde's thirty-six-page profile of Casanova de Villaverde. The profile acts as a prelude to *Apuntes biográficos de Emilia Casanova de Villaverde, escritos por un contemporáneo,* a book comprised of a collection of her private letters from 1869 to 1876. It was published in New York City in 1874, possibly a misprinted year, given the post-dated letters in the volume. The *contemporáneo* could only have been Cirilo Villaverde. In fact, some of the descriptive passages he pens about his wife in profile appear, as well, as characteristics of the fictional Isabel in his acclaimed novel, *Cecilia Valdés or El Angel Hill,* also published in New York in 1882.

In the profile, Villaverde sketches an overview of Casanova de Villaverde's life from birth until around 1874, the year following the *Virginius* incident. He offers the reader essential, biographical details about his wife that provide the skeleton on which I crafted the imagined Emilia. Short of becoming hagiographic, Villaverde's profile does allude to his wife's obstinacy, her unladylike love of athletics and adamant disinclination to compromise her political beliefs, characteristics that help to temper her many virtues.

Why was Villaverde compelled to publish such a positive profile of his wife? His motivation is clear. Villaverde wished to ensure Emilia Casanova de Villaverde's place in history. As an informed and esteemed revolutionary, his perspective on the woman demeaned and grossly caricatured in the pro-Spanish press for her activism, burned in effigy in her native city and criticized in writing by her enemies, would have been taken seriously. Villaverde wished to preserve her story for its significance to the political history of Cuba.

As he was no doubt aware, the strong-minded, sharp-tongued woman he married might never have received the well-deserved accolades she merited from her contemporaries. If we are to judge by the paucity of obituaries upon Casanova de Villaverde's death, his concern was warranted.

We will never know why Villaverde sought to gather her correspondence in secret, copying over two hundred of Casanova de Villaverde's letters for publication, but we can speculate that it was for the same reason. Villaverde needed to record his wife's meritorious deeds. The best way to do that was through her letters. He informs the reader that Casanova de Villaverde's treasure trove of correspondence was sent to important figures, like Giuseppe Garibaldi and Victor Hugo, to generals, heads of state and other public and private individuals involved in world affairs. Letters form the basis for detailing Casanova de Villaverde's organizational contributions. Letters to the editors of various newspapers document fundraising and personal activities. As such, the letters form a singular legacy, testimony to her agency and her sacrifices for the liberation movement. What Villaverde could not know was that the letters would also underscore a transnational community of people and ideas vital for understanding and informing present generations about a relatively unknown period in American Latino/a history.

It is in her letters that the historical Casanova de Villaverde comes to life as my imagined Emilia. Here the historical woman reveals the intrigues, petty jealousies, rivalries and disillusions connected with the liberation politics of Cuba and Puerto Rico. She writes to *paisanos* in the Carolinas, Philadelphia, Boston, New Orleans and Ybor City, but it is primarily in New York City where much of the action takes place. As such, her correspondence sheds light on New York's active and diverse Latino/a community of expatriate intellectuals, workers and refugees over an eight-year period, a time when American Latinos/as are barely visible to the broader society.

We learn of Casanova de Villaverde's intimate involvement with the war raging in her native land and the efforts she makes to keep the army provisioned. We begin to uncover and understand the uncompromising woman in all her strengths and faults, a woman who acted on principle and stood firm on her decisions. And from the quintessential patriot, organizer, activist, visionary and intellectual that was Emilia Casanova de Villaverde, the imagined Emilia takes form.

"The Memorandum of the Wrongs and Acts of Violence which, Since 1868, the Spanish Government in the Island of Cuba Has Done to the Person, Family and Property of Inocencio Casanova, A Naturalized Citizen of the United States of America" (1871) and its companion piece, "Memorial, & C. of Ynocencio Casanova" (1873) provide another perspective on which to build the imagined Emilia. These documents offer ample evidence about Inocencio Casanova's incarceration, loss of property and goods at the hands of colonial administrators in Cuba. We find insidious reference to his daughter and implications that she might have been the reason for the elder Casanova's imprisonment.

Along with snippets of information about the lives of his American-citizen sons, we learn the extent to which the harsh conditions in a rebellious Cuba debilitated the family at the start of the revolution. The imagined Emilia takes shape under such circumstances, informed by documented glimpses into the lifestyle of the Casanova family. The embargo and confiscation of the family's land and business ventures, poignantly related by Inocencio Casanova, an American citizen himself, brings the imagined family to favor the rebel cause.

In this regard, the detailed descriptions found in the *New York Times*, in 1902, of the Casanova Mansion on the Long Island Sound, home to the Villaverdes and the Casanovas for more than a decade, support an allegiance to the rebel cause. Its role as the launching site for ships carrying men and munitions to the Cuban war front and the involvement of the Casanovas and the Villaverdes in the *Virginius* incident as well as other failed expeditions, finds verification in the correspondence. Casanova de Villaverde's story begins to bear a more direct relationship on international affairs than previously imagined when the *Virginius* incident brings the United States to the brink of war with Spain.

Indirectly, Cirilo Villaverde's novel, *Cecilia Valdés or El Angel Hill,* provides the imagined Emilia with a cultural timeframe against which we can plot her activities. We learn Casanova de Villaverde played a supporting role in the novel's writing as a reader and editor. While descriptions of the Villaverde marriage and life in New York are scant, the imagined Emilia grows in proportion to the wealth of information given in the prologue about Villaverde's own life and the writing of his book.

Based primarily on the above, I created a story for the imagined Emilia from childhood, adolescence and young womanhood in Cuba, to her life as a wife, mother, writer and revolutionary in New York. Her actions and conversations are suggested by her correspondence, but much of it is imagined based on the historical progression of her life. With the exception of a few of the ladies of Las Hijas and minor characters she encounters that help to move the story, many of the people she meets and interacts with are themselves historical figures. The story of Ana Otero's New York recital, which actually took place the week of August 20, 1892, is changed to move the narrative along. And Lola Rodríguez de Tió arrived in New York in 1896. She was not in the city for either Inocencia Martinez's club meeting (1893) or Villaverde's wake in 1894.

There is also an abundant literature to be found in secondary and primary sources on the Ten Years' War itself, which helps to set the stage for the imagined protagonist. Among those pivotal for developing the story of Emilia were César Andreu Iglesias' *Memoirs of Bernardo Vega: A Contribution to the History of the Puerto Rican Community in New York,* Rodrigo Lazo's *Writing to Cuba: Filibustering and Cuban Exiles in the United States,* Louis A. Pérez, Jr.'s *Slaves, Sugar & Colonial Society: Travel Accounts of Cuba, 1801-1899,* Josefina Toledo's *Sotero Figueroa, editor de Patria: Apuntes para una biografía* and Cirilo Villaverde's *Cecilia Valdés or El Angel Hill.*

Newspaper accounts and journal articles in *El Demócrata, Patria, The New York Sun, The New York Herald, La Verdad, Harpers Weekly* and *The New York Times,* among others, helped to set the tone for the period. Census, birth, death, ship's manifests, naturalization and passport records were vital in searching for dates, residences and other information relating to Casanova de Villaverde and the Casanova family.

Online internet sources, some of which drew upon *Epistolario familiar de don Inocencio Casanova* and Emeterio Santovenia's *Vida y obra de Emilia Casanova,* as well as Dania de la Cruz Martínez's "La Junta Patriótica de Cubanas en Nueva York," proved invaluable. Others offered a wide range of information, among them, Cubanet, Historyofcuba.com, OpusHabana, Ancestry.com, Latinamericanstudies.org, Cubaliteraria, Familysearch.org, individual blogs, newspapers, newsletters and numerous historical sites dedicated to the period provided the initial historical accounts needed to reconstruct the imagined story of the Villaverde family.

My interpretation of Casanova de Villaverde's life as a child in Cuba, her education, adolescence and young womanhood, as well as her life in New York and her senior years, are culled from copious reading of secondary sources and my background as a historian who researches and writes about the Puerto Rican and the Latino/a experience. These readings helped me spin the tales of her immediate family and her children.

I would be remiss if I did not address my initial encounter with this historical figure. Emilia Casanova de Villaverde's story was a biographical entry in *Latinas in the United States: A Historical Encyclopedia*, a three-volume encyclopedia that I edited with my colleagues, Vicki L. Ruiz and Carlos A. Cruz. Fascinated by the lives of American Latinas in the nineteenth century, I found myself returning, again and again, to Casanova de Villaverde's narrative and wondering about the hidden details of her life in a city in which I've lived much of my life. I never ceased to be delighted with the surprised looks on my students' faces whenever I mentioned that in the nineteenth century, a Cuban patriot, Emilia Casanova de Villaverde, lived in a mansion in the South Bronx!

My fascination with the lives of American Latina women was reflected among the audiences I encountered on my lectures who always wanted to know more about them. This book is my gift to them with the hope that they and generations of young adults will find the stories from our American Latino/a heritage as compelling and inspirational as I did.

Virginia Sánchez-Korrol, 2012

Glossary of Spanish Terms

Aya
English governess hired as tutor for the Casanova children.

Bambolinas
Backstage rigs, ropes, pulleys and other stage set equipment used in mounting theatrical productions. Behind the scenes.

Bibijagua
A species of large ants found in Cuba destructive to agricultural production.

Brindis
A toast, as in to offer a toast to one's health.

Cosecha
The harvest.

Cocuyos
West Indian Fireflies.

Curandera
A woman practitioner of the art of herbal healing.

Danza
A genre of Puerto Rican music most popular during the nineteenth century. The venue and cultural styles associated with this music were similar, in many respects, to European counterparts.

Guardia de la Bembeta
The name of a battalion of volunteers recruited and financed by Emilia Casanova.

Guayabera
A shirt for men's formal wear popular in the Caribbean and Latin America.

Junta
A committee or board of directors. Also refers to a military dictatorship.

La borinqueña
A Danza. The national anthem of Puerto Rico.

Las viejitas
The old women.

Mambíes
The name of the Cuban Army of Liberation that fought against the Spanish Colonial Army during the Ten Years' War.

M'ijita
Popular term of endearment. Diminutive for "my little daughter."

¡Qué vivas!
A toast to life.

Quintas
Referring to landed property, holdings or an estate. A villa or country house.

Treaty of Zanjón, 1878
Treaty between Cuba and Spain that ended the Ten Years' War, 1868-1878.

Villa
An encompassing administrative status accorded to a collection of communities in recognition of their growth and progress.

Volantes
A two-wheeled carriage popular in Cuba and Puerto Rico in the nineteenth century where the body is in front of the axle and the driver rides on the horse.

Voluntarios
Paramilitaries attached to the Spanish Army during the Ten Years' War.

Yuca
Cassava root vegetable popular in the Caribbean.